Book Two

Deadly Revenge

Deadly Triad

Book Two

Deadly Revenge

By

Nancy Kay

Deadly Triad

Deadly Reflection
Deadly Revenge
Deadly Encounter

Desert Breeze Publishing, Inc.
27305 W. Live Oak Rd #424
Castaic, CA 91384

http://www.DesertBreezePublishing.com

Copyright © 2012 by Nancy Kay
ISBN 10: 1-61252-940-2
ISBN 13: 978-1-61252-940-0

Published in the United States of America
eBook Publish Date: February 1. 2012
Print Publish Date: February 2013

Editor-In-Chief: Gail R. Delaney
Editor: Theresa Stillwagon
Marketing Director: Jenifer Ranieri
Cover Artist: Jenifer Ranieri
Photography Credit: Nancy K. Schneider and Joseph V. Schneider
Photographed On Location:
        Bob's Gun Shop and Indoor Range -- McKean, Pennsylvania
Cover Model: Joseph V. Schneider

Cover Art Copyright by Desert Breeze Publishing, Inc © 2011

Dedication

With respect and admiration I dedicate *Deadly Revenge* to The United States Marine Corps, The Pennsylvania State Police, Volunteer Firemen, and Emergency Medical Service.

Chapter One

Damn. *What was the matter with him?*

Rich McConnell rearranged and realigned with a covert tug. He wasn't sixteen anymore. Truth be known, he was a few notches past the half century mark. Regardless, when Ada Blaine bent over to tend her plants, *his* body snapped to attention.

After parking in front of Ada's sprawling cottage, he'd caught sight of her amidst the neat pathways crisscrossing her vast gardens. Several acres covered with emerging herb plants stretched from the front of her place, wrapped around the side, and covered most of the rolling slope stretching clear to the lake.

Rich sauntered forward.

Ada glanced his way. "Ah, Rich, you're early. I didn't hear you arrive." She straightened and paused to brush loose bark from her pants.

"Ada," he acknowledged, and tucked his hands into his pockets. "Good-morning."

"And a fine one it is." She peeled off her gloves and studied her lush herb gardens.

Rich agreed. Sunlight speared through scattered clouds, chasing morning mist from the surface of Pine Shadow Lake. Pine Bluffs, Pennsylvania was in for one spectacular day.

"Spring seldom lingers around here, but this recent warm spell gives me reason to hope." She brushed a wisp of hair aside and lifted one hand to shade her eyes. "What do you think? Is the snow done?"

"Ummm, what?"

Lowering her hand, she stepped closer. "Are you getting hard of hearing, Rich McConnell? I asked if you thought the snow was done. You know as well as I do we've been known to see Canada's chill edge south in May." She turned back to her gardens. "I hope it stays warm. My plants are hardy, but they do better if they've had spring rains and plenty of sun."

His hearing was fine, but his heart stuttered when she'd asked if he was "getting hard." Then she'd rambled on about cold Canadian air, and Rich heaved a mental sigh of relief.

He forced his attention to the herbs. "Your plants look good. Maybe Mother Nature will spare us this season."

"Maybe." Ada rolled up the sleeves of her denim shirt. "Have a seat and visit." She swept her hand to the steps of her wrap-around porch. "I need a break. Want some coffee?"

He followed her around to the front and lowered himself onto the steps leading to the wide covered porch. "Coffee? I thought tea was your brew of choice," he teased, placing his booted feet on the bottom step.

Ada laughed. "Nick McGraw is responsible for broadening my choices. In the morning, or when he needs to think, Nick claims there's nothing like a cup of strong coffee. I learned this even before he married my niece."

Rich leaned back. He smiled, resting on bent elbows. "He must take after his uncle, Tom. Tom McGraw is one of my best friends, and when he retired from the force I highly approved of Nick stepping into the position. When will Pine Bluffs new chief of police and his lovely bride be back from their honeymoon?"

Ada's face softened. "Not for at least three weeks. They've only been gone a few days. I miss them. I think Cassi's dog does too. Rufus has been moping around since they left."

Edging past him, she climbed the steps. When her leg brushed him, he jerked. Tart lemon joined forces with the scent of woman, lingering in her wake.

"What's on your mind today, Rich? You seem fidgety. On second thought, we'll both have tea. Coffee might just make you jump out of your boots." The storm door bounced shut behind her.

Rich squinted into the sun topping the trees along the lakeshore. Best to quit thinking about what he'd like to jump out of, and it sure as hell wasn't his boots.

Months ago the bottom dropped out of his comfortable, predictable world when Ada strolled into Tom and Mary McGraw's annual Christmas Eve gathering. Damn. He'd known Ada for years and always pictured her as trim, and... well, sturdy.

That night she'd looked sleek, all curvy in some kind of clingy getup. Not her usual chinos and denim. Plus, she'd done something to her eyes that made her look drop dead gorgeous. Hell, he'd never noticed her eyes before. Nor had he gawked at her extremely attractive backside. This morning while watching her pull weeds his gawking had gotten him in deep shit.

The door creaked open. Ada returned, carrying a tray. "Here." She moved forward. "I'll set our tea on the table against the wall and--"

The tray flew apart like an exploding grenade!

Scalding hot liquid stung his face, and thick cream arced like a fireworks display. Cups, saucers, and teapot crashed to the floor. In one fluid move, Rich pushed off the steps.

Frozen, Ada was staring at what remained of the tray in her hands when he slammed into her. He twisted, taking the impact as they hit the floor. Together they rolled across the porch and crashed into the wall of the cottage. Pinned beneath him, she lay motionless.

"Are you hit?" Rich scanned the woods north of the cabin. He ran a quick assessing hand over her body.

"No... I mean, *hit*? What are you talking about? You hit me," she accused in a tense whisper, and began to struggle.

"Lie still." He ordered, blood pounding in his ears. His words halted

2

her frantic efforts. He laid a hand on her cheek and turned her head, forcing her to look at him. "That was rifle fire."

Like a snared rabbit, her eyes grew wide.

"Don't move, Ada," he repeated, softening his tone. "We're protected here, and I've got to find out what the hell is going on before we stand up like targets."

She nodded, lying rigid and unblinking beneath him. Inside the cottage, Cassi McGraw's dog, Rufus, scratched at the door, whining between bursts of rapid fire barking.

"Rufus, shut up." Ada flinched, but Rich's harsh command worked. Aside from the rustling undertone of leaves fluttering in a stiff breeze, there was silence.

"Uh... Rich," Ada gasped.

He scrutinized her face. Had she been hit after all? She grimaced, wriggling beneath him. Another time, another place, he'd have welcomed the sensation, but her eyes radiated pain, and he feared the worst.

"My back. Something is cutting my back."

He lifted away from her. "Roll over, slowly," he cautioned. "Face the wall and let me get a look at you." Moving gingerly, Ada pushed onto one side.

"Oh, damn." Rich clenched his teeth. Pieces of broken glass covered her back. Thank God she wore thick denim. Nonetheless, jagged broken pieces penetrated her shirt, and blood seeped through.

"I've got to get you inside." He scrambled up and knelt by her side. "Can you move?"

"Yes, I'm fine."

Brave, yes. But she sure as hell wasn't fine.

"Okay. Move fast, keep low." Shielding her with his body, he whisked her inside.

Rufus danced at their feet, whining and woofing soft greetings. Rich nudged the dog aside and snatched up a portable phone. He punched in 911, and while relaying succinct facts to a Pine Bluffs PD dispatcher, he steered Ada away from the wide expanse of windows overlooking her gardens. Tall trees and thick brush formed a natural barrier bordering her property on two sides with the main road in front and the lake to the rear.

"Stay down," he cautioned. "The police are on their way."

Ada sank onto a low stool by the fireplace, and within seconds a distant siren began to scream. Rich moved to a window near the front door where he watched and waited, keeping out of sight until a marked car swept up Ada's driveway. Lights flashing, it rocked to a stop. The siren cut abruptly. He recognized Marcy Evans, the town's only female officer, at the wheel. Beside her, Officer Jake Montroy clutched the dash.

Rich cracked the front door, signaling to make them aware of his position. Weapons drawn, using the car as cover, Marcy and Jake exited the unit. The cruiser's hot engine clicked, cooling in the brisk, morning air.

Spattered cream, a crystal trail of sugar, and drops of blood adorned the porch floor. The wide covered porch flanked three sides of the structure. It stretched across the front, wrapped around, continuing alongside the cottage till it reached the rear, then wrapped again and stretched across the back facing the lake. Rich shook his head, how close they'd come to disaster.

He closed the door and returned to Ada. "Marcy and Jake are here," he said, crouching down to relay the news. He assessed her condition. "After they check the area, we'll get you to the Health Care Center."

Ada moved to stand. "Rich, I don't think my injuries are serious." The look he directed at her never wavered, prompting a tight smile. "All right," she admitted. "I feel like I've been napping on a bed of nails." She frowned, adding, "And I may need a tetanus booster. But I'm not going anywhere until I find out what happened out there."

"That makes two of us. I'll damn well *know* what happened out there." He placed his hand under her elbow and helped her up. "Though, before we do anything, you take off that shirt and put on something loose fitting."

Rufus glued himself to Ada's leg, panting as if he'd run a race. She rubbed his ears. "It's all right there, fella. Come on, you can keep me company while I change."

"Keep away from windows," Rich reminded.

She nodded, easing away, her movements stiff and measured.

"Do you need help getting that shirt off?"

Ada turned around very slowly. Brows raised, she speared an indignant queen-of-the-manor look at Rich. Her cool reply was directed at the dog. "Come Rufus, *you're* all the help I need."

Sexy dignity. Unable to resist, Rich grinned at her departing back.

At that moment, Montroy knocked and identified himself, redirecting Rich's attention. He opened the door and asked Jake, "Do you see anyone?"

Jake shook his head, then pulled a pen and notebook from his pocket. "You're sure there was only one shot?"

"Only one." Rich was adamant. He stepped onto the porch and closed the door. "I caught the echo as Ada and I hit the deck."

Jake stopped writing and looked up. "Is she all right?" Sharp eyes ran over Rich. "Are you?"

"I'm fine, but Ada may need medical attention. She's changing clothes." Careful to avoid the debris, Rich stooped down and ran his hand along the outside wall of the cottage. "The round knocked a tray right out of her hands. I knocked her out of the line of fire, but we rolled through all this broken shit on the deck in the process. Unfortunately, she faired the worst."

Squinting, Montroy leaned in closer. "Right there." He used his pen to point. "Just up and to the right of your hand."

Rich inched his fingers along. Sure enough, there a barely discernable hole. "Damn," he muttered, gauging the trajectory from the tree line with narrowed eyes.

He got to his feet and rubbed his hand against his jeans. "Whoever pulled that trigger was either a lousy shot, or one hell of a good one who wanted to scare the shit out of us."

"Rich, I think that's the foulest language I've ever heard come out of your mouth. And all in one sentence to boot." Marcy clomped up the steps and paused to tuck her weapon into its holster. She turned to Jake. "There's nothing out there now. I did find a spot where someone could have been standing, kinda trampled down, but it's hard to tell."

Jake frowned. "You're sure of the direction, Rich?"

"Without a doubt. I was leaning back, turned slightly away, when I detected the crack. Then the tray blew apart"

The door to the cottage opened. Ada had combed her hair and changed, but she looked shaken, her face devoid of color.

"Ada!" Marcy strode across the porch. "Are you hurt?" She threw a fast look at Rich. "Was she hit?"

"I'm not hit," Ada insisted. "I can speak for myself," she muttered as Marcy pushed into the cottage. Jake and Rich followed.

"Do we need an ambulance?" Jake pulled out his cell phone.

Rich stepped forward. "Marcy, Jake and I will go outside. You take a look at her. If you feel we need an ambulance we'll make the call. If not, I'll take her to the Vineyard Center."

He and Jake left Marcy and Ada alone.

"I'll do another sweep of the area before we leave," Jake said while they waited. "We'll talk to you both later. Right now, Ada comes first."

Within moments, the door opened. "No ambulance," Marcy said, "but she needs medical attention. Now."

Jake walked with Rich to his truck. After opening the truck's door, Rich paused. "You're a smart cop, Jake. I know you'll be thorough." His gaze flicked over Ada's gardens, on to the lake, and then back to Jake. "But be careful. If that round's what I suspect, and had hit either one of us, we'd be calling the coroner."

Chapter Two

Shadows crawled across the road, swallowing up patches of light sifting through the trees as the sun dipped low in the sky. For their return trip to Pine Bluffs, Ada propped one shoulder against the seat and faced Rich, eyes closed. The position appeared awkward, but Rich suspected it kept her injured back from rubbing the rough surface.

By the time they'd reached Vineyard Medical Center in North East, blood dotted the back of her clean shirt and a nurse whisked her away. Her injuries turned out to be superficial, though, meticulous treatment took several hours.

Ada's silence on the return trip sent a clear message. The day had taken a toll.

Rich swung into her driveway and cut the engine. Her eyes fluttered open. She pushed upright, wincing. "Ah, we're home." She heaved a sigh and reached for the door.

"Wait." Rich's hand closed on her forearm, and his sharp gaze probed twilight shadows. The annoyed look she directed at her entrapped arm made him loosen his hold. He gave her a quick pat. "I'll come around and help you."

The broken glass and shattered tray were gone and, in the fading light, faint blood spatters were a grim reminder. He nudged her through the door. "I talked with Marcy and Jake late this afternoon. They'll come back and follow up tomorrow."

Once inside, he breathed easier. She was safe for now, but nightfall was imminent, creating a big problem for Rich.

He didn't want to leave Ada alone.

Harley Phillips worked at Rich's hardware store. He agreed to cover and take care of closing the store after Rich finally tracked him down. For some damn reason he was late for work that morning. Planning ahead, Rich instructed him to open up the following day.

Call it dated chivalry, or just his overprotective nature, but Rich refused to leave an injured woman alone. He couldn't shake the feeling Ada was still in danger. So he'd made up his mind on the way back from North East that she'd not be alone that night.

Once inside her cottage he searched every room, checking windows and doors. Ada waited. She sat by the fireplace with her feet propped on an ottoman until he'd done what he had to do. For Rich, the process was as natural as breathing.

He scooped up a quilt from the sofa and draped it over her legs. Color had returned to her face, but he didn't like how vulnerable she looked huddled deep within that oversized chair.

No sense dragging his feet, he might as well make his intentions known. "I don't want to leave you alone tonight."

"I'll be fine," she declared with a dismissive flip of her hand. "Besides, I've got my watch dog here."

Rufus lay at her feet. His tail thumped when she rubbed a sock clad foot over his back, and Rich bent down and gave him a brisk rub. The watch dog rolled over, exposing his belly.

"Mind if I make some coffee?" Rich asked.

"I can--"

"No," he said, repositioning the quilt she'd started to remove. "You can't. Or, more to the point, I won't let you."

Ada stiffened. Clearly, a woman *not* used to taking orders.

Softening his voice, Rich laid his hand on her shoulder. "Let me take care of you, Ada."

She smoothed her hands over the quilt, meeting his steady gaze with a determined one of her own. "All right, but since you're making coffee, put on water for tea, please. There's cut up fruit in the refrigerator, get it out with some cheese. Oh, and some of my fresh bread. I don't know about you, but I'm starving."

Rich moved about her spotless kitchen, biting back a smile and following her succinct, detailed instructions. She was wise enough to know she should rest, yet stubborn enough to dish out orders and make sure things were done *her* way. He was at home in the familiar surroundings, and smug, knowing he'd prolonged leaving her alone.

*****

Ada's back stung. Before removing what seemed like a million tiny pieces of broken pottery, the doctor had injected painkillers. Their pain-blocking effect had worn off.

The aroma of perking coffee filled the room, soothing her and settling her jangled nerves. Rich looked quite comfortable moving about in her kitchen. He kicked off his boots and placed them by the door before removing his shirt-jacket and draping it over a chair. Nicely housebroken, she concluded, for a man who lived alone. In worn jeans and sock clad feet, he was a welcome diversion from her prickly back.

"There's a teapot in the cupboard beside the range," she offered, noting his determined search.

He turned and pointed, questioning brows raised.

"That's the one," she assured.

He rolled up the sleeves of his pullover and, as he reached up, her eyes wandered down the long length of him. Tucked into a trim waistline, the soft cotton shirt clung to broad shoulders.

Impressive.

Especially for a man who must be, oh, a few years east of fifty. When Rich bent to retrieve a dropped spoon, her eyes slipped lower. Faded, threadbare denim clung to firm hips.

Oh, my.

What was it Cassi's quirky friend Lanie, would say? Great butt? Ada pulled her reluctant gaze from Rich McConnell's backside. How long had it been since *she'd* rated a man's butt? Must be the aftereffects of the pain meds.

Amid Rich's protests, she cleared the long, low table in front of the sofa, gathered up napkins, and got out small colorful plates. Moving around actually soothed her discomfort.

Rich settled on the sofa, and she sat cross-legged on an oversized floor cushion across from him. Practically drooling, she dug into the assortment of cheese, fruit, and leftover sliced beef he'd laid out. When the platter was almost bare, Ada eased to her feet, ignoring Rich's frown. She retrieved a heaping plate of home-made, white chocolate chunk and macadamia nut cookies. His frown slid into a boyish grin, and together they made a sizeable dent in the mountain of goodies.

After dunking a cookie and savoring the tea-drenched bite, Ada swallowed and looked at Rich. "Your quick reaction caught me by surprise today. Law enforcement background?"

"Close," Rich said. "I was in the Corps, the Marines. A rifle crack, a shattered tray." He shrugged. "I didn't need a road map. Training kicked in, and I reacted."

"You certainly did." She sipped, eyeing him over the rim of her cup. "When you asked if I'd been hit, I couldn't focus. I was still trying to figure out how I ended up on the floor, and why I felt as if a dozen needles were stuck in me."

She straightened, reached around, and gingerly lifted her shirt. Every once in a while the fabric caught a tender spot. Sitting here talking with Rich helped take her mind off the discomfort. "Tell me about the Marines. How long were you in, when did you serve? Where?"

Rich slouched into the sofa and stretched out long legs. "My stint was between Vietnam and Desert Storm, mid seventy's to early ninety's. In many ways I was lucky. I never saw combat, but in the military there are always risks."

Puzzled, Ada said, "If you didn't see combat, what was the danger. What risks?"

"I was twenty-one when I joined the Corps. After basic, about three years into my stint, I was chosen along with close to sixty other marines for special duty at a little known naval ammunition depot on the east coast."

"Secret stuff?"

"Very." His eyes lit with humor. "We called it 'secret squirrel duty'."

"Some tough Marines," Ada scoffed.

"Actually, the duty required top secret/cripto clearance and, almost to a man, the group exuded the best of the Corps."

Ada waited, expecting to hear more, but Rich just scooped up another cookie. He studied it for a long moment, took a bite, and pushed off the sofa. Sipping coffee, he circled the room. At each window he paused and, like a silent sentinel, peered out into the deepening twilight. Physically, Rich was but a few feet from her, but Ada suspected his mind was far, far away, in the distant past.

Almost to a man? She reflected, recalling his words. He may not have seen combat, but something happened while Rich McConnell served his country.

*****

Thinking about the *Group*, stirred bittersweet memories. In order to distract Ada, to take her mind off her discomfort, he'd dredged up past history. Now he regretted the direction her questions had taken them.

He peered into midnight darkness surrounding the cabin. Ada more than likely sensed his mood change and let the conversation die. Smart woman. Maybe someday he'd tell her why he walked away from an exciting career and bought a hardware store in remote western Pennsylvania.

Ada gathered their empty plates and cups. "It's getting late, Rich." She moved away, balancing her load. "I'd like to know more about that secret squirrel stuff, but the day's catching up with me. I'm sure you need rest too."

Rich rubbed a hand across his face. Coarse stubble rasped beneath his palm. How in the hell was he going to convince this stubborn, independent woman he was going to spend the night?'

Chapter Three

Ada groaned aloud. Except for a narrow path of light across the floor, her bedroom was cool and dark. The lowered shade allowed only a sliver of sunlight to penetrate the room.

She'd been exhausted last night, half asleep when Rich came into her bedroom. Moving silently on sock-clad feet, he lowered the shades and retreated, leaving the door slightly ajar.

Figures, she mused, folding the covers aside. The first time a man enters her bedroom in years he's there to pull the shades.

She pushed to a sitting position. Testing, she rolled her shoulders and sharp needle-like prickles made her wince. Nope, yesterday was not a bad dream, and the man who'd toured her bedroom last night was still in her home.

Not in her bedroom. That thought was... intriguing, but no, he'd spent the night on her sofa after somehow convincing her she shouldn't be alone. Clever man. In the light of day, she was surprised by how easily he'd persuaded her, *and* how quickly she'd agreed. Being bone-deep tired probably had something to do with it.

She drew up her knees and hugged them close. The stretch to her back felt good. Not a youngster any more. She was east of fifty, just like Rich, and she mentally thanked her niece Cassi for pushing her to stay fit.

Though the business she started years ago kept Ada in shape, Cassi was an educated fitness instructor who insisted Ada needed to do more than lift forty pound bags of organic fertilizer.

Cassi designed an individual fitness regimen for her and, after a few weeks, Ada could tell the difference. Now lifting those forty pound bags and moving mountains of shredded bark seemed less of a struggle.

Along with her herb gardens, Ada owned a half acre of fruit bearing bushes. Her plans to expand came to a screeching halt yesterday shortly after Rich delivered a rented tiller. She worked hard to make her organic herb business successful, and some idiot taking potshots at her was damn annoying. Producing gardens took years to establish, and plans to expand with the addition of more berry bushes where in the works. Lost time for a serious gardener could be disastrous.

Ada swung her feet to the floor. She paused, further assessing her injuries. Fortunately there'd been no need for stitches. Strips of tape covered the worst cuts and, though she felt them when she moved, the discomfort was tolerable.

A rich, potent smell wafted into the room. Ah, coffee. Although she seldom drank the stronger brew, for some reason this morning its rich, tantalizing smell made her mouth water.

Best get dressed and face the day.

Ada slipped on her robe and headed for the bathroom. She spied a damp towel hanging next to hers and grinned, picturing Rich drying his rugged face with her fluffy, apple green towels. Before retiring, she'd had the presence of mind to lay the towel out for him along with a washcloth and a spare toothbrush.

Unfortunately, she didn't stock men's shaving supplies.

Fortunately, she did have a vivid imagination. And took a moment to indulge in the brief fantasy of a bare-chested Rich wielding a razor on his lean jaw.

Then reality struck.

She gawked at the image in the mirror over the sink.

Oh. My. God.

The vision staring back at her was no fantasy. It was a nightmare. She bore a scary resemblance to the witch in Snow White, *Queen Grimhilde.*

Flat on one side, her hair drooped limply over her forehead. Dark circles ringed her eyes. She looked like a hung-over, sleepy raccoon having a bad hair day.

Injured or not, she was hitting the shower.

Rich looked up when at last she strolled into the kitchen. After luxuriating in a long shower, she spent considerable time repairing her appearance. His gaze did a slow sweep, head to toe and back.

When his eyes finally met hers, she smiled. "Big improvement since last night, huh?"

Rich returned her smile, and she moved to a simmering kettle. She added several tea bags to a porcelain pot and filled it to the brim. Steam bellowed, and a rich aroma filled the air as she retrieved a cup.

She shot a glance at Rich. He sipped coffee, leaning against the counter with his long legs crossed at the ankle. Dark circles beneath his eyes were telling. Yet, despite obvious fatigue, he looked rugged and rakishly handsome.

"How's your back this morning?"

"It's fine," Ada replied, spoon clinking as she stirred a hefty amount of cream into her tea. "The shower did sting a bit, but after coming face to face with myself this morning, I had no choice. My goodness, Rich," she admonished. "Why didn't you tell me what a fright I was last night?"

He shrugged, and chuckled as she grinned at him over the rim of her cup. Lifting a brow, she was about to comment when Rufus woofed softly and scrambled from beneath the table. His tail whipped side to side as he dashed to the door. According to Rufus, whoever had arrived presented no threat. Ada set her tea aside and moved to the kitchen window.

"Oh, no." She sighed. "No secrets in this town."

Resigned, she grasped the dog's collar and opened the door.

Mary McGraw, Molly Hirtzel, Lois Farrell, and Katy Kunzelman clamored up the steps. Molly led the pack. "Ada, oh my goodness." She paused to catch her breath. "We overheard you'd been shot!"

Lois crowded up behind Molly. "Not shot," she said, giving Molly a gentle shove. They both squeezed inside. "Shot *at*."

"Girls," Ada began, releasing Rufus. "I'm fine, and--"

Katy burst through the door. Barely stopping, she shot right past Lois and Molly. She grasped both Ada's hands, and with dark, worried eyes assessed Ada head to toe. "Were you hit?" she demanded.

Ada cast a glance at Mary, Lois and Molly, her peers. It occurred to her Katy was at least two and a half decades younger. She was new in town, and the attractive, dark haired girl, had recently joined their exercise group. Her presence in class was like a shot of adrenalin at each session. They welcomed Katy's bubbling exuberance. At the moment, she bubbled with concern.

Mary joined them and together, tightly packed against one another just inside the door, they faced Ada.

"I'm fine," Ada repeated, squeezing Katy's hands. "Where did you hear about the uh... problem we had here yesterday?"

No one responded.

Distracted, their eyes fixed beyond her, looks of surprise, concern, puzzlement, and one tongue in cheek smile, crossed their faces. Without turning, Ada knew what grabbed their collective interest.

Rich McConnell.

Katy stood stock still. Ada released the younger girl's hands and turned around. Her gaze met Rich's amused eyes. Leaning against the counter, hair mussed, tee shirt untucked, Rich looked quite at home.

From the corner of her eye she saw Mary McGraw step forward and wrap one arm around Katy's rigid shoulders. "Why, Rich," Mary said, her voice smooth as butter. "What a nice surprise. I thought I recognized your truck outside."

He smiled, tipping his cup in greeting. "Morning, Mary, ladies. How did you find out?"

"At the hardware store this morning," Katy piped up. "Harley told me. I called *everyone* and we rushed right over."

Ada wasn't surprised. Harley, an intense man with a propensity for gossip, often put work on hold to catch up with what was goin' on in Pine Bluffs. He'd wasted no time spreading the news.

"Figures," Rich muttered. "Can't be found when I need him, yet manages to know everything going on in town."

Rufus squeezed past to greet Jake and Marcy as they came through the door.

Marcy's eyes widened. "Good-morning, everyone."

Jake nodded a greeting to the assembled group and, typical Jake, got right to the point. "Ada, Rich, We're here to finish getting your statements and tie up any loose ends."

Ada herded her friends toward the door. "How about we meet at the Brown Cow tomorrow? We'll know more by then, and I'll share whatever turns up," she promised, as she guided her concerned friends through the door.

Once they'd departed, Jake set about questioning Rich and Ada.

"That covers the time right before and after the shot," Jake said, concluding the interview. He turned to Rich. "I'd like to recon the area again. I could use a fresh pair of eyes, Rich."

"I'll stay here with Ada," Marcy said. "I can check inside her cottage since we didn't get to do that yesterday."

Jake nodded agreement, and Rich followed him out the door.

"Do you mind if I take a look around, Ada?"

"Of course not. But if you don't need me, I think I'll take Rufus and sit on the porch."

Marcy scrutinized her carefully. "I think that's a good idea. You still look a little pale. If I have any questions, I'll come and get you."

Ada called Rufus. She grabbed a light sweater from a hook by the door, draped it gently over her shoulders, and stepped outside. Rufus looked longingly after the departing men, but she called him back and made him sit by her chair.

She took stock of her gardens. Early shoots, a green haze against the fading browns of winter, reached for the sun's life-giving rays. She vowed to put the shooting incident behind her, to move forward, and concentrate on expanding her gardens. Newly purchased berry stock would arrive soon, and her spirits lifted thinking about how they'd mature and hang heavy with fruit in a few short years.

Along the wood line bordering her land, she regarded Jake and Rich. They moved in and out amongst the trees, stopping every so often. She fixed her gaze on Rich's tall, broad shouldered outline and something inside her tightened. The same reaction his scruffy sleepy-eyed appearance induced when she'd watched him in her kitchen last night.

How long had it been since a man's closeness stirred sexy thoughts? Thinking of Rich that way unsettled her. It also excited her.

*****

When Rich and Jake returned, the two women were sitting on the porch. Ada considered their grim expressions as she looked from one man to the other. "Any luck?" she asked, leaning forward. The movement made her wince, a sobering reminder.

"No." Jake raked a hand through his hair. "I was hoping we'd find a shell casing, something to go on. The only clue we found was a roughened spot on the bark of a tree."

Ada frowned. "Which tells us?"

Rich propped his backside on the porch railing. "If someone sighted in and braced against a tree, when they fired it might disturb the surface."

Someone used one of *her* trees to take aim at them. Ada shoved out of her chair. The very idea sent an icy chill rushing over her.

She crossed her arms and gave them a brisk rub.

Rich undid her arms, and took her chilled fingers between his hands.

It felt good. She'd forgotten how comforting a masculine touch could be.

A quick look passed between Marcy and Jake. Ada gave Rich's hands a squeeze and pulled hers away. He stepped back and, tucking his hands into his pockets, resettled his hip on the railing. It occurred to Jake and me it could have been a hunter's wild shot."

When Ada raised a questioning brow, he explained, "Spring Gobbler season runs from late April through May twenty-fifth. We've both seen hunters around. I talked to a couple not far from here last week."

Ada wasn't buying it. Her gaze swung from Rich to Jake.

Turkey hunting, indeed.

Marcy pushed out of her chair and pointed to the wall behind Ada. "Jake, you and Rich claim this was the point of entry. Let's go inside."

Rich pushed away from the railing and all three trailed Marcy into the kitchen. She pointed across the room to the sliding door at the back of the house.. "Over here," she said, crossing and indicating a neat little hole in the wide oak trim surrounding the door. "I figured a round fired from about two-hundred yards would lose little altitude. So while you were gone, I followed the path of trajectory and bingo."

Jake leaned in close. He'd barely touched the edge of the hole when something hit the floor with a soft clunk. He fished in his pocket and produced a small plastic bag. Marcy handed him her pen. Using the tip of the pen, he slid the small piece of metal into the bag and held it up.

"Damn," he muttered, handing the bag to Rich.

"M-14." Rich's voice came out flat, his eyes turned hard. He handed the spent bullet back to Jake. "The round's intact, except the tip mushroomed upon final impact."

"They don't hunt gobblers with 7.62 millimeter rounds." Jake examined the misshapen object closer. "I was in the Corps too, Rich. In some circles the M-14 is a trained snipers best friend."

Ada's breath caught.

Sniper?

Chapter Four

Ada drizzled scented oil into the rumbling flow and swirled her fingers through the frothy water. Every muscle in her body ached. She eased into the liquid warmth, and a lemony vapor enveloped her. At first, the tiny wounds on her back prickled and burned, but as she sank up to her chin the silky water soothed.

Marcy and Jake had been there most of the day. They'd gone over details until she was ready to scream. To be honest, she was getting more than a little annoyed by the repetition. When all was said and done, all their hard work produced nothing except a spent rifle round. Jake must have a notebook full of details, but the slightly flattened bullet was the only hard evidence they possessed.

They'd also questioned anyone who might have been passing by or in the area when the shot was fired. No luck there. Whoever pulled the trigger that morning seemed to have arrived undetected and then vanished into thin air.

Rich, of course, kept checking on her. In exasperation, she'd finally pointed out firmly that he had a store to run, and that the Pine Bluffs patrols promised to keep an eye on her.

At the end of the day, he arrived on her doorstep one last time. He appeared satisfied to find a marked patrol unit parked at the entrance to her driveway and promised to come back the next day. Then finally... *finally*, he went home.

She appreciated everyone's concern, but Ada was more than ready to be left alone. Maybe then she could relax and get back to normal. With the end of the long, arduous day in sight, all she wanted was to pamper her tired, abused body and let her frazzled mind rest.

So, Ada escaped. Eyes closed, chin deep in airy bubbles, she settled into her private spa.

She'd splurged on the old-fashioned porcelain tub. Deep and spacious, it was surrounded by a ledge holding soaps, lotions, and sponges. Depending on the degree of desired stress relief, candles, and a glass of chilled wine often joined the assortment. Tonight, the aroma of vanilla scented votives mingled with the lemon-scented oil, and within easy reach was a tall, brimming, glass of chardonnay.

An eye level window provided an unobstructed view of her gardens and Pine Shadow Lake. A golden path, paved by the sun, rode on the lake's glasslike surface as twilight blanketed her domain, and her tension ebbed away.

Two days of being buffeted about in a whirlwind of stress triggered unexpected feelings. Long forgotten feelings which rose like bubbles in a stirred cauldron of emotion. Could she risk exposing herself to long buried passion? Could she trust, or maybe even love again?

She sponged her arms and legs, letting the scent of citrus tickle her nose and the warm water soothe her injuries. Lifting one leg high, she stroked the smoothness and trailed her hand up to gently sponge her breasts. Her nipples drew tight and she clenched her thighs.

Behind closed eyelids, she imagined intense tawny eyes, a mussed head of sandy hair, and strong hands with long, lean fingers. Imagined making love. Something Ada hadn't thought about in a very long time.

John had been her first lover. She married him, and their lovemaking had been lusty and fulfilling. Tears formed and she blinked them away, forcing herself to concentrate on soft candlelight, flickering and dancing on the bathroom ceiling. Back then, she'd been insatiable. But physical desire had died along with John in a fiery car crash, or so she'd thought until, like petals of a flower unfolding, once again something stirred within her.

Her tight reign on emotions, kept locked inside for many years, eased when Cassi came back into her life. On her deathbed, Ada's estranged sister, Alison, begged her to care for her newborn baby. But John's death had crushed her, leaving her unable to care for her tiny orphaned niece, and Cassi had been adopted. Years passed and Ada healed, though she'd never lost track of her sister's child. A child everyone *assumed* was the only one Alison gave birth to all those years ago. Besides Alison, no one knew Cassi had a twin. The existence of another child, ill, damaged, and abandoned, was a secret Ada's sister took to her grave.

When Cassi's adoptive parents perished in a plane crash, Ada was given a second chance.

She welcomed Cassi with open arms, and in return, the young woman opened her heart. The circle widened when Cassi fell in love and married a man from Pine Bluffs. Upon returning from their honeymoon, Pine Bluffs would be Cassi and Nick McGraw's home.

The water turned tepid, and several candles sputtered out. Ada closed simple bifold shutters over the window. She got to her feet, skimmed her hands over her skin and, grabbing a thick towel, stepped from the tub. Goosebumps sprung up, and she rubbed them briskly away, continuing to reflect on the recent past and how random events paved a rocky, dangerous road for Nick and Cassi. For when Alison's abandoned baby, Cassi's twin, aka Sadie Mitchell, discovered Cassi, she set out to destroy her.

She'd have succeeded, too, if not for Nick and TJ McGraw.

Nick met Cassi while on vacation in Pine Bluffs, where his cousin TJ was a member of Pine Bluffs PD. Nick arrived just in time to meet Cassi, who had journeyed to town after her parent's death in order to meet Ada. A strained, cautious meeting at first.

Nick and Cassi's meeting was quite unconventional, too, Ada recalled, bending down to blow out the remaining candles.

While walking silly Rufus, her newly adopted pup, the dog led Cassi to Robert Burch. Unfortunately, Mr. Burch was dead. Nick stumbled on the scene and immediately determined the man had been stabbed to death. Though on vacation, Nick *was* a detective for Philly Pd and had no choice but to turn Cassi over to the local police.

One thing led to another and, though eventually cleared, Cassi was questioned about the murder which resulted in the news story that caught Sadie's attention.

Nick fell in love with Cassi, and TJ's astute, determined police work saved Cassi's life when a deranged Sadie tracked her down and tried to kill her. Sadie didn't survive. Ada suspected Nick would be forever grateful to his cousin, TJ, for saving the woman he loved.

Shivering, Ada's thoughts returned to the present. She finished drying, dropped the towel, and slathered on cream. Her reflection in the free-standing mirror at the end of the room caught her attention. She gazed at the lean line of her body, and a flush of warmth rushed over her. Lifting the long-stemmed wine glass, she toasted her naked self and finished the golden chardonnay.

Thank God for this second opportunity with Cassi. Was it possible what she felt while watching Rich move about her kitchen yesterday was another layer unfolding? Until now, making love was a remote, forgotten sensation.

But Rich McConnell made her body tighten and her blood heat.

*****

Rich stepped onto the balcony overlooking the long, narrow expanse of lawn behind his apartment. He'd purchased the carriage house when he moved to Pine Bluffs, at a good price, too. Over the years, he'd renovated the tall narrow structure he now called home.

Initially, the building was several rooms above a two-stall garage and storage area which had once been a large stable. He'd enlarged the overall structure, knocked down walls, opened spaces, and refitted doors and windows. Backbreaking work. But in the end, he'd created a spacious area that spilled onto the second floor balcony where he now stood sipping a cold beer and watching the sun set.

Beside him were a tiny table, two swivel chairs, and a folding lounge which could easily hold two. Not that he ever shared the lounge. His short lived marriage had failed miserably long before he moved to Pine Bluffs. Since then he'd been leery of entanglements, and any relationships were discreet.

Calling his ships-in-the-night encounters relationships was stretching the truth. Lately, the only ships in *his* night were freighters he watched entering the city of Erie's harbor when he occasionally dined at Smuggler's on the bayfront.

His property stretched to Pine Shadow Lake. From the balcony he could see his inboard, a sleek sixteen footer, tied to the squat, square dock beyond the cattails. Like Ada's , his view of the lake was unobstructed. Though she lived on the other side of town, he suspected she valued her privacy and isolation from lights and traffic as much as he did his.

Life was good. Didn't he have everything a man could want? His business thrived, so he lived comfortably. He'd splurged on a boat and restored a classic Volvo, which he only drove on perfect days.

Then two days ago an M-14 round barely missed a woman he cared about, very much. More than once that day she'd sent his hormones into overdrive. If not mistaken, she'd been aware of him, too. Where the hell did all this awareness leave them?

His phone jangled and, stepping through his patio door, he scooped up the receiver. "Hello."

"Rich, how ya been, bro?" Gary Wilson's voice was unmistakable. Deep brown eyes, fanned by tiny lines, and a lanky body came to mind. The body, in all probability, was draped across a comfortable chair.

"Hey, you old son-of-a-bitch, what's up?"

Rich and Gary had served in the Corps together many years before, though it seemed like yesterday. The tall, thin, black man had been an anchor through some rough times.

His raucous laughter rang out as Rich plopped onto a tall stool.

"Not much," Gary said. "Just wanted ta hear your sorry-ass voice. Not cuttin' in on a hot session with a wild woman, am I?"

"Hell, no. One just left and the next one doesn't get here for another half hour."

A rush of memories hit Rich. Hot summer nights and endless long-necked bottles of beer when off base. Catching night duty together at the depot, they'd stop on rounds of the perimeter, park, and, in silence, watch the star studded sky.

"God, it's good to hear your voice. How are Latisha and the girls? Hell, they must be in college by now."

"College? Dumb white boy, I'm a granddaddy. Rene graduated last month and is off to law school, and Suzette presented me with my first grandson in January." Pride bubbled in Gary's voice.

Rich rose and strolled back onto the balcony. A stiff evening breeze had sprung up and he settled against the railing, absently watching ripples on the water as the light faded. "That's great. Gary. You've worked hard to raise those kids, you deserve some pay back."

For a very long moment, he listened to the early evening chorus from the cattails on the shore. One by one, tiny hairs on the back of his neck rose. "Gary, something tells me this isn't purely a social call."

Another long moment passed in silence. "He's out, Rich. They let the bastard out."

"I'm not surprised. He only got fifteen to twenty, and I figured he'd walk before the twenty was up." Rich frowned into the darkness as the waterfront chorus increased.

"I figured as much, too. But Sam, you remember Sam? He spotted

18

Steiner recently in Asbury Park. If he's hooked up with his old pals that could mean trouble."

Rich recalled Sam. The guy was regular Navy and had been stationed at the base the same time as he and Gary. It had been tricky when Will Steiner had suddenly been pulled from the Group. Sam and Will had hung out occasionally, took weekend leave, and hitched up to New York City.

Then it had hit the fan, and Steiner was whisked away before anyone knew what had happened. His actions were a major security risk, and unfortunately, Rich had been the one to blow the whistle. Now, a shiver ran up his spine as he remembered the silent, narrow-eyed look Will gave him as two men from the Office of Naval Intelligence firmly, but quietly, led him from the barracks just before dawn that day. He'd never forgotten that moment. To his knowledge, Sam had never seen his drinking buddy again, and it had been tough for Rich to pretend he didn't have a clue where the guys from ONI had taken Will.

Rich switched ears and walked back inside. "Hey, don't sweat it. He doesn't know where I am. Besides, if I know Steiner, it won't be long before his ass is right back in the slammer."

They continued to talk. Rich got more updates from the new granddad, and elicited a promise to have pictures via e-mail soon. They caught up with mundane details, and hung up promising to try harder to keep in touch.

He made a pot of strong coffee. It was way too late for ingesting caffeine, but Rich needed the jolt. He wanted to feel it snake through his system while he watched the night.

As he watched and listened to the sounds of life along the shore, every nerve in his body was on alert.

Chapter Five

Ada turned the corner onto Lake Street and caught sight of the ice cream parlor, fondly referred to as *The Cow* by locals. She'd decided to walk into town, taking the shorter route along the lakeshore and breathing in the smell of spring from breathtaking azaleas along the way. As she drew closer, she could make out her friends seated before one of two bow windows flanking The Brown Cow's entry.

She quickened her step. She loved the popular spot, a charming combination of old and new. The glass tabletops were a showcase for items displayed for sale. While sipping sodas, or scooping up mountainous sundaes, customers could view the quaint assortment of watches and fancy pens. Lois Farrell and her sister inherited the parlor when their parents passed away soon after Ada moved to Pine Bluffs. The unchanged ambiance pleased her every time she walked through the door.

Through the window Ada noticed Katy -- hands waving, dark, curly, head bobbing -- seated next to Mary and Molly. She stepped inside, breathing in the sweet smell of butterscotch. From behind the counter Lois waved, and overhead fans turned lazily, stirring the sweet smell as Ada crossed the room.

Chrome and glass fixtures behind the counter gleamed, a stark contrast to the old fashioned octagon-shaped wooden tables. The chairs around those tables matched the chrome, except for a tiny band of wood serving as a backrest and seats which bore a striking resemblance to the hide of brown and white cows.

Eclectic? Definitely, but it worked.

"There you are." Katy leaped up. She pulled out the chair next to her. "Get over here, we've been waiting forever!"

Ada glanced at the clock on the wall. The smiling cow face indicated it was ten minutes after two. *Forever* must equal ten minutes.

"Oh Katy, sit down." Molly exclaimed.

"I'm a few minutes late," Ada confessed, winking at Molly Hirtzel over Katy's head. She sat and her eyes swept the table. "What a perfect spring day. I passed your place, Molly, and your azaleas are gorgeous."

"They are," Katy declared eyes wide. "The colors are unbelievable. But I don't want to hear about herbs and flowers." She flipped her hand dismissively. "I want to hear about the hunky hardware guy."

A tall milkshake-filled glass plunked down in front of Ada. "Thanks, Lois," she said, and touched the hand her friend placed on her shoulder.

Lois gave her a quick pat. "Vanilla, right?"

"As always." Ada sipped, then pulled a napkin from a tall two-sided holder and wiped away a foamy white mustache.

She glanced around the table. "I'll get to Rich in a moment. First, I want to clear the air about what happened at my place so everyone can quit worrying."

The gathered group grew silent, and she began, "Someone fired a shot on my property. I'll not tell you I wasn't scared," she declared. "I was terrified when I figured out what happened. But thank God it missed us."

"What do the cops say?" Katy slurped her root beer float.

"Not much to say. They recovered the bullet, and they know what kind of gun was used." She shrugged. "So far that's it. The trail ends there."

Ada turned her attention back to the impatient Katy. "As for Rich being at my place that morning," she continued. "He's a gentleman, and, as a gentleman, he was concerned for my well-being. I'd been injured and he insisted on staying the night. He slept on my couch and he made tea for me the next morning. Nothing any good friend wouldn't do."

She placed her hand on Katy's arm. So young. The girl was so young and ready to see love at every turn. She leaned in, close to Katy's ear and whispered "That's *all* there is to my night with the hunky hardware man."

Katy grinned. She turned and placed an unexpected kiss on Ada's cheek. "I know chemistry when I see it, and there was chemistry in your kitchen that morning."

Much later, after chatting over their indulgent treats, they spilled out onto the sun drenched sidewalk and prepared to go their separate ways.

Having left Rufus home alone longer than expected, Ada accepted Mary's offer to drive her back to her cottage. She knew from past experience impatient dogs could shred screen doors. She also sensed something was on Mary's mind.

"Mary, you're too quiet. Has Tom mentioned something about the shooting I should know about?" She asked as she fastened her seat belt.

Mary lowered her window, looked out, and pulled onto Lake Street. "He and I are concerned, honey. It wasn't that long ago they found Robert Burch's dead body not far from your place. Or, how in the line of duty TJ had to shoot Cassi's psychotic twin sister to save Cassi right in your back yard."

Two dead bodies in about as many weeks had been a record for Pine Bluffs. Ada recalled the night Mary's son saved Cassi from Sadie Mitchell.

Anxious, she shot Mary a swift look. "Tom's retired, but he *was* chief of police in Pine Bluffs and I suspect he keeps his finger on the town's pulse. What does he know?"

"Tom spoke to Jake. But there's nothing to tie the shooting to what happened before. Believe me, my friend." Mary glanced her way. "They don't know more than what they told you."

"Hmmm." Ada gazed at small shops slipping past. There hadn't been an obvious connection to Burch's murder and her niece either, until Sadie Mitchell came after Cassi that horrible October night and they discovered the connection *had* been Burch's body.

"Ada?"

"Sorry, mind's wandering."

"Don't go there."

"I can't help myself, Mary. If not for your TJ, I might not have Cassi in my life." She paused, shaking off the past and asked, "Speaking of TJ, how is he? Does he like being a state trooper?"

Mary's eyes brightened as she brought Ada up to date on her only son. "He's in a patrol unit out of Erie headquarters and seems very happy. With his education and background, he's hoping to get transferred to a crime unit. I think Pennsylvania got a deal when they hired Thomas Jacob McGraw," she concluded proudly, and slowed to turn up the lane to Ada's cottage.

Ada began to gather her things. "Pine Bluffs *lost* a good policeman and *gained* a great new chief. It's what they both wanted, and that's what matters."

Mary parked and turned to her. "I'm wondering about something, though."

"What's that?"

"I'm afraid I agree with Katy. Rich looked very much at home in your kitchen. Maybe you should invite him for dinner, explore the possibilities."

Ada opened her mouth, closed it. Her cheeks grew warm.

Mary's one brow shot up. "You're blushing," she exclaimed. "Are you sure you told Katy the whole story?"

Ada opened the door, "Stay a while. I'll make tea and we'll talk."

They settled on Ada's sprawling back porch. Mary sniffed the air. "Ah, your herbs are thriving this spring. Smell that mint, and your parsley's early. Everything looks gorgeous."

Ada placed a tray on the table between them. Her gaze swept the wood line and down the path to the lake while Mary looked on. Off to the left a barnlike storage shed held her tools, everything she needed to run her business. Restaurants from all over the county relied on her supply of fresh herbs and berries. She'd learned how to grow and maintain her plants at the knee of her grandmother years ago, and the thought of having her very livelihood being threatened chilled her through and through.

"You're still uneasy."

"A little," Ada admitted. She poured their tea and settled into a chair. "I'm so used to doing this." She swept her hand over the cups and serving items. "Now I wonder if every time I do, I'll remember that day."

"Did you hear the shot?"

"I honestly don't remember. Rich grabbed me, and I was on the floor beneath him before I could think."

"Well," Mary remarked. "That situation could have been exciting in itself."

"You're as bad as Katy," Ada scoffed, and pushed the shooting incident aside. "Just because you and Tom still act like teenagers, it doesn't mean everyone craves..."

"A little nookie?" Mary suggested.

Ada laughed aloud. She relaxed and stretched out her legs. How blessed she was to have a friend like Mary who softened the bad things and helped her deal with them.

Rufus appeared at the screen and whined, his soulful eyes begging to join them. She rose and opened the door. He brushed past her and shot straight to Mary for attention.

"I've been keeping him close to the cottage," Ada admitted. "If anything happened to him, Cassi would never forgive me." She groped in a battered wicker basket, retrieved a tattered tennis ball, and tossed it into the yard. Rufus bounded after it, but he soon tired of the game and headed for the lake. Ada returned and stood by the railing, keeping a watchful eye on him.

"Can I ask you a personal question, Ada?"

"You can ask me anything."

"Your husband John died in a tragic accident. You've never talked much about him, is it to painful?" Mary's eyes grew dark with compassion.

Ada glanced at Rufus prancing along the lakeshore. A large stick protruded from his mouth, his tail a banner in the wind. Satisfied he was safe, she returned to her seat. "You've often told me Tom still takes your breath away."

Mary smiled. "That I can't deny."

"I know in my heart if John were alive today I'd still love him. From the moment we met, he swept me off my feet. He was the love of my life, there's never been another."

Mary's expression turned thoughtful. "You've never been involved with another man since John? Surely there's been someone."

Ada set her rocker in motion. "Before I moved from Erie to Pine Bluffs, all my friends, my well-meaning friends," she avowed, giving Mary a tiny smile, "would set me up. You know the deal. I'd like you to meet my cousin, brother, dentist, you fill in the blank."

Mary cocked her head to one side. "Did you ever oblige them?"

"Oh, once and a while. When I moved away, and that was over twenty years ago, I lost touch with most of them. They meant well, but I needed to restart my life. To move on."

Rufus burst from tall grass along the shore and loped onto the porch. He headed straight for his bowl and, after gulping water with noisy gusto, collapsed in a heap beside her chair. Absently stroking his fur, she fixed her gaze on Mary. "There's never been anyone since John. I've had dates. I guess that's what you'd call them. I even had a weekend fling once." She folded her hands in her lap. "Does that surprise you?"

"I'd be surprised if you hadn't," Mary admitted. "Tom can still make me, uh..."

"Smile, giggle, blush?" Ada teased.

"You know what I mean." Color flushed Mary's cheeks as she sipped her tea.

"Multiple orgasms?"

Mary sputtered, grabbing a napkin to blot her dripping chin.

Ada shook her head. "We are so pathetic. Younger girls have no qualms asking one another how many times their partners 'got them off' or made them 'come'. We've experienced it, Mary. We just never talked about it."

Mary grinned. "So, how was your 'fling'?"

"Disappointing. Humiliating. Wrong. All of the above. It was also a long time ago," she added. "Since then, I've built a comfortable life. Do I miss having someone who loves me, someone I can love in return? Yes, sometimes I do. But I have wonderful friends." She took Mary's hand and squeezed. "And family. Since Cassi's come back into my life I feel more alive, more aware."

"Um hmm. Then I'm sure you've noticed Rich is an attractive man."

"He is. Though something tells me, warns me, he comes with complications. Do you know what happened to his first marriage?"

Mary shook her head. "When Rich bought the hardware store and moved here, at first he was very withdrawn. We knew he was retired military, and since Tom had been in the service, eventually he and Rich became friends. I asked Tom once if Rich ever mentioned his ex."

"What did he say?"

"Rich dedicated his life to his military career. According to him she didn't like coming second, so one day she just walked out."

Ada frowned. "Just like that, he let her go? That doesn't sound like Rich," she mused. "He's very attentive around women."

"I've always thought so, too," Mary continued. "I think he's dated, but I've never met anyone he's taken out. And I think... Ada?"

"Huh? Oh, sorry. I was thinking about what you said."

"About never meeting any of Rich's dates?"

"No, about how attentive he is, *and* how handsome. His eyes, did you ever notice his eyes? They're a unique shade of golden brown, like dark clover honey. Except the day of the shooting," she mused. "I was on my back trying to figure out what happened. I looked up and his eyes turned hard and tawny gold like the eyes of a jungle cat.

"You noticed his eyes while someone was shooting at you?"

Heat crept up Ada's neck. "Strange, huh? He's kept himself in shape, too. Probably his background. There's not an inch of extra flesh on him," she said half to herself. "He's solid, all muscle."

Mary fanned her face. "I think it's time you took Katy's advice. Ask him over for dinner. You're a marvelous cook. Encourage him, maybe he's shy."

"*Shy*?" Ada croaked, "I don't think so, Mary."

Mary's brow shot up. "Really? Maybe you've triggered something in the man. Ask him to dinner," she repeated. She placed a hand on Ada's knee, gave a rub and a pat, then rose, preparing to leave.

Ada got to her feet. She was about to walk Mary to her car when a low growl came from behind them. Rufus walked stiff-legged to the edge of the porch. Ada latched onto his collar. Her gaze swept over the yard where a gentle breeze ruffled her herb plants and rippled the surface of the lake. Shadows shifted within the trees beyond the berry patch.

Rufus rumbled out another warning, and goosebumps sprung up on her arms.

"Take him inside," Mary said urgently.

Tugging Rufus along, she managed to get through the door. Inside when she released her hold, he dashed from door to door stopping to listen at each one.

What set him off?

Mary's arm came around her, steering her away from the sliding glass door. Rufus continued his frantic pacing and growling, and Mary reached for the phone.

Paralyzed, her knees threatening to buckle, Ada sank into a chair.

Maybe the shot hadn't been random, or accidental.

Chapter Six

Jake searched Ada's property for the second time in less than three days. Though by the time he'd arrived, Rufus was chomping dog biscuits and seemed to have forgotten whatever set him off.

Feeling a bit foolish, Ada sent Jake and Mary on their way. She prepared a simple dinner and retired early. Evening passed without further incident and her previous urgency faded.

Early the next morning Cassi called. She sounded so happy, and said they were having a wonderful time. Ada didn't want to ruin their long-delayed honeymoon, and assured Cassi all was fine at home.

She rationalized that omitting wasn't lying, and spent the remainder of the morning tilling her garden. After showering, she loaded the tiller in the back of her CRV and returned it to the hardware store.

"Morning Harley," she called.

Harley paused from sweeping the entry and strolled forward. "Mornin' Mrs. Blaine, here, let me help you with that." He removed the tiller, slammed the rear hatch shut, and wheeled it into the store.

"Is Rich around?" She asked, shouldering her purse and following him.

"He'll be back shortly," Harley called over his shoulder, maneuvering the tiller toward a rear door. "He went to the bank. I have to put this out back, just make yourself ta home."

After dragging the machine outside, Harley pulled a cigarette from his shirt pocket. He cupped it with one hand, lit the end, and took a deep drag. Ada shook her head. If Rich saw him smoking within sight of customers she suspected he'd not be happy. She wasn't sure he'd forgiven Harley when he couldn't find him the morning of the shooting. He'd hit the ceiling. Lately Harley seemed to rub Rich the wrong way.

She turned and surveyed the store's neat, organized aisles. The building's old, wooden floors creaked, yet those floorboards were spotless. Neat rows of shelving lined bright walls highlighted by sunlight spilling through high windows. Overhead, several ceiling fans turned lazily.

Each department was well marked, and inviting displays were scattered throughout the store. Ada frequently shopped here, had for years, but today she noticed things... differently.

The neatness and order reflected a man who took pride in his responsibilities. She strolled down the aisle lined with bins of nails. Rich was no ordinary man. To her surprise, he was at home in a kitchen as he was selling the latest power tool.

"Need some nails?" A deep voice startled her.

"What?" Ada clasped her hand to her heart. "Oh, Rich, I didn't hear you come in."

His eyes warmed as his gaze swept over her. The look made her self-conscious, while at the same time, glad she showered and changed from her work clothes.

"How'd the tiller work?" he inquired.

"The tiller worked fine," Ada responded. "I've enlarged the garden. I'm going to give mesclun a try and I've cleared a spot for more berry bushes, got them on order."

"Good choice. Mesclun is a fast crop, about thirty-five days from seed. With our climate, you might squeeze out two harvests in one season. You'll wait a season or two for the berries to come, though."

"You're right," Ada agreed with a touch of surprise. "If my greenhouse was larger, I'd get an even earlier start. As for the berries, they're just an addition. I'm set with plenty now, just looking ahead."

Rich reached around her to straighten a display sign, and a clean, spicy scent swamped her senses. When his arm brushed against her, for a brief moment, she lost focus.

"Just the two I'm looking for." Tom McGraw strode down the aisle toward them. His russet hair looked shaggier these days and was sprinkled with gray. The former Pine Bluffs Police Chief seemed more relaxed since retiring and handing the reins over to his nephew, Nick. Mary used to call creases bracketing her husband's mouth his tension barometer. Today a broad, relaxed smile deepened those lines.

"Tom." Rich chuckled. "What brings you in today? You own every tool I sell, and you can't be out of the materials you purchased just last week." He turned to Ada. "Here's the man who could enlarge your greenhouse. He's starting a whole new career."

Ada laughed."Mary mentioned your ambition, Tom. She couldn't be happier."

"Why were you looking for us?" Rich asked.

"When was the last time you had wings at The Corner Bar?"

Ada rolled her eyes. Just thinking of the cozy bar in North East and its famous spicy chicken wings made her mouth water. Rich caught her eye and they laughed. No doubt their minds ran down the same path.

"That's what I thought." Tom's voice was smug. "You're both coming with Mary and me tonight. How about it?"

Rich looked at her. His brows rose questioningly.

Why not? Her plan had been to invite him for dinner at her place. Maybe her first dip in the dating pool would be better with two of her closest friends.

Chapter Seven

The aroma of spicy chicken wings made Ada's mouth water. All around them customers young and old laughed as they consumed heaping plates of wings and washed them down with cold, foam-topped pitchers of beer.

Tom McGraw led the way. The wooden floor beneath their feet creaked, announcing their arrival, and upon reaching a four-top tucked beneath a window on the far wall, he pulled out a chair for Mary. Rich did likewise for Ada.

Despite the rustic interior and well worn furnishings, the table was clean and equipped with an assortment of condiments and a holder bulging with napkins. The Corner Bar -- a staple in North East since long before Ada moved to Pine Bluffs -- boasted of mouth-watering chicken wings and drew a variety of clientele.

A tall, busty girl maneuvered her way across the room to greet them. She wore a T-shirt bearing the image of a chicken with a band aide where its wing should have been. "Evening, folks. Welcome to The Corner Bar. What can I start you off with?"

"A pitcher of Molson okay?" Tom inquired, glancing around the table.

Rich nodded and turned to Ada. "Sounds perfect," she responded.

Ada couldn't remember the last time she'd been so relaxed, and a top notch, ice cold beer to wash down the wings she'd been anticipating all afternoon qualified as 'perfect.'

Her relaxed state continued as the evening progressed. The wings measured up, and then some, as well as the company. Tom kept them entertained relaying unusual, oftentimes hilarious stories of his years on the job. He left out pertinent details -- such as names and exact locations -- but many of his stories brought tears of laughter to everyone's eyes.

Then, as if a switch had been thrown, Tom's face changed. Mary paused, a brimming glass of beer midway to her lips. Ada knew her friend, and she'd obviously picked up an unsaid vibe from Tom. Something was definitely amiss.

"Tom?" Mary set her glass down and laid her hand on his arm. "What is it?"

Tom placed his hand over Mary's, his gaze locked on the man behind the bar. He cast a brief glance at Ada, then back to the bar.

Ada swung around and her heart jumped in her chest.

The man behind the bar appeared frozen in place. With his jaw rigid, his eyes narrowed as he returned Tom's gaze.

"Tom." Mary's impatient tone made Tom blink and, heaving a deep sigh, he gave her a weak smile.

Ada couldn't look away. A hand waved in front of the bartender's stony face, making him blink. He sucked in a startled breath and jerked around to face a customer. "Andrews, can we get a refill here?" The shaggy-haired man's voice carried across the room. He thumped an empty pitcher down on the bar.

"Sorry," the bartender muttered, grabbing the pitcher and refilling it. He gave a little cough and, with a grim smile, handed over the brimming pitcher. "Lost in thought there, this one's on the house."

"No problem." The man's brow unfurled. "Thanks."

The bartender grabbed a towel and sopped up the moisture left behind, moving it in slow circles on the ancient wood.

Tearing her gaze from the man behind the bar, without pause, Ada downed the remaining contents in her glass. Rich peeled Ada's fingers from around her empty glass. "I'm not sure what just happened here, but would someone catch me up with the program?" Rich folded Ada's hand into his. "Ada, are you all right?"

When she nodded, returning the pressure of his grip on her hand, he seemed satisfied and turned his attention to Tom. "Okay, partner, what gives?"

"Let's get our check. I'll fill you in on the way back to Pine Bluffs.

The bartender's pointed, silent gaze followed her to the door. When they stepped outside, balmy night air wrapped around her. Despite the enveloping warmth, she shivered all the way to Tom's car.

Rich wrapped his arm around her, guiding her into the back seat and followed close behind. No one spoke as Tom eased onto the street and turned south on Lake Street. As they approached the ridge south of town, Ada glanced back. Darkness shrouded the usually picture perfect view of Lake Erie and she drew in a shaky breath. "Is that who I think it was, Tom?"

"Yes, damn it," came his clipped reply. "Rick Andrews, a man I hoped I'd never lay eyes on again." Tom glanced in the rear view mirror at Rich. He cleared his throat. "Sorry about the mystery back there, Rich. I apologize, but I just wanted to get us the hell out of there."

Ada turned to Rich. "You weren't there the night my niece was shot, or a least didn't know until later, but Sadie Mitchell, Cassi's twin, had a boyfriend. He showed up sometime before dawn the next day. Came right to the hospital and demanded to see Sadie. I thought Nick was going to rip the guy's head off."

"So Andrews didn't know Sadie had been killed," Rich surmised. "A hell of a shock, regardless of the circumstance."

Tom shrugged. "Tough break, I guess. After the hospital, his next stop was Pine Bluffs, PD. I had a hard time dealing with the SOB. On one hand, Andrews acted like a jackass, demanding to know who killed his woman, but, I couldn't help but notice the raw pain, real pain, etched on his face."

"Do you think he recognized me, Tom?" Ada shivered and Rich

shifted closer. "He stared daggers at all of us when we walked out the door."

"Slim chance he remembered you, Ada. But I've no doubt he remembered me. I threatened to throw his ass in jail when he stormed into the station like a madman. At that point, we didn't know if Sadie Mitchell was connected to the man whose body Cassi found in the bog. To this day, we still don't know for sure. We questioned him that morning, but eventually had to cut him loose."

"Was there any follow up? Did he ever come back to Pine Bluffs?" Rich asked.

"The authorities from Ohio were more interested in Rick Andrews than our department. They'd been shadowing him, and Sadie, for quite a while. They took it from there, and that's the last I saw of him. Seeing him tending bar in North East shocks me. There's nothing specific though, no reason to feel alarmed." Tom cast a reassuring glance into the mirror at Ada. "He may not be the most upstanding citizen, but nothing points to him being a threat to anyone, except maybe me."

Mary shot him a hard look.

"Don't worry, darlin'," He reached over and gave her knee a pat. "When I told him Sadie was dead, he accused me of having ice water in my veins. I don't consider that a viable threat."

"Well," Ada concluded, giving herself a shake. "We've relived enough tragedy for one night. The man tends bar in North East, which proves nothing except maybe he needed a job." Her eyes met Tom's in the rearview mirror. "I'm sure you'll be having your spies check him out."

"You're one smart lady." Tom grinned.

Chapter Eight

As they rode along Rich studied Ada, half listening as she relayed highlights of her most recent call from Cassi. It appeared she'd dismissed the incident at The Corner Bar. Not only smart, she was resilient. Fearless, too. Maybe to a fault. One moment she'd been visibly shaken, then, smooth as glass, she segued into an account of her day.

Her eyes sparked when she talked about her niece Cassi. Her hair reminded him of light brown sugar and brushed her cheeks as she talked, framing her animated face. He was used to Ada wearing a hat, or having her hair pulled back from her face. Tonight soft waves hung free. His fingers itched to touch the silky strands.

He tamped that itch down, for now.

Tom dove on in silence, and Mary's hand rested on his thigh. The simple, intimate gesture between his two friends caused an ache of loneliness. An unfamiliar mood for Rich, but one that recently plagued him.

Ada fell silent, as if sapped of energy, and Tom switched on the car radio surrounding them with soft music. They'd almost reached Ada's when Mary swung around and came out with, "How's Rufus? I was surprised to hear him growl so fiercely yesterday."

"Growling? At what?" Rich straightened in the seat, glancing from Mary to Ada. "Ada, what happened yesterday?"

"Mary gave me a ride home from town yesterday. We had tea on the porch, and Rufus was with us when out of the blue he looked out beyond the gardens and started growling. So, we took him into the cottage."

"Did you call the police?"

Ada laid her cool hand on Rich's arm. "Rich, you're overacting."

"Maybe." He relented, but mumbled, "Seeing a teapot blown apart in your hands tends to stick in my mind." He glanced down at the soft fingers touching him. How can she be so calm? Every damn day, it seems, fate throws something new at her. And she's comforting me?

"I appreciate your concern," Ada assured, giving his arm a gentle squeeze. "I *did* call Jake, and he found nothing. Since then, Rufus has been his goofy, normal self. My guess is the ground hog who's been taunting him was eyeing up my garden."

Rich relaxed. With a laugh, he took hold of her hand. For the remainder of the drive they listened to the soft music, her fingers within his grip.

When he walked Ada to her door, Rufus greeted them. He waited while she took him for a brief outing, and then shooed him back into the house.

"Thanks for a great evening, Rich. I'll have to work hard after eating all those wings." She patted her trim waistline. "But, they were worth it."

"My pleasure, Ada, I'll see you soon." He laid his hand against her cheek and placed a gentle kiss at the corner of her mouth. Reluctantly, he drew away. "Lock the door," he advised, and waited until she closed the door and he heard the deadbolt slide into place.

Pausing on the steps, his gaze swept over her gardens. A fine mist hugged the ground all the way to the lake. On the way to Tom and Mary's car, he faltered, overcome by a sudden chill, a sharp sense of awareness.

He stopped and wheeled around. Nothing moved. Even the treetops, pointing skyward high above the shrouded gardens, were motionless against the night sky. He continued toward the waiting car, unable to shake the feeling unseen eyes watched and waited.

But who were they watching, and what were they waiting for?

Chapter Nine

Ace Hardware customers were early birds. Contractors, plumbers, and the every day do-it-yourselfers usually showed up shortly after Rich unlocked the doors. He stepped out into the morning sun, toting a couple of wooden high-backed rockers. An old fashioned railing bordered the store's porch, wrapping around and framing wide steps that lead to the street. Rich strived to create a look more homey than business, a friendly, accommodating place. The railing he'd help design and install did the trick.

At the sound of footsteps on the wooden steps, Rich turned, breaking into a smile when he spied Tom ambling toward him. His friend grasped two cups, one in each hand, both sporting The Brown Cow logo. A small bag was tucked beneath one arm.

"Aw, Brown Cow coffee." Rich grinned, reaching for the cup Tom offered. "Thanks, McGraw. I thank Lois often for her coffee and breakfast biscuits."

"Since I've retired I'm afraid I've put on a few." Tom patted his flat stomach as he held out the bag. "I can't stop for coffee without grabbing a couple of biscuits, but, what the hell." He plopped down in one of the rockers and, balancing his coffee, dug into the bag.

After spreading sweet-smelling raspberry jam on a biscuit, he took a hefty bite. "Have some jam," he offered, when Rich dug for a biscuit.

"I'll pass on the jam." His mouth watered when he inhaled the rich berry scent. "Don't tell Ada, I turned down one of her finest. I missed my run this morning and those wings last night are sitting in my gut, so today I'll be good."

"Speaking of last night," Tom began. "I agree with Ada."

"About what?" Rich said absently, prying the lid from the steaming cup.

Before Tom could answer, Harley opened the screen door and strolled out. Tugging his cap into place, he turned to them. "Hey, 'morning, Tom, looks like a good one," he drawled, squinting into the morning sun.

"Morning Harley," Tom bit into another biscuit.

"Harley," Rich directed, aggravated by the interruption. "Make sure all the new lawn chairs are out today. The weather's improving, they'll start to move."

"Sure thing, boss, I'll get right to it."

Rich gestured to Tom. "Walk with me. I want to show you the new composite deck material down back." Tom looked confused, until Rich cast a meaningful glance at Harley's disappearing back. He nodded, popped the last of the biscuit into his mouth and, coffee in hand, followed

Rich.

Harley currently topped Rich's shit list. He hadn't addressed the matter yet, but the morning of the shooting when he had to take Ada for treatment, he'd played hell finding someone to cover the store. Granted, Harley eventually showed up and offered to close, enabling Rich to stay with Ada, but he'd yet to explain where the hell he'd been that morning. He was supposed to be at work. Soon, Rich vowed, he'd address that little stunt. At the moment, he wanted to talk to Tom in private.

The converted barn behind the store rose amongst tall maples. A generous, paved area inside provided plenty of room for loading. Wide double doors allowed trucks to drive into the building, load, and then exit and circle back to the street.

Rich inhaled the pungent scent of new wood, loving the earthy smell. Tom followed him through the barn. They moved to a shady knoll a short distance away and just outside the rear doors. The smell of wood faded, and the sweet fragrance of a nearby azalea bush bursting with color filled the air. A short distance away the morning sun glistened on Pine Shadow Lake.

Rich turned to Tom. "Agree with Ada about what?"

"Your overreaction last night." Tom raised a hand, halting the objection on the tip of Rich's tongue. "I've known you a good many years, and you don't jump at shadows. What's going on in your life?"

Rich valued Tom's friendship. Had from the day they'd met. He'd respected the policeman, and he still respected the man. Yet, he kept parts of himself well hidden from his friend.

Recently, his life reached a turning point. He resented the fact that just when he was about to let his guard down and maybe, just maybe, get close to another human being, one phone call stirred up all the sludge from his past.

If the gunshot had been random he could let it go. But the call from Gary came too soon after a freakin' bullet whizzed right by his head. Coincidence? Maybe. Regardless, Rich didn't like the implication.

He moved to the nearest tree and leaned against the rough bark. He took a deep swallow of his coffee. "What I'm about to tell you stays here, Tom. If you can't promise me that, tell me now." He turned his head, contemplating his friend.

"I'm here as your friend, Rich. I'm not the chief of police anymore. But I care about Ada, and you're looking at her with more than passing interest. Am I right?"

"You're right. You'd have to be blind not to have picked up on that," Rich admitted. "She's not rushing into my arms." He shot Tom a quick grin. "But she's not running away either."

Tom chuckled. "I noticed your preoccupation months ago. At our Christmas party you weren't at all interested in our manly discussion about the upcoming ice-fishing season."

Rich wasn't surprised, Tom didn't miss much. Turning serious, his gaze wandered to the lake and followed the wake of a large boat far out on the water. "I've got some history," he began. "Some things happened when I was young that could come back to haunt me. Until I caught the sound of that M-14, I thought the past was just that, past. Now I'm not so sure."

Tom waited. He finished his coffee and placed the empty cup on the ground by his feet. "I'm listening," he said.

Rich took a deep breath. He pushed away from the tree, moving about the small space as he talked. "I had the world by the ass back then. I was a Marine with first rate duty doing something I believed in. I was married to a girl who'd swept me off my feet. Life was sweet, a little hectic at times, but overall, good."

Tom crossed his arms. "So far, sounds pretty normal."

"Yeah, almost." Rich planted both feet, shoving his hands into his pockets. "Then strike one hit. The hand-picked group, the security detachment I served with, had a flaw. One man's actions put not only my fellow Marines, but the whole damn country at risk. To this day I sometimes wonder if anyone else saw what I did and just kept their mouths shut."

"I take it you didn't."

Rich leveled his gaze on Tom. "No, I didn't. Drugs weren't widespread in the service back then. There were some who experimented, but booze was the vice of choice. All of us were guilty of getting totally wiped out on occasion. But we never, ever let it keep us from doing our jobs. When on duty, we didn't screw around."

"You're not going to tell me you're feeling guilty because you ratted out a no good druggy all those years ago?"

"Guilty? Hell no. I felt relief when ONI hauled Will Steiner's ass out. But I wasn't ready for strike two." Rich turned away. A truck rumbled into the barn behind them, followed by the slap of boards being loaded.

"Which was," Tom prompted quietly.

"I could hear her sobbing before I got inside. We had a tiny place on base, kind of a row type apartment. At first I thought there'd been a family emergency. Dodie didn't talk about her family, so I had no clue what could have happened. Then she started yelling at me." Rich crushed his empty cup and hurled it to the ground. "There was no fuckin' emergency. My wife's lover had just been arrested."

Tom closed his eyes and shook his head, then asked, "Did she know you were responsible?"

"I'd been sworn to secrecy, but she knew something had been bothering me. I didn't say one word. When I tossed her out on her pretty ass, she must have put it all together. I didn't give a shit at the time. My darlin' wife, Dodie, left that day. I plowed through the next couple of months, taking extra duty and spending my weekends off getting shit-faced. If it wasn't for a fellow Marine, one of the best friends I've ever had, I'm not sure how I would have ended up."

"Would that be the friend you recently heard from?

"That's him, Gary Wilson." Rich's shoulders relaxed. "Gary was in Group with me. He saw me through the Steiner incident plus a nasty, miserable divorce."

"Christ Rich, why didn't you ever talk to me about this?"

"Tom, it just wasn't important. I left the whole mess behind years ago. Will Steiner was behind bars and until recently, I've been gun-shy about any emotional attachments."

Tom placed a hand on Rich's shoulder. "So just when you'd decided to explore your attraction to Ada, your friend calls and tells you--"

"Steiner's out. An old acquaintance from Group saw him. I guess I wouldn't give it much thought, except for one tiny detail which I can't seem to forget."

"What's that?"

"In my mind he failed as a Marine in all respects except one." He stepped around Tom, scooped up the two cups from the ground, and they began to walk back to the store.

"He could take out a target at three hundred feet without blinking with an M-14."

Tom stopped. "Son-of-a-bitch."

"Exactly," Rich agreed, and they continued on in silence.

After Tom left, customers began arriving and Rich didn't have time to dwell on the past. He'd call Gary later and see if there was any more news about Steiner.

Just before noon, the clatter of shoes caught his attention. Katy Kunzelman burst through the door leading to the room above the hardware store. Ada, Mary and several others followed. He'd forgotten Ada taught Cassi's aerobics class in her absence, and the morning session had just ended.

Katy, Mary, and the others called greetings as they moved off down the street, and his determination to distance himself from entanglements dissipated as Ada walked toward him.

"I was hoping to see you before I left." She tugged a colorful headband free, and raked fingers through her damp hair. "Would you be available for dinner tonight?"'

Chapter Ten

Ada chopped parsley and sliced basil leaves into tiny slivers. While tossing them with fresh greens, she inhaled their pungent fragrance then set the colorful bowl aside and shook a jar of her homemade dressing. Salad plates were chilling, and fresh rolls were warming. All she needed was her guest.

Before class that morning, Mary cornered her, and bluntly asked exactly when she planned to invite Rich to dinner. Ask him soon, Mary prodded, 'strike while the iron's hot.'

Strike while the iron's hot?

The clichéd phrase cast a glaring light on the generation gap when compared to Katy's description, which labeled Rich the Ace 'Hot-ware' man.

Ada laughed and pulled marinating chicken from the fridge. She had to admit Rich stirred her up. All it took was a brief kiss to set her pulse pounding and weaken her knees. This wasn't like her. She was sensible, down to earth, mature, *boring*.

Her life was in order, her business thriving. Why would she want to change anything just because her hormones had been given a nudge. No, not a nudge, more like a jolt. She couldn't deny her attraction to Rich. If she ended up succumbing to that physical pull deep inside when he touched her, she'd be sure and thank Cassi for insisting she keep in shape.

She turned to her mirror, twisting left, then right, studying her reflection. Workouts paid off, no doubt about it. Of course there was always candlelight.

She checked the time and slipped the chicken into the oven. A quick look around assured her everything was ready, so she scooped up two wine glasses and stepped onto the porch. June was a full week away, yet warm evening breezes played across the water. Usually, it was too cool this time of year to sit outdoors after sunset. This spring was not the usual.

She placed the glasses on a table and returned to the kitchen. Rufus woofed and scrambled to the door. When she swung the door open Rich's gaze dropped, and then climbed to meet hers. He gave a long, low whistle.

"Why thank you Richard." She took the chilled bottle of white wine he offered. "For this, too," she added, and lifted the bottle to study the label. "Perfect," she exclaimed, "Sauvignon Blanc goes with anything."

She carried a tray with pita triangles and humus outdoors. Rich followed and uncorked the wine. Not a leaf stirred, keeping the air warm and comfortable as the sun balanced on the horizon. Ada placed the snacks on a table between them, and Rich filled long stemmed glasses to the brim. "Perfect wine, perfect setting," he said, and touched his glass to hers.

After dinner, Ada suggested they wander down the winding path to the lake. The shadowy outline of trees and the rhythmic lap of water on the shore defined the night.

Rich took her hand and paused as they left the porch.

"Afraid of the dark?" she teased.

"Not at all." He stopped, turned, and eased her into his arms. His lips brushed hers, a brief touch, almost polite. Then he came back for more, pulling her tight against him.

She pressed her body against him, felt the heat, and breathed in his spicy aftershave. Her fingers slid up his back, down again. His touch was gentle, but demand hovered just below the surface. He eased back and cupped her face between warm hands, tilting her head until she gazed into his clear, amber eyes.

"Well," she murmured. She lowered her gaze and pressed her cheek to his chest. His heart thundered beneath her ear and a swirling concoction of want and lust fizzled through her.

How long had it been since she'd wanted someone, or felt the rush of pure, simple lust?

And, she *wanted* this man.

Wanted to melt against him, curl around him, and run her hands over him. Her pounding heartbeat matched his, goose bumps erupted on her skin. She shivered, and he wrapped both arms tightly around her.

Then a sharp, ice-cold, poignant stab of guilt hit her.

All those feelings had once been exclusively reserved for John, who'd been ripped from her life all those years ago.

"Ada," he murmured, and tipping her head back he took her lips again.

When the kiss ended, she took a deep breath. Cool night air whispered over her heated skin. She wanted to say something, anything, but his nearness scattered her thoughts. Like leaves skittering ahead of a storm, her emotions tossed and rolled over her in waves. She untangled herself from his embrace and they returned to the porch.

In silence, he helped her gather their after dinner wine glasses and followed her into the cottage. As she rinsed glasses, placing them in the dishwasher, Rich came to stand behind her. She leaned back when his arms encircled her, resting against him. "Are you surprised?" he asked.

She tilted her head, slanting a look over her shoulder. "No." His tawny gaze studied her. "No, I'm not. Things become locked inside a person over time. I've managed to build an emotional wall around myself. Tonight you shook that wall's foundation."

"Good." he smiled down at her. "Don't let guilt stop that wall from crumbling." His words held a wealth of understanding. "There are many ways to want a woman," he continued, pulling her close again. "It's been a while since my wants encompassed more than a physical itch."

His frank admission amused her, melting away some of the tension, pulling her thoughts back to center.

"You take my breath away, Ada. Sometimes I wonder how I overlooked you for so long. I'm not a shallow man, but something came alive in me when you showed up at Tom and Mary's looking totally different from the lady gardener I knew."

"You don't like my gardening attire?" she teased, shifting her weight. "I actually kind of like you in your snug, red Ace T-shirt."

"Are you flirting with me, ma'am?"

"Hmmm. Maybe." Unless she was prepared to invite this man into her bed right now, she'd better stop. Stop and make sure this is what they both wanted.

Her eyes searched his face. She turned and, placing both hands on his chest, gently pushed him away. "I'm in danger of being swept off my feet," she admitted, and slapped her palm against him when he grinned and started to lean in again. "I need time to think about this, about us."

Rich tucked a wayward strand of her hair behind one ear, tracing his finger down her neck. "Don't look back. I've found it only complicates the road ahead. Good or bad, the past is just that, the past." He cupped her cheek and dropped a fast hard kiss on her lips. "How about we take things as they come and see where this goes?"

Before Ada could reply, he moved away.

Jingling keys indicated he was preparing to leave.

"Rufus and I'll walk you out," she offered, and shrugged into a sweater.

Rich snapped a leash on the wriggling dog and opened the door.

Fireflies dotted her garden, and a spring chorus played to the stars as she accepted one last tender kiss before he got into his truck.

The engine hummed to life, and his window slid down. "I'll wait until you're inside before I leave."

Ada led Rufus back to the cottage. She turned and waved, then stepped inside and closed the door. The sound of Rich's truck had barely faded when Rufus rushed to the sliding glass door. He froze there, and a growl rumbled low in his throat.

Chapter Eleven

Ada rubbed tense fingertips against tired, burning eyes. She forced them shut, hoping by some miracle she'd drift into a deep, pre-dawn slumber.

The move was futile.

Blinking like a sleepy owl, she tossed aside tangled sheets and sat on the edge of her bed. Where the horizon met the mist-shrouded lake, a vivid pink sky announced a new day.

Her bare feet brushed against Rufus. He stiffened his legs in a stretch and noisily licked his lips. His eyes remained closed, and his breathing resumed its deep even tempo.

She wanted to poke him with her toe. After all, he was the reason for her sleepless night.

The whole blessed night she'd been awake. When was the last time that had happened? After she'd managed to calm Rufus, and quiet his stubborn growling, she thought she'd fall asleep immediately. But her mind would just not shut down.

She headed for the shower, angry for getting caught up in what was probably some kind of canine anxiety. Pounding water cooled her temper and cleared the grit from her eyes. After dressing and running a comb through her hair, she entered the kitchen. Rufus waited by the glass door.

She'd refused to call the police last night, though she'd come close, *again*. "How many times can I call 'wolf', and then face the embarrassment of another false alarm?" she mumbled.

Fear evaporated, much like the morning mist, in the light of day. Rufus, the silly pooch, appeared quite normal.

As a precaution, she attached his leash before venturing outside. She usually took her morning tea and did a walk about the garden while he cast about freely, reading messages left during the night. This morning she kept him under her control. Thank goodness for retractable leads.

Morning dew dampened his paws and covered the toes of her canvas slip-ons. As a rule, damp feet didn't bother Ada, but today she was running on zero hours sleep and as yet, no morning tea. Wet feet pushed the irritation level over the top.

"Crap," she muttered, toeing off the soggy shoes before reentering her cottage.

Then something caught her eye.

A piece of paper was tucked under the tabletop lamp on the porch. She glanced around before pulling the neatly folded paper free. Her name jumped out, printed in neat block letters. Had Rich left her a note?

A tiny smile touched her lips. The smile disappeared and her lips clamped tight after she lifted the edge and read the single word printed inside.

Payback.

Payback? For what? From whom?

Ada shoved Rufus in the door, slid it closed with a bang and flipped the lock. Her gaze raced over her gardens and beyond. She swung around, checked out the kitchen and peered into the shadowed hallway. The sound of Rufus lapping water from his bowl eased the tension. If someone was near, on her property or in her home, he wouldn't be so relaxed.

Her heart pounded, thundering in her ears. She began to shake, despite warm, morning sun spilling into the room, the soothing sound of her teapot simmering and the steady tick of her mantel clock. All familiar, all normal.

She should have felt safe!

Rufus approached and cold wet drops hit her bare feet. She yelped, jerking with a gasp. Water dripped from his whiskered face and her sharp voice made his ears flatten.

Kneeling down, she pulled him close. "Come here, you. I'm not mad at you." Her grasp loosened when he whined and wriggled. "Sorry fella, a bit too tight, huh?" She got to her feet and moved away from the door. She rummaged in a drawer, remembering how Jake had bagged the spent bullet.

After carefully slipping the note into a plastic zip bag, she zipped it shut, and dropped it on the counter. She crossed her arms, tucking her shaking fingers beneath them.

Calmer, after having moved in a positive, proactive direction, cold fear gave way to percolating anger. How dare someone trespass on her property and threaten her.

Chapter Twelve

Officer Frank Infantino glanced up when Ada and Rufus entered Pine Bluffs PD. "Mornin' Frank."

"Mrs. Blaine, it's nice to see you. Hey fella!" Rufus shot around the desk. "What brings you to the station?" Frank asked, laughing as Rufus bumped, nudged, and whined. "Okay, okay, calm down big guy."

Ada glanced around, hesitating. Should she just hand the note over to Frank?

Footsteps echoed down the hall and Marcy swung around the corner. "Whoa!" she yelped, laughing when Rufus deserted Frank and lunged toward her. She leaned down and caught him before he bowled her over. "Ada, what a nice surprise. What brings you two in?"

"Do you have a moment?" Ada asked.

Marcy giggled, dodging wet, sloppy kisses. She gave Rufus a final pat, and straightened. "Of course, the break room is empty, and I could use a cup of coffee." She turned and slapped her thigh. "Come on, boy, maybe there's some leftover donuts."

Rufus trotted happily after her, and Ada followed.

Marcy closed the door behind them. She dumped the remnants of the morning's coffee and refilled the pot. When the coffee maker began to squeak and sputter, she turned to Ada. "What's going on?" She looked closer and frowned. "You look like you need some serious sleep. Sit down, Ada, before you fall down."

"Tell me what you think of this." Ada pulled the bag from her pocket and laid it on the table. The note, visible through the plastic, displayed her name. When flipped over, the cryptic message could easily be read.

Marcy lifted the bag. Her brows snapped together. "Where did you get this?"

Ada paced as she told Marcy how she'd found the note, and about her restless night. "I didn't take my walk along the lake this morning," she concluded. "Instead I walked Rufus into town. Damn it, Marcy. I'm spooked." She stopped abruptly and tapped a blunt finger next to the bag on the table. "This is... disconcerting. I don't like being spooked, or disconcerted."

The coffee machine beeped. Marcy selected two clean mugs and filled them. She added a generous shot of half and half to Ada's. Nodding a thank you, Ada sipped. Warmth spread through her. Maybe the caffeine would sharpen her muzzy mind.

She settled across from Marcy. "I've been alone in my cottage over twenty years. Never, ever, have I been afraid to sleep at night, or walk along the lake at dawn. Then last night I panicked. I was scared. This morning, after I found this," she exclaimed, giving the bag an irritated poke. "I couldn't bring myself to take my morning walk. I locked the doors before I took my shower, for God's sake!"

She jumped up, pacing again. Rufus sank to the floor. He laid his head on outstretched paws. She stopped and swung around. "Look, now I've upset poor Rufus." Kneeling down she ran her hand over his head. "Why would someone do this to me?"

"As your friend, I understand how you feel, Ada." Marcy picked up the bag and studied it. "As a police officer, I can't ignore facts. An M-14 round took out your tea tray."

"So you think someone is what, harassing me?"

"I wouldn't say harassing, more like a warning."

Ada got to her feet, only to collapse on a chair. "A warning?"

Marcy touched her arm. "Give me a moment, I'll be right back." She returned clutching a folder. "This contains facts concerning the first incident, the shooting. Plus our search when you and Mary called us a few days later. Tell me exactly what happened last night and how you found the note this morning. Then I can update your file."

"Oh. My. God." Ada covered her face with both hands. "I have a file." She gave her cheeks a brisk rub, and then watched Marcy write 'Blaine evidence' on a plastic evidence bag. "Can you test for fingerprints?"

Marcy shook her head. "Hard to get prints from paper, next to impossible. If whoever handled the note had something oily on their fingers, maybe. This note is neat and clean. Whoever wrote it used caution."

She gave her best account of the night before, and as Marcy organized the file contents, several rapid knocks sounded on the break room door, followed by muffled giggling.

"My little angels." Marcy rolled her eyes, tucked everything back into the folder and threw open the door.

Mark and Robbie Evans burst into the room. "Hi Mom," they chorused. "Where's Rufus?"

"Where's your father?" Marcy demanded.

"He's talking to some guy out front," explained Robbie, the older of Marcy's young boys. "Officer Frank told us Rufus was here," Mark added. "Can we play with him?"

Rufus sprang to his feet.

"There he is! Hey, Rufus! Come here boy!" Mark crouched down, exploding into wild giggles as Rufus bowled him over. Trying to shield his face from the darting, wet tongue he curled into a ball.

Ada stepped forward, and Marcy placed a hand on her arm. "Let them go." She chuckled. "They love that dog. In fact," she said, tapping one finger on her chin. "Why don't you let Rufus spend some time at our place? You need some rest, and I'll make sure patrols keep a close eye on your place. Our yard is fenced, and it's my weekend on duty. Rob is repairing the front porch and it will keep them out of his hair. What do you say?"

"Oh please, Mrs. Blaine!" Robbie bounced as if on springs, and Mark joined in.

Marcy's brows shot up.

"Stand still Mark." The older of the two squared his shoulders and met Ada's eyes. "May Rufus come home with us to play?"

Mark tried to mimic his brother, but all he could manage was a desperate, "Please!"

Amidst scrambling and wild laughter, a hastily made plan came together. Her personal plan was to sleep, and to let her jittery nerves settle. The prospect appealed on so many levels.

Rob agreed to take Rufus home with him and the boys. They swung by the cottage. She gathered up dog food, bowls, and treats.

"Rufus lives for the treats." She handed Rob a bag full of bite sized miniature bones. "Perfect bribery tools," she whispered for Rob's ears only.

She waved goodbye, almost guilty by how thrilled she was to be facing a blessedly long, hopefully stress-free, weekend.

Hours later, Ada drifted awake. After checking the time, she yawned and closed her eyes. Three solid hours of sleep felt like heaven after the night she'd put in, pacing, checking doors and windows. Her hand slid down and rubbed her tummy when its unladylike rumble reminded her she'd skipped breakfast. The tiny throb just above her right eye threatened to expand, moving from throb to pound unless she dragged her butt out of bed and got some food.

She devoured a sandwich heaped with lean turkey, sliced tomatoes, and mayo. The much needed rest improved her mood considerably, and with each swallow, her energy level rose. Her first impulse was to call Marcy, but the day had evened out, and she hated to stir up stress about the note again. She'd wait. Marcy would call when there was something to tell.

Though recharged from the nap, her peak time for work was early in the day. After her crappy, sleepless night, and then discovering the note this morning, her day got kind of screwed up. Gardening chores could be put on hold for today. No sense digging and planting when she'd just wear herself out and do a half-assed job to boot. Better to start fresh tomorrow.

She lounged on the porch sipping iced tea. Her gaze wandered to the path leading into the woods. She'd be wise to avoid the shadowed trail for the time being. How long before she'd feel comfortable strolling there alone again?

On the other hand, the lake was wide open. Not a soul in sight she concluded after scanning the horizon. She had a wonderful kayak. Time spent on Pine Shadow Lake would accomplish two things. Relieve lingering stress and give her some much needed exercise.

While she collected her boating gear, a Pine Bluffs patrol car cruised slowly by.

Her mobile guardian angel.

The cruiser car rolled out of sight. Alone at last, she turned to the beckoning, rippling lake waters.

*****

The roll of youthful laughter, punctuated by several sharp barks, drew Rich to his office window. He recognized Rob Evans' truck and caught sight of two small bobbing heads and a wildly waving tail through the truck's rear window.

Rob and Harley were loading, sliding a variety of two by fours and six wide planks on board. A dog's head popped through an open window, and after giving two quick, excited yips, the head disappeared. Wild giggles followed.

Rich shoved his hands into his pockets and enjoyed the show. God love him, carting around Rufus and two rambunctious boys. Rob exchanged a few words with Harley and slid into the driver's seat. With a tap on the truck's roof, Harley waved them off.

Rich shuffled back to his desk, prepared to retackle his neglected paper work. A cup perched on the window sill half-filled with coffee long gone cold caught his eye. "There's where I left you." As he backtracked and reached for the cup, movement in the lumber yard below made him pause. "Son-of-a-bitch," he muttered. "How many times..."

He burst through the double doors leading to the loading area.

Harley's head jerked up, and he ripped a smoldering cigarette from between his lips.

"Damn it. One spark and all this wood goes up like a giant friggin' torch. Tell me what part of no smoking on store property you *don't* understand?"

Harley shot him a look that made Rich pull up short. Something not quite threatening, but... The attitude shifted as fast as it flashed, and the cigarette hit the ground. "Sorry, boss. Bad habit." Harley's eyes lowered and, using his heel, he ground out the unfinished smoke. "I've a lotta' shit on my mind, guess I forgot.

Rich gave a disgusted snort. "Well, leave that particular habit at home, will ya'?" He turned to leave.

"How's Mrs. Blaine?"

Rich wheeled back around. "Ada? She's fine. Things have settled, and I hope it stays that way. Which reminds me," he said, recalling another bone he had to pick with his employee. "Where the hell were you the other morning? When I called, Nelson told me you hadn't come in yet. You were scheduled for the early shift. What happened?"

"Ah, yeah. Sorry. Damn truck conked out. Made me late."

"Next time, call." Rich turned and stalked away.

He glanced over when Harley caught up with him and, reaching around, opened the door. As they began the climb to the sales area,

Harley blurted out, "How about that note left on Mrs. Blaine's porch?"

Rich stopped dead. "What note?"

Harley grimaced, rubbing one side of his face. "Sorry again, thought you'd be one of the first to hear about it."

"Damn it, what note?" He was ready to toss the irritating little shit back down the stairs.

"Somebody left her a message. Some kind of note. They put it on her porch sometime last night."

Rich took off, leaving Harley behind, and charged up the remaining stairs to his office. His fingers drummed a nervous, steady rhythm on his desk while waiting for Ada to answer her phone. "Come on. Come on, Ada. Pick up."

When her machine picked up, Rich disconnected and hit speed dial for Pine Bluffs PD.

Chapter Thirteen

Ada's kayak glided through the tranquil waters of Pine Shadow Lake, barely causing a ripple. Midday sun beat down, the lake's surface sparkled. With each stroke of her double-edged paddle, ripples spread like a wide river of diamonds.

Well away from shore, she pulled her paddle. She leaned back and drifted, gazing at the cloudless sky. Tension slipped away.

Then the rhythmic slap of paddles off to her left caught her attention, and another kayak appeared from shadows along the shoreline. The sleek craft zipped through the water with surprising speed, heading straight for Ada. A man propelled the one-man craft. His paddle dipped rhythmically, strong, even strokes closing distance between them.

Stay calm, appear unconcerned.

Prey to predator flashed with chilling reality in her mind. She straightened, taking a white knuckled grip on her paddle. He was almost upon her and her nerves jumped in time with each slap of *his* paddle on the lake's surface.

A green cap sat low on his brow, hiding his face. The sleeves of the black T-shirt he wore were rolled tight, revealing strong, well defined biceps. Strangely, those well developed arms were pale, ghost like, and *that* image made her shudder.

"Hi there," he called, waving a hand. "Hope I didn't startle you. I was heading out from up the shoreline," he said, gesturing vaguely, "and fell in behind you."

She glanced in the direction he'd pointed. Using her paddle, she turned her craft to face him. "I'm afraid I don't know you."

He drifted closer. The deliberate way he studied her had icy fingers skipping up her spine. He adjusted his cap. "Uh, I'm from up near Buffalo. A little town called Angola. Lake Erie's a challenge, especially when the wind's up. I heard tell of this little spot and decided to check it out."

He tipped his cap back to wipe his brow. "This is beautiful. Lake's smooth as a baby's butt and crystal clear."

Ada examined his rather ordinary face. Nothing distinctive grabbed her attention. Except, like his arms, his broad forehead and lean, hollow cheeks were untouched by the sun.

She dug into her duffle for sunscreen. Anything to keep her hands busy, keep them from shaking. "I'm Ada Blaine," she offered. "I live down the lake." She nodded in the direction from which she'd come and began to briskly slather the protective cream on her bare arms. "I agree with you. Pine Shadow Lake is beautiful, perfect for kayaking."

She exchanged the sunscreen for a water bottle and gulped down a hefty slug. Her throat tightened, and she worried the lukewarm liquid would come back up.

"Bet it gets crowded as the weather warms." He took in their deserted surroundings. When his gaze swung back and landed on her, she flinched, and he drawled, "Looks like we're the only two out here today."

Ada stuffed the water back in her bag, straightened, and adjusted her glasses. "Hmm, well. Enjoy your day on the lake," she said. Her paddle cut in, moving her away.

Her kayak shot through the still water. Inside her, turmoil crashed like wind-whipped waves. With each stroke she surged forward, leaving the stranger from Angola behind. Not until she rounded the spit of land near her cottage did she pause and look back.

He was nowhere in sight.

She *hated* the cold fear rearing its ugly head and destroying her peaceful time on the lake. Vehemently despised the suspicion fast becoming part of her life.

Any other time, she'd have chatted about the area, or the weather, for Pete's sake. Encountering the stranger coiled her insides tight as a spring. Worse yet, after that lame, stilted conversation, she'd run like a scared rabbit.

Her kayak bumped the dock. She tossed her duffle onto the wooden surface and heaved her paddle up beside it. She levered up and out of the kayak, then pulled the craft from the lake and tipped it over to dry.

While gathering her gear, a barely audible sound and slight movement made Ada glance up. She reeled back, nearly toppling into the lake when she spotted a man on shore. He stood erect with arms crossed and widespread legs.

"What part of Marcy's advice to lock your doors, stay inside, and rest wasn't crystal clear to you?" Rich stepped forward and, reaching out, grabbed onto her before she toppled into the lake.

She clutched her chest. "My God, Richard, don't sneak up on me like that. You're the second man today to almost give me a coronary."

"Second?" Rich's grip tightened. He guided her from the dock onto solid ground and she frowned at the hand clutching her arm. Then she lifted her gaze and came face to face with a seething angry man.

Well, she wasn't exactly feeling all warm and fuzzy at the moment either.

With a deft twist, she broke free, turned, and stomped up the bank. Rich followed, close on her heels. As if on cue, a marked patrol car cruised by her cottage and her blood pressure soared. Did everyone presume she needed round-the-clock baby sitters?

Initially, all the attention had been comforting. Now she couldn't *breathe.* Her friends were smothering her, and she refused to be cast as a damsel in distress. Was Rich there because he wanted to be, or was he just looking out for the helpless little lady?

Rich skidded to a stop when she whipped around. She tapped a rigid finger against his chest. "I am not a helpless female! Some jackass is getting his kicks leaving stupid notes," she sputtered out, and added, waving her hand toward the lake. "Then, some man in a kayak says an innocent 'hello' and I run like a damn scared rabbit. I don't *like* feeling this way!"

Astonishment flicked across Rich's face. She lowered her head and closed her eyes, letting the adrenalin rush subside. He touched her. His warm hand cupped her arm, and he gave it a gentle squeeze.

She placed her hand over his and heaved a shuddering sigh. "I'm sorry." She regarded his amber eyes. Eyes no longer angry, but dark with concern. "I'm so sorry. Everything's twisting me around, too many things. You just happened to be in the line of fire when my fuse burned down."

He wrapped an arm around her. "Come inside, we'll talk about the note, and you can tell me about what happened on the lake today." She leaned on him as they climbed the porch steps. Ada dropped into a chair, and Rich settled against the railing, waiting.

She gathered her thoughts and filled in the blanks, beginning from when he'd left her the night before, right up to her encounter with the stranger on the lake.

Calm and relaxed, Rich listened. His stance settled her nerves and soothed away the rough edges. "I *do* appreciate what everyone's doing for me," she insisted, rummaging in the duffel she'd dropped by her chair. "I'm not ungrateful, what I am, is embarrassed." She lifted a water bottle and drank deeply.

Rich crouched down. His hands curved gently over hers. "You're right. I was mad, and maybe it took your explosion to knock some sense into my head. More than mad, I was scared."

She paused, the water half way to her mouth. He slowly shook his head. "Like it or not, Ada, while you're dealing with your independence, fighting things you can't control, I'm trying to stifle the outdated macho reaction to protect you." He tightened his grip on her hands. "I'm sorry, too."

She pulled one hand free and touched his face. "Aren't we the pair?" Her gaze met his, and she smiled. "I'm used to being on my own and looking out for myself. I didn't mean to snap at you for caring. Throw in a healthy helping of plain old fear, and it's clear I'm not dealing well at all."

Rich got up and pulled Ada to her feet. "Rob Evans stopped to order more supplies for his project," he explained. "I noticed he had Rufus and the boys with him."

"So, Rob told you about the note?"

"No. Actually, Harley told me. He was helping Rob with his order."

He shrugged one shoulder. "I assume Rob told him. I tried to reach you. When that failed, I confronted Marcy and she caved when I pressed her for details. When I came looking for you, your car was here and the place was locked up. I couldn't find you."

"And that worried you"

Ada wrapped an arm around him, absorbing his warmth. Her world began to settle.

"Yes, at first I *was* worried. I was about to call Marcy when I saw you out on the lake."

"Then you got mad."

"Then I got mad."

"Why?"

"Haven't you ever been scared, Ada? Really scared something awful has happened, and then it turns out you were all churned up for no reason?"

Ada sensed tension mounting in Rich, and she wasn't so sure he was referring to what had just happened. "Go on," she encouraged softly.

"There you were, docking your kayak, acting like all was great with the world, and I felt like I'd taken a sucker punch to the gut."

Ada rested her head on his shoulder. "How dare I not lock my doors and hide away in my room."

"Be careful." He chuckled, and gave her a squeeze. "Or you'll tick me off again."

Turning serious, he gripped her chin, lifting till she stared into his eyes. "I'm sorry I let my temper deal with unfamiliar feelings. I think, in many respects we're alike. I'm not used to looking out for anyone but myself, and you're not used to anyone looking out for you."

The lake shimmered in the sun while a gentle breeze stole through her herbs. Right then, at that moment, Ada felt safe. "The man I saw on the lake was friendly," she mused. "He claimed he was from Angola. Looking back, I was borderline rude."

"Don't let 'friendly' fool you. Under normal conditions, I'd say he was exactly what he claimed to be. Facts are facts, and wouldn't coming on your property from the lake be an easy thing to do?"

Rich's words made sense. The day the shot was fired neither of them had considered the intruder arriving by boat. Maybe those investigating had, and if she'd known that today, that man would have really sent her packing. Yes, how easy it would have been for someone to come up from the lake and leave that note on her porch.

"I can't live in hiding, Rich. I'd eventually go crazy." She lifted a hand, anticipating his objection. "Look, I'll take precautions and pay more attention to people and things around me." She thought a moment. "I know how to use a gun. Should I think about getting one for protection?"

Rich left her side. He walked the length of the porch and stopped. Linking his fingers behind his head, elbows akimbo, he raised his eyes to the fast darkening sky.

"Serious question," he commented. "One that deserves some serious thought."

Ada waited, plucking spent flowers from a nearby hanging basket. Their pungent smell clung to her fingers, and she rubbed her hands briskly against her pants.

When Rich returned, he took her hands. Lifting them he dropped a quick kiss on the back of each one. "You smell like everything in nature all mixed together."

"Is this a diversion, Richard?"

He pulled her in, wrapped his arms around her. "I don't know how to answer your question. Part of me says 'yes', she needs to have protection when she's alone."

Ada waited. The feel of his arms banded around her made everything fade away, only the here and now existed.

He continued. "Yet, part of me says 'no', guns kill."

She pulled from his embrace. "I need to think," she declared. "I can't do that when you hold me."

Rich's smile spread slowly.

She tapped his cheek lightly. "Don't look so smug."

He caught her hand. "I'll somehow manage to get my smugness under control. In the mean time, come home with me."

She carefully withdrew her hand. The unveiled invitation caught her off guard. "Rich... I don't know, I..."

"For *dinner*, Ada. I'm asking you to come to my place for dinner. You cooked for me, now I want to cook for you."

Amusement flicked across his face, but gentleman that he was, he remained silent.

"Dinner?" She considered a moment. "I think that would be nice. Can I bring something, maybe a dessert?"

"Just you, Ada." He walked toward his truck, pulling her along. "I'll take care of everything, but you have to make me a promise." They stopped. He crossed his arms and leaned against his truck. "Steps need to be taken to assure your safety."

"Such as?"

"Leave lights on in your cottage. Either I'll follow you home tonight, or we'll get one of the night patrols to escort you. I'm sure I'll come up with more, but for now, it's a start. Agreed?"

He looked so serious, jaw set, eyes intense and dark. The breeze whipped his thick hair into tousled disarray. His litany of safety precautions barely registered as she fought the urge to nuzzle right in where his unbuttoned shirt exposed his neck.

Ada didn't want to fight urges anymore.

She placed one finger on his tan, muscled arm and traced the firm line from elbow to wrist. "*If*, I come home tonight, I'll take your suggestions under consideration. See you between seven and seven-thirty." She turned and walked into the cottage, leaving Rich leaning against the side of his truck.

She didn't have to look. She could *feel* those tawny brown eyes boring into her retreating back. The screen door bounced shut behind her and, after a long moment, Rich's truck roared to life and pulled away.

Nerves, along with anticipation, danced in her belly. She savored the moment he'd wrapped his arms around her. He wanted to protect her, and that was fine. What woman wouldn't cling to a big, strong, handsome man?

But Ada wasn't used to clinging to *anyone*. She managed to reach this point in her life all alone. At times, not an easy journey. She'd often been scared, panicked actually, and ready to give up.

She'd made mistakes.

Those times passed, trampled down and left behind over the years. Emerging strong, independent, and successful on her chosen path, up until now Ada had been content with her life. Or so she'd thought, until that comfortable, well-traveled path took a sharp turn, and Rich McConnell interrupted her smooth, comfortable journey.

She found herself poised to reopen an emotional door. One she'd slammed shut all those years ago. Granted, she hadn't made any promises, but she'd left a crack wide enough that a determined, confident man would have no trouble marching right on in.

Rich McConnell had confidence to burn, along with stubbornness, charm, and a healthy dose of determination. Add those traits, to the chemistry sparking between them, and any doubts she harbored they'd end up in bed together that night simply vanished.

Locking the cottage door behind her, Ada glanced at her watch, just enough time for one quick stop. With luck, anyone in Pine Bluffs she knew was having dinner and not roaming the aisles at the local Rite Aide Pharmacy.

Ada entered the store and, after a couple furtive peeks around, headed for her target aisle. While engrossed, studying the label on a personal feminine product, a familiar voice behind her made her juggle, and come close to dropping, the tiny bottle in her hand.

"Whoops!" Mary McGraw cried, her hand shot out and caught the teetering item.

"Mary. What a surprise," Ada exclaimed. She took the small blue-capped bottle from Mary and hastily returned it to the shelf. Her nerves did a jittery twitch. She attempted to steer Mary down the aisle. Maybe she could divert her friend and avoid further embarrassment.

No such luck. With one eyebrow quirked, Mary gave her a look. "Hmm. Hot date tonight?"

Ada's cheeks flushed, like a kid caught stealing penny candy. She huffed out a short breath and lifted her hand, only to let it drop to her side. "Well. Well, I..." she stammered.

Understanding bloomed on Mary's sweet face. Ada just shrugged.

Mary took Ada's arm and tugged her back in order to study the display on the shelf. "Ah, here it is, "she murmured, and plucked a small container from the shelf. She held it up, tapping the front as she handed it to Ada.

"Sensation naturelle?" Ada inquired, taking the bottle. Mary nodded and winked. In silence, Ada read the claims on the label and instructions on the back.

She lifted one hand and covered her eyes. "Oh, Mary." Her shoulders shook with laughter. "I feel like a nervous virgin on prom night. And trust me, I'm no virgin and I'm not going to any prom tonight. I'm having dinner with Rich at his place, and I'm bringing dessert."

They hugged one another, bursting with laughter. Their outburst earned a disdainful glance from the young girl manning the check out.

Mary swiped away tears and asked, "Do you mean you're actually bringing a dessert, or you *are* dessert?"

A short time later they parted in front of Rite Aide. Mary gave her a brief hug. "Have a wonderful evening," she advised. "Don't overthink things, just let whatever happens, happen." Mary slipped into her car and departed.

Ada tucked the tiny bottle promising 'sensation naturelle' into her purse and headed for Rich McConnell's.

Chapter Fourteen

The glow from a copper lantern over the entrance cast a halo of light on a curved pathway. Ada paused to admire the building's brick exterior. She'd been by Rich's place numerous times, yet tonight marked the first time she'd venture inside.

Faint chimes echoed when she pressed the button beside the door. Footsteps approached. The door swung inward, and Rich filled the entry. "Ada." His gaze did a quick head to toe sweep. "Come in."

She entered the high-ceilinged foyer. Stairs flanked by a gleaming, wood railing curved upward, and against the wall to her right sat an oak bench. "This is extraordinary, Rich. The exterior is attractive, but this is unique."

"All part of the original stable," he explained. "I sectioned it off to create an entry and storage." He pointed, drawing her attention to several doors along the far wall. "Two are for storage, the other leads to a laundry and workshop."

He opened the first door and switched on a light revealing a washer and dryer. She followed him and, while passing through the laundry into another room, admired lush solitude visible through a bank of windows framing his back yard.

"This is my workshop." At the flick of a switch, fluorescent lights illuminated a true man's paradise complete with a wall of tools, a sturdy, scarred, work table and a serious looking table saw. "That's my gun cabinet," he said, indicating a locked door on the back wall.

Ada took time to express appropriate admiration. Upon returning to the foyer, she remembered the wine and dessert she'd brought and detoured to retrieve them from her car.

"Just come on up," Rich started up the stairs. "I'll leave the door open."

Moments later she climbed the curving hardwood staircase and stepped into another segment of Rich's domain. The entire wall facing the lake was glass. Counters of earth-toned granite wrapped around to form a u-shaped work area, and hickory cabinets lined the walls. The built in range top looked functional and well-used.

Rich turned, knife in hand, and deftly whipped a utility towel over his shoulder. She noted his sock-clad feet, causing a brief flash of déjà vu'.

"Well, what do you think?"

"I'm... well, surprised would sum up my reaction so far." She nodded to several thriving pots of herbs on the windowsill. "Those are something I never thought I'd see in your kitchen."

"Really?" A pleased smile stole over Rich's face. "Quite frankly, not many have seen my kitchen."

"Why keep it a secret? Men can be excellent cooks and, from the way you wield that knife, I'll bet you rank right up there in the cooking arena."

"Why thank you, Ada." He placed the knife on the counter, leaned in, and kissed her cheek. "What have you there?"

"It's a Pinot Grigio. I hope it suits your dinner selection." She handed him the bottle and set aside another container. "I know you said I didn't need to bring dessert, but I'm quite proud of my fresh berry cobbler."

"Glad you overrode me." He nodded toward a colorful array of vegetables and a bowl filled to the brim with marinating shrimp. "Wild caught gulf shrimp and fresh vegetables on skewers should provide a perfect match for the Pinot."

The rich aroma of the marinade drew her. She moved closer, brushing against Rich. His woodsy, spicy aftershave overrode the marinade.

Overhead, a rotating ceiling fan stirred the air. Standing so close to Rich made Ada's cheeks flush. She figured the backwash from a jet prop wouldn't dispel the heat his nearness generated. Savoring the moment, she stared at the shrimp, speechless.

Rich's voice broke the spell. "Never seen shrimp marinate before?" Humor lit his eyes.

She canted her head, speculating if somehow he sensed her reaction to his nearness. Her pulse quickened. Looked like they'd reached a definite turning point.

So why not test the waters?

Her gaze locked with Rich's and she moved. He leaned down, accepting the challenge and this time his lips went straight to hers.

Emotions surfaced, bubbling and churning through her veins like uncorked champagne. She feared her knees were about to fold by the time he lifted his head.

"Yes," she rasped out.

He ran his thumb gently across her moist lips.

"Yes?"

"Uh, yes, I have seen shrimp... marinating."

His laughter made her grin, and he reached for a nearby frosty mug of beer.

Ada gave him an affectionate poke. "What can I do to help?"

He wrapped one arm around her and pointed with the dripping mug. "There's a loaf of bread. Cut up some herbs, toss them with oil, and then slice the bread and coat each piece. We'll grill 'em."

Ada went to work, happy to do something familiar. She couldn't help but feel she'd just jumped head first into that very murky dating pool.

Rich polished off the beer and, using a simple corkscrew, opened the chilled wine. He crossed the room and flipped a switch. Soft music surrounded them.

Ada snipped oregano, parsley, and basil from the overflowing pots. While back-cutting the fragrant herbs, she took in her surroundings.

The décor was unmistakably masculine, though not overpowering. Furniture designed for comfort as well as function filled the space. A two sided fireplace divided the kitchen from the rest of the room, and its glass doors showcased realistic looking gas logs. The choices he'd made added layers to the man.

She coated the herbs with extra virgin olive oil and, while tossing them gently, her eyes were drawn to photos on shelves of a bookcase. Carrying the bowl she moved across the room.

The first picture showed Rich and a dark-skinned man. They gripped long-necked bottles of beer and sported wide grins as they toasted the camera. Both wore green fatigues, and through an open door behind them, several utilitarian buildings could be seen.

The second was of Rich with Tom McGraw bundled in winter gear and holding up a string of fish. A trail of footsteps visible behind them led to a dark hole in the ice of a snow-covered Pine Shadow Lake.

She studied the photos. In the first one Rich appeared younger, and was clearly from his Marine Corps days. The other, with Tom, seemed more recent.

"Ready to eat?" Rich's warm breath caressed her ear. She jumped. He reached past her, steadying the bowl of herbs still clutched in her hands.

"Yes, the herb mix is ready, too." She leaned back, settling against his chest. Strong arms closed around her. "I recognize Tom," she admitted, glancing over and up into his face. "Is the other man someone you served with?"

"Yes, we met at the east coast base I told you about, worked security together. His name's Gary Wilson. I still consider him one of my best friends."

Rich grew silent. She could feel the steady thump, thump of his heart against her. The picture of Rich with his friend caught the moment perfectly. Solid evidence of the bond between the two men.

"Do you keep in touch?" Ada turned her cheek into the warm, soft cotton of his shirt.

"As a matter of fact," Rich replied, shifting to settle her tighter against him. "I spoke with him recently. He's just become a grandfather, which I'm ashamed to admit was a total surprise. He and his wife, Latisha, have two beautiful daughters. When the girls were little I saw them, oh, every couple of months. Then I moved. They got caught up with family stuff and our relationship became one of cards at Christmas."

Ada sensed a kind of sadness. She placed the bowl on a shelf and curled her hands around the strong, sinewy arms enfolding her.

Then the feeling changed. She sucked in a breath as an unmistakable, steady, insistent pressure thrust against her from behind.

"Ada, did you hear me?"

"No, sorry," she replied, expelling a rush of air. She struggled to settle her racing pulse. "I got the feeling you were sad about Gary Wilson, or his family, or something... and then I felt..."

She grew quiet, unsure how to interpret what she'd *felt*.

"I said." Rich's deep warm chuckle rumbled in his chest. "I heard from him recently and we promised to keep in touch. But I'm losing focus here." He turned her to face him, lowered his hands to the curve of her hip, and pulled her against him.

Her mind went fuzzy. His scent surrounded her now, and she wanted to melt when her body molded against honed steel. She raised her arms, wrapping them around his neck seconds before he claimed her lips.

The kiss was hungry, demanding. Not the tempting, teasing enticements they'd shared earlier. Her surroundings spun away, like a pinwheel flashing bright spirals of color.

When at last he ended the straight forward assault on her eager mouth, he placed his forehead against hers and she struggled for breath. Desire spilled through her. Nerve-tingling waves of desire that made her want to satisfy all his touch had awakened.

"Darlin'." Rich's voice sounded rough, raspy. "I don't want to rush you." He kissed a moist trail over her flushed cheeks, ending at the sensitive curve of her neck.

Ada took a deep breath. "How long can shrimp marinate?" She felt his smile against her skin.

"A couple of hours won't hurt the little suckers one bit."

"Aren't you the confident one?" Her fingers teased the hair at the nape of his neck.

Rich nuzzled her. Reaching up, he took hold of her hands and planted a kiss on the back of each one. "Come with me, Ada."

She followed him down a cool, dark hallway. Her heart pounded, her insides quivered, and despite an outward calm, she feared her knees were about to buckle.

He led her to a room with creamy walls set off by warm touches of wood. Windows showcased the lake beyond and soft light poured in, drawing her eyes to a large bed with a curved iron headboard. A chocolate-colored quilt draped across the king-sized mattress, and pillows in multiple shades of green were strewn across the surface.

Ada stepped through the doorway and stopped.

Rich released her hand and moved silently to the windows. He pulled a transparent shade, engulfing the room in shadows. The setting sun became a hazy outline visible through the delicate weave while soft evening breezes sifted around the edges, gently lifting the shade.

Ada remained motionless until Rich returned to her. He placed one finger beneath her chin and lifted, forcing their eyes to meet.

"Getting cold feet?"

A long moment passed and his eyes darkened. He cupped her face with gentle hands.

"Richard." She took a deep, calming breath. "If my feet are cold, they are the only part of my body that is right now." She raised her hands, mirroring his gesture, framing his handsome face. Then she touched her lips to his.

His fingers slipped beneath the edge of her shirt. When they touched the bare skin of her back, awakening needs surged to life. His kisses edged past tender, staking a claim, exuding confidence.

The gesture fogged her brain like a sensuous drug. Somewhere in the background, Dean Martin crooned about 'Memories.'

Rich swayed in time with the distant refrain. He molded her body to his, moving his hands, caressing and soothing her. Every bold, yet gentle touch to her naked skin stoked simmering needs.

Her legs brushed the chocolate quilt and Rich stilled their movement. Passion spilled from his eyes, melting her heart. He dipped his head and pushed her collar aside, then placed his warm lips against her neck. "Relax, darlin'," he murmured against her heated skin. "Any time you want to slow down, or stop," he said, drawing back and looking into her eyes. "Just tell me."

Ada smiled up at him. "Slow is fine." Then she glanced away, nerves jittering. "Though I'm afraid I'm a bit out of practice. It's been a while, Rich."

"I like slow." He kissed her forehead, her cheeks and rubbed his lips slowly across her mouth. "I prefer a long, slow drive in the country, with frequent stops to enjoy the view, to racing headlong down a damn mountain." He went back to the sensitive spot on her neck. "I guarantee my way will prove to be incredibly satisfying at the end of the ride."

One by one, Rich undid the round, pearl buttons of her shirt, placing moist kisses on the emerging skin.

Ada shivered as he slid the garment from her shoulders and tossed it aside. Cool air rushed over her skin.

"Scenic stop number one," he murmured, nipping the swell of her breast.

At the last moment, she'd chosen a soft, lacey bra the color of sea foam. A gift from Cassi. Now, with Rich's eyes all but burning holes in the fine fabric, she thanked her lucky stars for that last minute decision.

"One of my favorite colors." His hand closed over her breast. Ada shut her eyes, giving herself over to the long forgotten feel of a man's touch. She arched into his caress, wanting more. How good it felt to be stroked. Intimately, boldly, and with the skill of a treasured lover.

Sliding his arm around, with one hand he unhooked the filmy undergarment and pulled it from her body as if unveiling a precious work of art.

Ada crossed her arms. Her fingers gripped her shoulders, and her folded arms hid her bare breasts. She quivered when Rich gently pried her hands free, loosened her arms and admired her. Holding her breath, she closed her eyes. Muscles, low and intimate clenched.

"Aw, Ada, you're beautiful," he murmured, releasing her hands and dropping a kiss on the swell of one breast before wrapping her in his arms.

She buried her flushed cheeks in the warm curve of his neck. Pressing against him she inhaled alluring, masculine heat. Mesmerized by the feel of his hands and the soft words he whispered against her skin, she let him gently ease her onto his bed. At some point he'd moved the quilt aside and with deft hands he slid her slacks and lace edged panties down her legs. Soft, cool sheets caressed her bare skin.

Standing beside his bed, he slowly unbuttoned his shirt. Heat poured from his eyes. Ada fought the urge to cover her exposed body, struggling not to behave like a startled maiden. She curled onto her side, tucking one bent arm beneath her head. His scent, now so familiar, rose from the pillow cradling her head.

Rich shrugged his shirt off and peeled a snowy white t-shirt over his head. He pulled a leather belt from the loops of khaki slacks and dropped it. The slacks slipped low on his hips.

In her mind, Ada begged him to pick up the pace, to speed up this long, tempting drive. She craved the return of his hands to her body. Her eyes trailed over him, following a thin arrow of dark hair, admiring the way coarse strands swirled around a sexy navel and disappeared beneath the tab of his zipper. Though a mature man, Rich remained fit and toned. When she looked up, his honey brown eyes appeared almost black. They locked with hers, gleaming in the shadows.

Placing one knee on the bed he leaned down, and with infinite care, tucked a strand of her hair behind one ear. "May I join you?"

The totally sweet, considerate question coiled around her pounding heart and squeezed. This man. This virile, handsome man had just shattered the wall surrounding her soul, making her want him with every fiber of her being. Her juices flowed again, her insides quivered, demanding what words could not describe.

By giving in to the needs of her body -- needs firmly intertwined with more than just physical pleasure -- did she risk heart-wrenching emotional pain?

Segments of an often lonely past flashed vivid and bright in her mind. Maybe this time love wasn't in the mix. Regardless, she craved, desired, his presence in her life. Could she turn away now, away from insistent urges and buried feelings his touch awakened?

In answer she raised her arms, opening to him.

Discarding his remaining clothes, Rich went to her. He pulled her trembling body close. The heat of his arousal pressed against her flesh and his lips covered her eager mouth. She shuddered, releasing a long, low moan of pure pleasure. Her soft intimate flesh throbbed and her whole body jerked when his hand sought and found her.

He stroked. Soothing her. Exciting her. His kisses covered her breast, making her arch, inviting more. Hungering for that which she'd been so long without, she rubbed against him, greedy for more of his touch, more of *him*.

"I want to make love to you, Ada," he rasped out. His fingers trailed up her thigh. Her legs opened to his bold caress. "You have a beautiful, woman's body, and I want you. I need to have you, now."

"Yes," she whispered. "Yes, take me Rich, I'm yours."

Barely visible in the encroaching twilight, he skimmed over her, a minute rubbing of tantalizing, heated flesh. A quick brush of coarse hair on her soft belly. Gentle fingers tested, spreading her moisture, and heightening her sensitivity.

And as she pressed her heels down, gently thrusting against his questing hand, the tiny bottle tucked away in her purse popped into her mind. At that precise moment, Ada decided, her clever lover brought about her own 'sensation naturelle.'

He shifted and began to enter her, shuddering with his need, exerting pressure, intense, stimulating, and arousing. She closed around him. Her hands tightly gripped muscled hips to pull him tight against her.

He moved, testing. She responded, easing into a rhythm, being touched where she craved to be touched. The exquisite friction increased until her body tensed, and bowing beneath him, her world exploded.

"Oh, Oh Rich," she cried out as his thrusting fed her pleasure. Rolling spasms, never ending pleasure, swept her away. Her muscles strained. Her starved body couldn't get enough.

At last, she collapsed.

The sheets beneath her were damp and the man above her -- his skin slick and moist -- braced on strong forearms lifted a hand and gently stroked a damp curl from her flushed cheek.

"Shhh, easy," he crooned against her moist parted lips. Inching down he nibbled her breasts. Then tucking his face into the curve of her neck, quivering head to toe, he began to thrust in and out, moving fast, breathing hard.

She knew the moment of his release and, much to her surprise, the sounds of his pleasure once again sent her to a shattering climax.

Awareness returned as cool air whispered over their heated bodies. The evening breeze lifted the drawn shade and slapped it against the window frame.

His lips touched her forehead, then her cheek, and she sighed when his hand skimmed her naked breast in a lingering caress. He untangled himself from her, from the sheets, and carefully covered her. The soft fabric floated down, settling over her.

Naked and dimly outlined in the twilight, Rich moved across the room. He disappeared into an adjoining bathroom, closing the door with a soft click.

Ada squeezed her eyes shut. She stretched her aching muscles. Raising her arms above her head, she pushed her heels into the mattress, lifting her hips. Her body quivered.

He'd given her intense, scream-inducing climaxes. Not once, but twice, maybe three times.

Had she screamed?

She blushed, scrunching beneath the sheet and rolling over to curl her tingling body into a tight ball.

The bathroom door opened. Rich's tall frame filled the doorway with a towel wrapped around his lean torso. She struggled to read his face, but light from behind him made it impossible.

"I left a clean towel for you." His voice rumbled softly. "Take your time. I'll pour the wine and start the grill." He crossed the room, gathered his discarded clothing, and quietly disappeared down the hallway.

After making use of the bathroom and putting herself back together, Ada made her way to the kitchen. The door to the balcony stood open. Through the open door Rich could be seen facing the lake and sipping wine. She joined him, accepting the chilled glass of Pinot he pressed into her hand. Silence loomed between them. She accepted the wine he offered and, turning to him, she murmured softly, "Richard, you're a spectacular lover."

Ever the gentleman, his simple "Thank you" made her blush

The evening breeze stirred her hair, and Rich tucked a wayward strand neatly behind one ear. His hand trialed downward, a soft brush of knuckles against her face.

A night chorus rose from the cattails, and leaves on the trees rustled in accompaniment. He hooked his arm around her, pulling her against his solid warmth.

Together they sipped chilled wine and watched night fall.

Chapter Fifteen

Rick Andrews downed his third mug of beer, followed by a stiff chaser. He'd made his way to The Corner Bar, as usual, but this night as a customer.

"Hey, Ricky," the young man tending bar rasped out. "The boss sees you gettin' toasted he'll shit bricks."

"Jim, mind your own business," Rick shot back. "Hit me again." He nudged his empty shot glass forward.

"How about I have Angie get you some food? You're goin' to be on your ass, buddy."

"Sure, why the hell not?" Rick relented. "How 'bout one of them double burgers, with mayo and a side of fries."

He spun around, studying the half-empty room.

It was early. The dinner crowd lingered, but soon the Saturday night regulars would spill in. Couples makin' out in corners, dancin' plastered up against each other. Every damn weekend they came. He ached with loneliness while watching them.

Ached with loneliness for Sadie.

He swung back as Angie slapped a plate of fries and a king sized burger on the bar.

Jim topped off the shot glass.

"Thanks," he mumbled.

"Last one." Came the warning.

He devoured the sandwich, picked at the fries, washing it all down with beer. When he tossed back the last shot, the mixture formed a greasy lump in his gut.

The hum of voices, clatter of dishes, and bursts of laughter intensified. Jim refused to refill his mug, and the turn-down ticked him off. On the verge of pressing the issue, he caught sight of his boss moving amongst customers, chatting.

"Sell me a six, then," he muttered. Jim frowned, hesitating. Promising to leave got him the order. Jim handed over the chilled cans. Rick tossed a few more bills on the bar, hitched up baggy jeans, and weaved through the growing crowd to the door.

Unable to face another evening alone in his cramped flat over a garage, Rick drove to the lake. He popped the first can and rolled down the window of his truck. Cool night air rushed in.

One after another, he downed all six. The cold, foamy brews stoked simmering anger.

Crushing the last empty, he tossed it with the others cluttering the floor of his truck. He sped back through town, heading over the ridge toward Pine Bluffs. Alcohol coursed through him, fogging his mind.

Seeing that smart-assed Chief of Police in The Corner Bar the other night brought it all crashing back. Then he heard the name. Ada. He recognized the attractive, dark-haired woman at the table. Her relaxed laughter pissed him off. If all those years ago Ada Blaine hadn't tossed Sadie aside, maybe, just maybe, *he* wouldn't be suffering. Her selfish decision was the reason he painfully slogged through every fuckin' day alone.

Maybe his Sadie -- his spunky, crazy, Sadie -- wouldn't be lying beneath the cold, hard ground.

He slowed instinctively when he rolled into Pine Bluffs. Fog lay heavy on the ground around the Blaine cottage, its porch light a hazy glow. He didn't know why he waited, hidden in dense foliage. He hated seeing her friggin', cozy, safe world.

His eyes skimmed the dew laden grass. Was the spot under the young maple the place where Sadie had died? He knew it was on Blaine land, knew her blood soaked into the ground as her life drained away. Knowing tore at his heart.

Then crippling guilt choked him, for he'd walked away when she needed him.

A marked police cruiser approached and swung into Ada Blaine's driveway, its headlights illuminating the cottage. Two officers emerged and disappeared around the corner of the building, sweeping walkways, doors, and windows with high powered flashlights.

Rick quietly drove away.

At the edge of town he accelerated, swearing when the sound of a siren cut through the night. Flashing lights appeared in his rear view mirror, closing fast.

Chapter Sixteen

Rich eased his truck into the garage. He climbed out, passed through his workshop, and traipsed upstairs. Damn fog along the lake made the trip to Ada's cottage a slow go. He'd followed her home through a near-impenetrable haze just to make sure she arrived safely.

He shrugged out of his jacket and peered through the open window facing the lake. Like ghostly sentinels, the faint outline of trees speared through the haze and gentle, breaking waves whispered in quiet rhythm.

They'd dined on crisp salad, herb crusted bread, and skewered shrimp. His smile spread slowly. Exceptional shrimp, bursting with flavor because of the *extra* marinating time.

Rich turned away from the shrouded night, and wandered into the kitchen. A wine decanter, about one-third full, caught his eye. He grabbed a clean glass, tipped the carafe, and poured. Probably a bad idea, drinking wine so late, but he wasn't ready to crawl into bed just yet. He wanted to savor thoughts of an unforgettable evening along with his nightcap.

Wine glass in hand, he stepped out onto his balcony. He inhaled the moist night air and strolled to the railing. The memory of Ada, soft and warm in his arms, captured his thoughts.

Over the years, on occasion, Rich gave in to baser needs. No use denying it. Fact was fact.

Tonight held no comparison. Being with Ada had nothing to do with basic physical needs.

The unique combination of bold earthiness and sensuality, all wrapped up in one intriguing woman, turned need into *want*.

They'd come together, urgent with the passion of first lovers. He'd asked her to stay the night, but when she gently touched his face, and promised "another time" he didn't press the issue. He suspected she found the idea of someone discovering she'd spent the night unsettling.

Rich chuckled, a rather prim reaction from one sensuous, sexy lady.

He'd followed her home and walked her to her door. She didn't object when he insisted on checking every room, though raised eyebrows and a tight lipped smile sent him a clear message.

Alone now on his deck, surrounded by chilly fog, Rich tipped his head back and finished the dark, earthy wine. The empty glass dangled from his fingers and his eyes probed the night.

He wrestled with indecision, despite the perfect evening spent with a charming woman. Getting involved, sharing his life after so many years of *not* being responsible for anyone but himself could be a big mistake. Not to mention dangerous. He came with a past. Not one entirely of his making, but one that could rise up and bite him on the ass.

Will Steiner, like the proverbial bad penny, could turn up at any time and destroy the life he'd built. He didn't fear for *his* safety. Years of training and a well-oiled, fully functional .45 auto would thwart any such attempt. What he feared most was having someone he cared for become of victim of his past.

Being with Ada, making love to her, had left him in a satisfied, peaceful state.

Ingrained instincts yanked him back to reality.

A woman as strong and fierce about standing on her own two feet as Ada would push back if he pushed too hard, hovered too close. She'd admitted with reluctance that the incidents this past week had frightened her. An admission way out of character for her.

Rich suspected the note upset her more than the gunshot. Whoever pulled the trigger did so from a distance, but whoever left the note had trespassed.

Someone had walked onto Ada's porch and left a veiled threat.

Could *he* be the catalyst placing her in danger?

Stifling a yawn, Rich decided to examine the situation after a good night's sleep. He rinsed his glass, dumped the dredges from the carafe, and filled it to soak. After securing his doors and turning out the lights, he made his way to bed, foregoing a shower till morning.

He peeled off his clothes, tossed them into a hamper, and slipped on flannel sleep boxers. His weary body welcomed the feel of cool, rumpled sheets. He closed his eyes, willing sleep to come. A flash of warmth made him kick the sheet away. He tossed, punching his pillow into submission.

Then his eyes flew open. He lifted one corner of the mutilated pillow and inhaled the sweet scent of lemon. Grunting and repositioning, Rich gave his boxers a tug.

Damn, it was going to be a long night.

Chapter Seventeen

Ada bounded out of bed. Piercing rays of a glorious sunrise streaked through her window. Energized and ready to face the day -- though sore in a few *delicate* places -- she showered and pulled on work clothes.

Her mind churned out plans, visualizing her newly tilled soil, pulling together loose ideas. Some she discarded, others came together to form a cohesive plan for doing what she loved.

Working her land.

No stupid childish note, no stray bullet -- one she now fervently hoped *was* a turkey hunter's poor aim -- would dampen her determined spirit.

This morning extra zing, extra spark, propelled her into the kitchen. While she made tea, her blood pulsed warm and steady through her well-used -- *Thank, God!* -- pliant body.

Well-used.

She grinned, lifting her teapot to pour. How wonderful at this stage in her life to once more be desired by a man. Not just any man, but one she desired in return.

Ada scooped up a fresh muffin and stepped onto the porch. Sunlight shimmered on the lake and, with steaming mug in hand, she surveyed her herb gardens.

Hardy oregano survived the winter. Parsley, curly as well as flat, was coming back, too. Their bright green leaves poking through winter brown. She made a note to cut back the old in order to let the new growth flourish.

With Mother Nature's blessing, winter survivors and new plants she'd yet to set would soon fill every bed. From practical culinary herbs, to the greens, golds, and burgundy's of her more formal areas, new life burst forth. A quick shiver raised goose bumps, making her skin tingle. Would the feelings Richard reawakened grow and thrive like the gardens she nurtured?

Considering, she swung around the corner of her cottage, sipping hot tea. For a brief moment, the sun made her squint. She paused when the strong, heavy smell of turned earth reached her.

Had it rained last night? She raised one hand to shield her eyes, and moved down the porch steps to examine the land she'd prepared for her new venture. When she reached the bottom step, her blood which moments before flowed warm and steady, turned to ice.

No! Oh, my God, no!

Ada rushed forward, stumbling in her haste. Deep furrows gouged random patterns into the earth. Tender, young, berry bushes lined up in neat rows to await planting were ground into useless twigs. As if in a fit of madness, someone had crisscrossed her property and destroyed everything in their path. Her land was ravished.

She dropped to her knees, folding slowly back onto her heels she cupped her face.

And sobbed.

A small river of tea drained from her dropped mug, and the sweet muffin lodged in her throat. Ada fought for control. She crossed her arms, hugged her body and rocked in place.

Around her birds sang sweetly, claiming their space. Leaves rustled as ground squirrels foraged for food. Familiar patterns creating a background of soft melodies and eager chatter persisted unchanged.

But Ada's space was tainted and forever changed.

Wrung dry, she stumbled to her feet, swiping angrily at her moist cheeks. Spotting her empty mug, she scooped it up and stomped back onto her porch. She turned, hands on hips and glared at pure, senseless destruction.

"Why?" she muttered, through clenched teeth. "Why, and who?" She shook her head, fighting back a fresh round of tears. "What have I done to deserve this?"

She spun away from her plundered gardens and rounded the corner to the patio door. A whoosh of wings near the shoreline made her queasy stomach drop. Had something spooked them? Her sharp gaze scanned the path leading to the lake. Nothing.

Then several ducks returned, landing just offshore. Weak with relief she hastened inside. She closed and locked the door, then lifted her phone and speed dialed Pine Bluffs PD.

Someone had violated what was hers, and she'd be damned if they'd get away with it.

*****

Jake Montroy arrived at the Blaine cottage less then fifteen minutes after Ada called. She was one of the steadiest, most sensible people Jake knew, yet something about her voice set his nerves on edge when he took her call.

He feared this assault on Ada's property indicated a serious escalation of threats. With the Pine Bluffs Chief of Police on his honeymoon, Jake was acting chief. He'd do his best to measure up to Nick McGraw's reputation.

Jake's on the job experience with all three of the McGraw men, in his opinion, had been with the best. Considering he was about to get his degree in law enforcement, putting Jake in temporary control of Pine Bluffs PD made sense. Humbled by the honor, he'd vowed to make the small, efficient department run smooth as hot butter until Nick returned.

But, man when butter chilled, it got lumpy. Right now there was a definite chill crawling up Jake's spine as he frowned at the damage.

Ada hadn't exaggerated. The damn field looked like a friggin' tractor pull had taken place. He called the station for help, wanting to secure the area as soon as possible. Ada joined him on her porch and handed him a steaming cup of coffee.

"Thank you, Mrs. Blaine," he said, taking a sip while surveying the damage. Hot sun beat down and tiny trails of vapor rose from the moist overturned earth. Ada's beautiful garden resembled smoldering ruins.

"Have a seat, Jake. I imagine you want to hear what I have to say. Please call me Ada. Anything else just makes me feel old."

"Yes 'm," Jake replied, returning her tired smile. He removed his hat and, carefully balancing the coffee, eased into the chair.

Ada raised one eyebrow. "Yes, *Ada.*"

"Yes, Ada," he repeated. He grinned and sat his cup aside before pulling a notepad from his pocket.

Two cups of coffee and many full pages of notes later, responding Officer Chuck Long climbed the steps to Ada and Jake. Upon arrival he'd strung bright yellow tape around the crime scene as Jake directed. The perimeter formed a rectangle extending from the driveway to the wood's edge. A garish frame around broken and destroyed plants.

Stepping onto the porch, Chuck scowled back at the destruction. "Raspberry starts, weren't they?"

Expressionless, Ada nodded. "Yes, they were, Chuck. The best money could buy. I tilled the land myself, and then placed them ready to set." Shoulders slumped, Ada appeared beaten and discouraged. "Conditions were perfect," she continued. "Raspberry bushes take time to get established, they need a good start. Damned senseless."

Jake's hand formed a tight fist. 'Proper course of action' echoed in his head; be objective, control anger, process facts. He knew how to follow procedure. But *thinking* about slamming a clenched fist into the person who'd caused this lady such heartache didn't break any rules. If he ever came face to face with the bastard, all bets were off.

Ada turned to him. "Do you think this is all connected somehow?"

Jake studied her solemn expression. He didn't want to scare her, but he knew damn well placating evasions wouldn't work with Ada. He'd insult her if he made light of the situation.

"I'm very concerned," he said. "The shooting may have been a fluke, an accident. But the note," he shook his head, "that's tangible evidence." Using his pen, he pointed to the trashed garden. "That sure as hell wasn't a ground hog run amuck."

He dug out his notepad and flipped through several pages. Satisfied for the time being, he turned to Chuck. "We'll comb the area to find out if this character left anything behind. Then, if possible, we'll make casts of tire marks. I wouldn't hold my breath, though. Most tread patterns are pretty common. As soon as possible, we'll follow up to see if anyone saw anything."

The nearest house was barely visible through trees lining Ada's property. Jake calculated the distance at least a quarter mile. He didn't hold out much hope for any credible witnesses, especially on a dark, foggy night. He grabbed his hat, gave Chuck a nudge, and followed him down the steps. Upon reaching the bottom, he stopped. "We'll be here for a while, Ada, so just relax. Marcy isn't on duty," he added after a moment. "I'm sure she would come over if you need her to, or maybe you should go to Marcy and Rob's for a while."

"I could do that," Ada agreed. "Her boys are keeping Rufus entertained, or vice versa." She rose, gathering up empty cups. "Go. Do what you have to do, I'll be fine."

Jake nodded. He glanced at the sun, then put on his hat. "This coward likes to crawl out of his hole after dark," he said to Chuck. "Until we know more, I'm going to advise Ada not be here alone."

Chapter Eighteen

Rich whistled softly as he threw open the front door to Ace Hardware. Prepared to face the day, he stepped into the morning sun. Trucks idled in line, eager contractors waiting to load up and get to work.

He settled into a high-backed rocker on the wraparound porch and peeled the top from a take-out cup of Brown Cow coffee. Halfway through his pick-me-up brew, Harley swung into the side parking lot. The unfamiliar coup he drove kicked up a cloud of dust, and seconds later he bounded up the stairs. "Mornin', boss," he said with a cocky salute. He lifted his cap, and ran a hand through his shaggy hair. "Kinda surprised to see you sittin' here, all relaxed, sippin' coffee," he remarked, fidgeting and jiggling keys in his pocket.

Harley's arrival disturbed Rich's peaceful morning. A loaded half-ton exited the lot, and as Rich's gaze followed the lumbering truck, he commented softly, "In case you've forgotten, Harley, I own the business and can take a break whenever I damn well please."

The comment halted the jingling and Harley froze. He readjusted his hat. "Shit, Mr. McConnell. I didn't mean nothin'. But I kinda thought, with you bein' good friends with Ada Blaine and all, I thought maybe you'd be upset over what happened at her place last night."

Rich lowered his cup and pushed out of his chair, towering over Harley. "What the hell are you talking about?"

Harley stepped back. Giving a nervous laugh, he edged away. "Hey, boss. Calm the fuck down. Mrs. Blaine's all right, far as I know." He held up a hand when Rich shot him a furious look. "Somebody just messed up her gardens."

"Inside," Rich muttered and tossed the remains of his coffee into a trash can.

Once inside, he fired rapid questions at Harley. When he pressed for details, all he got were 'I don't knows' and nervous shrugs.

He dismissed Harley with a curt warning. "Watch your language." The employee's attitude was starting to piss him off.

Rich dialed Pine Bluffs PD. He gripped the phone like a vice and paced as he waited for someone to pick up.

She'd been fine when he left her, damn it. He'd checked every square inch of her cottage. What in the hell did he miss? He glanced at the time. "Come on, come on. Answer the damn phone."

"Pine Bluffs Police. Infantino speaking."

"Frank, what happened at Ada Blaine's place last night?"

"Rich?"

"Yes," Rich snapped. "What happened last night? Is Ada all right?" He needed facts, *now*, before he went off half-cocked and rushed over there like a damn fool.

"Ada's fine, far as I know, Rich, but I don't have much to tell you. Montroy and Long are there now, processing the scene."

Rich's throat closed up. *Processing?* He didn't like the sound of that. "How'd they get involved?"

"Mrs. Blaine called at the crack of dawn and--"

"An emergency call?"

"No, no. She called just past six to report some vandalism. Jake went right over. He called me back within fifteen minutes and told me to send Chuck over soon as he got here."

"That's all he said?"

"That's it," Frank said. "I wasn't surprised, though. When Mrs. Blaine called, she didn't sound so good."

"Thanks, Frank. Didn't mean to snap your head off. I appreciate you telling me. I'll check it out myself." He hung up and headed for his truck.

The drive to Ada's normally took about ten minutes, fifteen tops. Racing along, he caught glimpses of sparkling water between the trees. There was way too much crap bouncing around in his head, screwing up his concentration. Better slow down before he ended up in the lake.

He was within a mile of Ada's when he stopped, pulled over, and shoved the gearshift into park. Several cars blew by, buffeting the idling truck. Rich stared straight ahead, both hands locked on the steering wheel. One by one he methodically lined up facts, a skill his snarling DI drummed into his skull years ago.

First, the shooting. *He'd* been with her. Second, the note. *He'd* been at Ada's for dinner that night. And finally, last night. *He'd* been with her until past midnight.

Was he the link to all this crap?

"Shit" His flat-handed blow bounced off the steering wheel. Was Will Steiner's release just a friggin' coincidence or had the son-of-a-bitch somehow tracked him down? He wouldn't put it past Steiner to harass and frighten someone, especially someone Rich cared about. But how the hell far would he go?

Precious moments ticked by.

Long branches of a roadside willow brushed against his truck. Rich's gaze idly followed swaying clusters of pale green leaves. If someone was keeping tabs, rushing to her side was a lousy idea.

He shifted and made a sharp u-turn, heading back to the store. He'd call the McGraws, have Mary check on Ada, and then contact Gary for any updates on Steiner. For now, he'd stay away from Ada. He hated that idea, wanted to say the hell with it and turn right back around, but staying away from Ada now might keep her safe.

He floored it, arriving back at the hardware store in record time and in a miserable mood. He went straight to his office, slammed the door, and snatched up the phone.

First, he'd call Gary, then Tom, confident they'd agree with his theory. Then, soon as possible, he'd talk to Jake.

He dreaded the consequences of his decision. Ada would be hurt, and probably angry. Last night they'd connected, started... *something.* Backing away now would be pure hell.

But, by God, if staying away kept Ada safe, he'd do it.

Chapter Nineteen

Jake took one section, Chuck Long the opposite side. They crisscrossed Ada's damaged land, working together, covering the grid they'd created inch by meticulous inch.

Sun beat down, ducks along the shore splashed and muttered. Two policemen worked within shouting distance of Ada. She should have felt safe. She didn't. Early that morning the bottom dropped out of her world, and an alarming abyss yawned at her feet, like a black hole threatening to suck her under.

Last night she'd rediscovered intimacy. The pleasure of being held and cared for came crashing back in Rich McConnell's arms. Now, loneliness threatened to choke her.

For years she'd managed on her own, and old habits were hard to overcome. Much of her life hadn't been easy. When her grandmother died, she'd cried endless tears, and if not for John, her husband and anchor at the time, she may not have survived.

Within a few years, John and her beloved mother had been ripped away in a fiery head-on crash. It was then Ada withdrew and loneliness became her companion.

Until Cassi came into her life.

Reconnecting with her niece and being there when Nick and Cassi fell in love had reawakened something in Ada. Last night she'd let go, and, God, it had been wonderful. Not only the sheer joy of responding to a man's touch, but to trust someone.

So why shouldn't she call Rich? Why shouldn't she reach out and lean on someone she trusted?

She glanced at the two officers. They were crouched low, intent on studying some unknown find. Chuck rose and picked his way over the furrowed ground to the patrol car.

It looked like they'd be busy for a while, so Ada got up and went inside to call Rich and tell him what had happened.

If he insisted on coming over she wasn't going to argue. She'd call Mary, too, and of course, Marcy. For at some point, she'd have to reclaim Rufus. The world couldn't stop because some idiot decided to amuse himself at her expense.

Her pulse tripped up a notch as she punched in the number for the hardware store.

*****

Rich clicked a ballpoint pen, rapidly, repeatedly, waiting for Gary to pick up. He'd left instructions not to be disturbed. A move so out of character he'd glimpsed a few stunned looks before shutting the door to his office.

"Hello."

Latisha Wilson's soft drawl slipped past his irritation, a soothing balm for frayed nerves. He tossed the pen aside and leaned back in his chair. "How's the most beautiful woman I've ever met?"

"Richard, is that you?"

"None other. How are you Tish?"

"I'm great, honey. Life couldn't be better. I'm a grandma now ya' know, and that's pretty special." Not missing a beat, her tone changed. "What's wrong, Rich?"

Gary claimed his wife had a sixth sense, and Rich assumed her talent only applied to Gary. Guess he was wrong.

"You're a perceptive lady, Latisha. There've been a few bumps in my road lately." He grappled for the pen and resumed clicking. "Is that no good man you married around?"

"Somewhere, hold on." He detected her muffled call. "He's on his way, Rich. Take care, honey. You're one of my favorite people, ya' know, and we miss seeing you."

Rich strolled to the window, waiting for Gary to reach the phone. Memories filtered through the stress, good ones. Things had been difficult back then, pulling duty that kept them away from loved ones, sleepless nights. Yet Latisha and Gary kept him together when his marriage had gone to shit.

"Hey, what's up?"

"Hey, Gary. Latisha sounds good."

"Always." Gary chuckled. "I was out digging a hole. Tish drug home some kind of flowering bush and insists I get it in the ground ASAP. The weather's been perfect here, so I've got no excuse." Rich heard shuffling. "Christ, I'm covered with mud. I've tracked it all over the damn place."

"Planting a scrub sounds easy, facing Tish when she sees what you've done to her floors, not so easy." Rich envied Gary to be facing such simple problems. Though he'd seen the wrath of Latisha and was glad he'd never had to deal with it.

Rich plopped down at his desk. Resting one elbow on the desktop, he scooped up the pen and began to doodle as he asked, "What's the word on Steiner?"

Gary blew out a sharp breath. "Nothing. Nada. Not a damn thing. I'd have called you if I'd picked up anything."

"Figured as much," Rich retorted. "Since I talked to you about the shooting, there've been a couple of incidents I can't ignore."

He laid out what had happened with Ada, including his involvement with her. Gary would understand, and, he'd keep his mouth shut.

When he'd covered everything, he leaned back and heaved a sigh. "So, what do you think? Am I overreacting, or could all this be tied together? It burns my ass to think this is happening to Ada because of me."

Gary's first words took the edge off. "Rich, first I gotta say this. Damn, buddy, it's about time you loosened up and enjoyed life. Yeah, yeah, I know. You've been fine, yada, yada, but Tish isn't the only one with perception. Your voice tells all. That woman means something."

Gary'd nailed it.

"No argument," Rich admitted, "but until this mess gets cleared up, I'm backin' off."

"I understand. Let me touch base with a couple of guys back east. They'll know if Steiner's keeping his nose clean. Soon as I know anything, you'll know."

"Thanks. I appreciate your help. Now clean up the mess you made, and get the hell back out there and plant Tish's bush."

Gary's laughter rang in his ear as he disconnected.

He glanced at the time. Still early, but Tom was an early riser. He had to talk to someone, and it could be hours before he heard back from Gary.

Waiting would be pure hell.

Chapter Twenty

Ada hastened up the McGraw's front steps. The door swung open, and Mary's welcoming smile greeted her.

That smile dimmed when Ada drew closer. "Something's wrong." She placed her hand on Ada's arm, gave a quick rub. "Come in, I'll make tea."

Swallowing the lump in her throat, Ada nodded and followed Mary into her spotless kitchen. While Mary set water to boil, Ada attempted to soothe jumping nerves by gazing out the windows overlooking Pine Shadow Lake.

Her insides churned, and when Mary laid a gentle hand on her shoulder, she jumped. "Whoa, lady," Mary said. "I've never seen you so tense. Sit, and tell me what's happened."

Ada placed her hand over Mary's and squeezed. "I feel like an idiot, Mary." She dropped down at the well-used kitchen table.

Mary placed a steaming mug in front of her. "Why would one of the smartest women I know feel like an idiot?"

The scent of Darjeeling tea drifted up. She added cream, a rich swirl in fragrant amber, and took a fortifying sip. "You haven't heard?"

"Apparently not."

At first, words caught in her throat, but once she began, they poured out. "They might as well have driven over me," she concluded. "The damage tore up my heart, Mary. As sure as whoever did this tore up my land."

"Oh, Ada. What a mess." Mary's gaze sharpened. "Weren't you with Rich last night?"

Ada lowered her eyes. "I was. *That's* the reason I feel like an idiot."

"Why? What happened?"

"I had an amazing roll in the hay with a handsome, sexy man."

Mary's eyes opened wide. "Why would that make you feel like an idiot?" She shook her head. "Ada, you're confusing me."

"I gave in to the moment." She shrugged, and offered a sad smile. "We made love, drank wine, watched the sunset, and had a fabulous meal. All compliments of that sexy man."

Before Mary could respond, Ada pushed away from the table and, carrying her cup, returned to the window. A couple of deer paused on the McGraw's rolling lawn. She closed her eyes, shutting out their graceful beauty, squeezing back tears. "I let myself believe," she murmured. "I let myself want."

Mary's arm came around her.

She leaned against her friend. "This morning, after I discovered the damage I called the police. Then I called Rich." Ada's voice hitched. "Big mistake."

"Why? I lean on Tom when I have to, Ada. There's nothing wrong with needing help, or asking for it."

Ada straightened. She brushed away a stray tear and, with gentle hands, adjusted the crooked collar of Mary's blouse. "Last night was still fresh in my mind, so it felt natural to call the hardware store."

"Good," Mary declared, lifting her cup to sip.

"He'd left instructions not to be disturbed."

"*What*?" Mary shot Ada a startled look. "Who told you that?"

"Harley Phillips, and when I tried to tell him it was an emergency, he said Rich knew what had happened. Then he repeated, 'Mr. McConnell does not want to be disturbed.'"

"I can't believe this." Mary stalked to the sink. Water flew as she rinsed her cup. She snatched up a towel and studied Ada while briskly drying the cup. "You look tired, and pale as powdered sugar. I'm going to fix some lunch."

"I don't have much of an appetite," Ada rubbed her pounding temple. She hadn't eaten since last night, which could account for the headache.

Mary pointed to an empty chair. "Sit. I have to cook anyway. TJ's coming to lunch."

Ada's hand dropped. "Oh, then I should go. I have to get Rufus anyhow, and decide what to do next."

"Worry about that silly dog later." Mary slammed doors and drawers, muttering, "Stupid man. I don't know what's wrong with Richard, but we'll discuss *that* situation another time. In the meantime, we'll pick TJ's brain and see what he thinks about last night's vandalism."

She refilled Ada's cup and shooed her outside, insisting she get some fresh air.

Ada strolled along the deck, tilting her face to the sun. Mary was right. Maybe after getting something in her stomach, she'd be able to sort out the snarled mess in her head. A soft breeze stirred the air and a spicy aroma drifted out the window. From inside came the sound of Mary humming. Slowly, the snarl began to untangle.

At her age, after spending one night with a man, she should have known better than to build romantic fantasies. Teenagers had more sense. What man wouldn't back off when every time he saw a particular woman something bad happened?

Now she was making excuses. Regardless, he should have taken her call.

The sound of an approaching car drew her attention. She turned and waved as TJ's classy Camry sped up the driveway.

*****

TJ grabbed a napkin and blotted sauce from the corner of his mouth.

"Mom," he mumbled around a mouthful of food, "nobody tops your pulled beef barbeque." He took a long swallow of chilled Coors.

Ada smiled. She'd known Thomas Jacob McGraw, since he was a toddler. She'd watched TJ and his cousin Nick -- now her niece Cassi's husband -- grow and mature to fine young men, fine police officers.

Nick encouraged TJ to join the Pennsylvania State Police. Then, when Mary's Tom retired, Nick stepped in as chief and TJ left for the academy. Funny how things worked out sometimes.

Munching on a handful of chips, TJ tipped his chair back. He'd been aware of the shooting, but as they told him about the note, followed by the attack on Ada's property, his relaxed expression changed.

He asked questions, frowning and nodding as Ada answered.

Discussing facts and getting her concerns out in the open helped. After the first bite of barbeque, her starving taste buds woke up, and her queasy stomach unknotted.

She kept the fact she'd been out with Rich casual. TJ gave a considering look and acknowledged the information with a nod, but he pressed for details about the note and the damage. He was methodic, which she figured stemmed from being a policeman. Or, vise versa, he was a good policeman *because* he was methodic.

When he paused, quietly sipping beer, his silence tried her patience. She grabbed a napkin and, wiping sticky fingers, asked, "Any ideas, TJ?"

He pushed his empty plate aside. "Not off hand." His fingers drummed a rapid beat on Mary's table. "I'll make some calls. See if anyone patrolling this area last night noticed anything." He stopped drumming and glanced at his watch. "I'll talk to Jake, too. In fact, maybe I'll give him a call now before his shift ends. Something may have turned up at the scene. Excuse me."

While helping Mary clear the table, Ada asked, "Wouldn't Jake talk to the State Police?"

"Not necessarily. State patrols come through town, but their territory is broken down into zones in the county. They'll only assist if local departments ask for help. Tom had a good relationship with the staties, so I'm sure they'll work with Jake." She snapped the dishwasher shut and wiped her hands. "Let's wait on the deck."

TJ joined them shortly. He settled one hip on the railing and crossed his arms. "They found very little at your place, Ada. With all that churned up dirt, tread imprints left behind were rough, nothing out of the ordinary. It appears whoever did it drove right up your driveway. He came from the north and headed back the same way."

Ada shook her head. "That disappoints me, but I appreciate your time and effort, TJ."

He smiled. "For you, Ada, nothing's an effort. I did call the Corry barracks. Trooper Adamski was assigned to these zones last night. He wasn't there so I left a message. He'll call me."

Mary pinched spent flowers from a hanging basket. "Your dad

should be home soon. He's been in Erie fishing since early this morning."

"Good, I'd like to catch up with him." TJ pushed off the railing. He lifted the hanging basket down for Mary. "Oops, my cells buzzing."

He rehung the plant and, taking his cell from his pocket, strolled toward the end of the deck. Suddenly, he stopped. "No shit," he muttered. "Son-of-a-bitch."

Mary shot him a frown. His hand came up. "Sorry, Mom. Why don't you take Ada inside? I'll finish here, and then we'll talk."

The spicy barbecue in Ada's stomach turned over.

TJ's tight lipped expression when he joined them revealed nothing. She exchanged a look with Mary, waiting while he drew a glass of water.

Leaning against the counter, he drank down half the glass. "Here's what I've got." He swiped his hand across his mouth. "Close to midnight last night, Trooper Adamski nailed a truck on radar heading north out of Pine Bluffs. The guy was weaving all over the damn road, so he pulled him over. When he approached, the joker took off like a bat outa hell. Damn near knocked the trooper down."

TJ drained the glass and set it aside. "By the time he got back to his unit, the truck had disappeared. He radioed for assistance, but there weren't any patrols in the area to back him up. Trying to catch a speeding drunk would have been just plain stupid."

"So the man got away." Ada heaved a sigh. "He may have been my late night visitor."

"Maybe." TJ shrugged. "But there's good news. Adamski got the guy's plate number and ran it. His shift was almost up and when he checked with his supervisor he was told to follow up the next day. Adamski has a current address, he'll find the jerk. DUI wouldn't stick, but he has him for speeding and failure to drive to the right, along with fleeing and eluding which is a misdemeanor."

Icy fingers crept up Ada's spine. If this was good news, why had the frown between TJ's eyes deepened? Mary moved closer, and a quick glance revealed an identical frown creasing her friend's smooth brow.

In a low voice, Mary said, "There's more, isn't there?"

TJ nodded. "Now here's the bad news." His gaze locked with Ada's. "The truck is registered to Rick Andrews."

Chapter Twenty-One

It was late afternoon when Rich emerged from his office. Lucky for him, he kept a stash of snack bars and a good supply of coffee. The bars staved off hunger, but any more coffee and he'd launch into orbit.

His staff had left him alone, as instructed. To keep busy, he tackled a stack of paperwork and placed stock orders well into the next quarter.

He'd allowed himself one call, and if the chill in Mary McGraw's voice was any indication, she'd been talking with Ada. When he'd asked for Tom, she'd told him Tom had gone fishing. He'd cut the conversation short. No sense trying to make small talk when the woman's voice dripped ice.

All morning his decision to avoid Ada weighed on his mind. More than once he'd reached for the phone, only to stop short of punching in her number. He cursed the bizarre circumstance, and went back to his paperwork.

He didn't doubt Ada had gone to Mary. They were close, thank God. At least Ada didn't have to face this mess alone. He paused, pen in hand over an invoice. Had she told her best friend they'd become lovers?

At lunchtime he picked at the sandwich he'd ordered in, finally, after tossing most of the sub away, he emerged from his office. He stopped at a display of spray paints, absently moving a can of alabaster white from the barn red section, "Shit," he muttered to himself. "What kind of a man makes love to a woman and deserts her when she needs him?"

A man with his back to the wall, his practical, logical, mind deduced. Until he located that son-of-a-bitch, Steiner, he was plastered flat against that wall.

He scowled at the young girl working check-out. In the midst of chatting and ringing up a sale, she flicked a nervous glance his way and called for someone to haul paint out to the lady's car. When the door swung open, the paint lady followed the helper out, and returned TJ McGraw's cheerful greeting as he strolled in the door.

Rich couldn't help but stare. Tall and lanky, rusty hair cropped close, the young man coming through the door was a mirror image of his dad. The older McGraw's hair was now peppered with gray, but had once been the same rich red as TJ's. By God, Rich thought, it's like looking at Tom twenty years ago.

TJ scanned the room and zeroed in on Rich. He smiled and started down the aisle, his purposeful stride loose and limber.

"Ah, you've come out of your cave." TJ stopped in front of Rich and grinned while tucking his hands into his jeans pockets.

"Smart ass. I actually have to put in a day's work. Can't do that while socializin' and taking coffee breaks all damn day."

"I serve and protect, caffeine's a requirement. You got a minute? I'm guessing you know about this morning's incident?"

"Yes to both. Come on in, I might even have some coffee to keep you runnin'"

Rich closed the door to his office. He moved to prepare a fresh pot of coffee. TJ strolled around, touching an occasional gadget or picking up one of many tool samples scattered on shelves. "You did the same thing when you used to come here with your dad," Rich commented."

"What's that?"

"Put your fingers all over my tools."

TJ smiled as he carefully replaced the rubber tipped mallet he'd been examining. "It's been a while," he remarked, and shoved a heavy wooden chair nearer the desk. "I've been in the store. Even picked up a new set of wrenches last week, but I don't think I've nosed around your office since I was a kid."

"You may be right." Rich pulled out two mugs and poured fresh coffee. On the way to his desk, he handed one to TJ.

TJ propped ankle to knee and took a careful sip. "You use the same brew as Dad. When he was chief, the whole station, one after another, would stop in his office every morning to get a cup. He claimed it was the best way to find out what was going on without having to chase everybody down."

"Smart man. Between the two of us, we've probably made Lois Farrell a rich woman. Nothing like Brown Cow coffee." He took a healthy gulp, figuring, what the hell, who needs sleep. "So." he sat and wrapped his hands around the steaming cup. "Is this a friendly walk down memory lane, or did Mary send you?"

"You're sharp for an old guy."

Rich arched a brow.

"She *suggested* I pay you a visit," TJ admitted. "I called Dad and he's on his way back from Erie. Didn't catch a damn thing, but claims it's not all about the fish."

With a grunt, Rich turned his head toward the window. Mid afternoon sun poured in, creating a triangle of light on the wood plank floor. "He's right. Catching fish is a bonus, but just sittin' there amidst it all, that's what counts."

"He's going to come here." TJ shifted in his seat. "Jake Montroy and I put our heads together today, and after some checking, we've got a lead on who might be responsible for some of the crap involving Ada Blaine."

Rich swung around. "What kind of lead?" Tom knew about Steiner, knew the history. He wouldn't have betrayed a trust, even with his son. So who the hell was TJ talking about?

Two sharp raps announced Tom's arrival.

"Come on in," Rich called out and grinned when Tom, sporting a droopy brimmed tan hat, poked his head in the door.

After a coffee refill for TJ, and a fresh cup for Tom, they settled in to listen. Rich passed on more coffee and opted for bottled water.

He glanced out the window as they settled around his desk. Rain laden clouds were rolling in. The lined vest Tom wore meant temperatures must be plunging ahead of the storm. Not what Ada needed right now. Rain would turn her damaged land into a quagmire, delaying the repair. If he got his hands on the bastard responsible, heaven help the man.

Once settled, TJ told them what he'd found out from Jake and how he'd located the trooper on duty last night.

When he got to the part about the traffic stop and Rick Andrews, Tom burst out, "Damn it! The bartender at The Corner Bar. I meant to look into what that guy was doing in the area." He shook his head. "I never did."

"Wouldn't have revealed squat, Dad."

"Why not?"

"Other than driving drunk, which they can't prove, he's kept his nose clean. He moved to PA early this year after the place where he worked in Ohio booted him out. Seems he had a bad habit of overindulging and then pounding on anyone who looked cross-eyed at him. He pounded on a couple of good customers, so they fired his drunken ass."

Interested, Rich leaned in closer. "So, if they've hauled this guy in, did they check out his truck? Shouldn't be hard to tell if it was covered with mud from Ada's."

"When I spoke with Trooper Adamski, tracking down this clown was first on his list. I heard from him on the way over here."

"Let me guess," Tom said. "The truck was clean as a whistle."

"You got it, Dad. Mr. Andrews was all cleaned up, stone sober and polite as a little old lady. His truck looked recently washed, waxed, buffed, and polished. They nailed him for speeding, though. He'd been clocked fifteen miles over the limit, and for fleeing and eluding. The fleeing and eluding could have bought some jail time, but they ran a check and discovered this was his first serious offense. Not enough reason to lock him up. He'll pay a hefty fine, though."

"Christ," Rich shoved away from his desk and jumped up. "There's a connection there, between him and Ada. Did they question him about being in Pine Bluffs last night? Or take a closer look at his damn truck?"

"I hear you, Rich," TJ picked up a nearby pencil, fiddling with it. "Evidence. The key to any crime, and" he held up his hand when Rich sneered, "and, there was none. They went over the truck at his place, with his permission, and determined that going to the expense and taking time to impound it wasn't worth the trouble."

"Rich," Tom waited until Rich's gaze swung his way. "There's never enough manpower. It's better to pass this on to Jake. Our department's small, he can snoop around and maybe come up with a witness. Then the staties could be brought back and move on this guy. In the meantime, all we can do is keep our eyes open."

"This guy will be watched for a while," TJ added. "I've made headquarters aware of the situation, and I'll pass the word to guys on patrol. If Rick Andrews makes a habit of cruising down to Pine Bluffs, we'll know."

TJ tossed the pencil he'd been flipping around onto Rich's desk. "I've got to go. I'll follow up at work tomorrow and let you know if anything turns up."

As the door closed behind him, Tom refilled his cup. He plopped back down, yawned, and rubbed his whisker roughened jaw. "I thought I'd get more rest after I retired."

"Maybe if you didn't get up in the middle of the night to drop a line." As usual, Tom's calm nature settled Rich. "Hell, even when we go ice fishing we don't go at the crack of dawn."

Tom laughed, and nodding to a chair suggested, "Sit down and think this through. Maybe you're wrong. Maybe this guy, Steiner, has nothing to do with what's been going on."

Rich shrugged and sat. "Could be. I'm still trying to find out what he's been up to since he got out."

"What about Ada?"

Rich scrubbed both hands over his face. "Is she with Mary?"

"She is. I haven't been home, but Mary called me on my cell and, ah, suggested I stop in and see you."

"You, too, huh? She suggested TJ stop in earlier."

"Her suggestions were strong."

"I see." On his feet again, Rich crossed the room. His empty water bottle hit the recycle bin with a hollow echo. "I started over to Ada's place this morning, after I learned what had happened. All I could think about was her being in danger. Again. Then something made me pull over. I needed to take a breath, to think, and sitting there under a damn willow tree, a pattern I can't ignore struck me."

"A pattern?"

"Every time something happens with Ada, it involves me." Rich raised three fingers. "The shooting, I was with her." He bent one finger. "The note, I'd been there for dinner." Two fingers down. "And last night." He lowered the third finger and leveled his gaze at Tom. "I was with her last night."

Tom pursed his lips and nodded. "I understand. Your relationship with Ada has changed"

Rich's deep even voice turned rough. "She's more." He glanced at the window. Raindrops hit the glass, trailing down. The fading light reflected his mood. "Much more."

"We'll take care of her." Tom rose and laid a hand on his friend's shoulder. "Mary's going to try and get her to spend tonight with us. You could come home with me, stay for dinner?"

Rich shook his head. "Not until I know more. I've hurt her. She wouldn't complain, and she wouldn't expect me to coddle her. In fact, she reamed my butt when I had the nerve to question her for going kayaking alone. Which reminds me, she met some stranger on the lake.

"I'll tell Jake about that." Tom gathered up his things. "*You* owe Ada an explanation. Not going to her, offering to help, was wrong, considering." He raised his hand. "Wait, let me finish. She's no weak-kneed girl who expects a man to hover, but you should respect the woman she is."

"You're right. She'll bottle it all up inside. It wasn't easy for her to open up, to share mind and body. My actions must have cut deep. Above all else I respect Ada. I'll find a way to make it right, Tom."

"It's a good beginning for where I think you're heading." Tom winked, and walked to the door. "I consider you both to be close friends," he said, and turned to face Rich. "Do what you must do."

Tom left the door open. He called out to several acquaintances as he wound his way through aisles and out the front door.

Rich straightened his desk, stacking cups to be washed, and filing paperwork he'd completed. He glanced up when Harley stopped in the doorway. "Something I can do for you, Philips?"

"Just wanted to let you know I'm leavin' early."

"Are we covered?"

"Yeah, boss. My truck's in the shop and I need to go get it and settle up before they close."

Guilt made Rich stop. He halted his busy work to face Harley. The man fidgeted in place, jingling keys in his pocket. He'd been short with Harley of late. Granted, the man often had a piss poor attitude, but for the most part he worked hard. "Need a ride to get your truck?"

"No." His reply came quick and short. "I'm covered. They gave me a loaner. See you tomorrow." And just like that, he was gone.

"Huh, doesn't move that fast when he's working." Rich muttered, and turned to gaze out the window, vaguely remembering the coupe he'd seen Harley driving earlier. Must be the loaner.

Hard gusts whipped around the building, rattling the eaves. Closing time. He grabbed a light rain slicker on his way out. Maybe he'd hear something from Gary before this miserable night ended.

Chapter Twenty-Two

Ada drifted awake, her focus fuzzy. Someone had tossed a soft quilt over her and low flames danced on fireplace logs, casting a soft glow. Tilting her head, she squinted at rain coating the windows and then pushed upright, readjusting the quilt around her.

Across the room, stirring a pot on the range, Mary turned and smiled. "You're awake. Feeling better?"

"How long was I out?"

Mary glanced at the wall clock. "A couple of hours." She tapped the spoon on the steaming kettle and adjusted the heat. "You needed it," she declared, and crossed to Ada. "How about some tea?"

Ada tugged Mary down beside her. She wrapped both arms around her friend, breathing in cinnamon and spice. "What would I do without you?"

"You'd do fine." Mary rubbed her back and returned the hug. "The weather changed after you'd been down a while, so I got a fire going, along with a pot of soup. Now I'll make that tea."

Ada folded the quilt and lay it aside. She stretched and went to stand by the fireplace. "Is Tom home yet?"

"He's on his way. I hope you're not angry with me."

"Why would I be angry with you?"

"I made him stop and talk to Rich. In fact, TJ met him there and brought them both up to speed with everything that's happened."

"I'm not angry." Ada's gaze went to the window. Early twilight hid the lake and grey mist clung like a shroud. "I can take care of myself," she assured. "I've managed a good many years alone. One foolish mistake doesn't make me helpless."

"Sleeping with a man you care about doesn't make you foolish. Tom and I've known Rich McConnell forever. God's truth, in all those years I've never known him to hurt a living soul." She narrowed her gaze on Ada, "And I've never seen him wrapped up in a woman like he is with you."

Ada snorted. "It's easy to get wrapped up in a woman when getting her naked is your goal."

Mary choked on a laugh. "I have no first hand knowledge, but I doubt a single man who looks like Rich has trouble attaining that goal with any number of women." She passed Ada a steaming mug. "He's gentle with you, and protective. I noticed that when the four of us went out last week. It wasn't the first time he's gone out to eat with Tom and me, but it's the first time he wasn't alone."

"Really? You've never seen him date anyone?"

"He's been to our holiday gatherings, birthdays, lots of family stuff.

Always fit right in, always alone. I suspect somewhere in Rich's past there's something, or someone, that hurt him and he's never gotten over it."

Quite at home, Ada opened the fridge. She poured a dash of half and half into her tea. Regardless of what Mary said, she wasn't sure she could overcome the embarrassment of her expectation, followed by rejection, when she'd reached out to him. There'd been no mistaking the clear message he'd left in place. 'Hold calls, no interruptions.'

His complete about face after being with her demanded an explanation. A damn good one.

A fierce gust of wind accompanied Tom as he burst through the door. He slammed it behind him with enough force to rattle pictures on the wall. He pulled off his hat and shrugged out of a dripping slicker before glancing up to find his wife, hands on hips, frowning at the puddles in his wake. "I'll clean it up, soon as I get out of these wet things. Damn, what a day this turned out to be."

He toed off his boots, hung up the hat and, after removing the slicker, laid it on the floor. "I'll deal with this stuff in a minute. First, I need to get out of these wet clothes and get warm." Flipping open his belt, Tom was about to unsnap and unzip when Mary snagged his attention by clearing her throat.

His gaze followed the jerk of her head and met Ada's teasing grin. She raised her hand and wiggled her fingers in greeting. "Uh, hi Tom. Guess you didn't see my car out there."

"Can't see my hand in front of my face, let alone a car." He laughed and crossed the room, pausing to drop a fast kiss on Mary's cheek. "I'll just go up and change, then come back and clean up the mess I made."

After he'd disappeared up the stairs, Ada turned to Mary. "You are so lucky."

"It takes more than luck to housetrain a man, and I've had my moments with that one."

"You talk tough," Ada scolded, "yet the way you look at one another, all the little gestures, God, Mary. I envy your bond with Tom."

"You had that once." Mary poured fresh beans, followed by the whir of the grinder. She tapped them into the coffee maker and added water. "It's not impossible to have it again." In passing, she gave Ada's arm a quick rub. "Give my soup a stir, will you? He'll want biscuits with it and if you'll watch the pot, I'll whip some up. You're staying to eat, and if this storm doesn't pass by then, you're staying the night. No argument."

The ultimatum was okay with Ada. She wasn't stupid. A hot meal, a sound night's sleep, what better way to clear her muddled mind? Besides, sticking around presented an opportunity to pick one very sharp mind.

If she and Mary couldn't pry what was going on with Rich out of Tom over hot soup, homemade biscuits, and a couple glasses of wine, then they'd lost their touch.

"Red wine goes well with hot soup." Ada picked up the long handled soup spoon. "We'll soften the poor, tired man up, and then find out how his visit to the hardware store went."

Mary folded eggs, buttermilk, and baking powder into flour, her lips curving with a sly smile.

*****

Drumming rain ended sometime during the night, and a cloudless, robin egg blue sky lifted Ada's spirit. Determined, she shoved lingering doubts aside and rolled out of bed. Light streamed through the window, bouncing off the sunny yellow walls in the McGraw's guest room.

She'd slept like a rock, and as she made the bed, tucking and smoothing with quick efficiency, her mind analyzed. She'd trusted Rich enough to make love with him. Yet, after all his talk about looking out for her, hiding away in his office yesterday made no sense. His behavior not only confused her, it deeply wounded her to think his concern wasn't sincere.

Last night, during the soup/biscuit/wine fest, Tom let little snippets slip, which she'd fit together like a stubborn jigsaw puzzle until an 'aha' moment hit home.

"Stupid man code," she scoffed, giving the bed a final pat. Tom carefully switched subjects when she'd picked at the issue. So she'd let it drop and gone to bed.

This morning her thoughts were crystal clear. Rich either backed away because of guilt, or of some misplaced sense of responsibility.

But based on *what*?

She imagined it had something to do with his macho need to protect her. A flaw he'd admitted the night of the kayak showdown. Well, evidently Mr. Macho's brilliant idea for keeping her safe was to stay away from her, and she'd be damned if she'd put up with it.

She entered Mary's kitchen and inhaled the aroma of fresh brewed coffee. Water simmered on the stove, offering a choice. Ada chose tea. Too much caffeine tended to make her jittery and she needed nerves of steel to face the day ahead.

Through the window, she spotted Tom and Mary on the porch. White caps dotted the lake's surface, a reminder of last night's storm. Tom's nose was buried in the morning paper. Mary worked the crossword, balancing a cup on one knee.

"Morning," she called out, letting the screen door swing shut behind her. Mary's head popped up, and Tom lowered the paper. "Why didn't someone wake me? I feel like a rude houseguest, sleeping half the morning away." She crossed and bent down, giving Mary a quick hug. With a gentle pat to Tom's shoulder, she teased, "How's our champion wine drinker this morning?"

"Humph. I'm fine. It'll be a cold day when I can't handle a bottle of cabernet." He looked at her, squinting against the sun. "You seem awful chipper this morning."

Standing between them, Ada rested a hand on each of their shoulders. "First, I want to thank you both. I needed last night. Needed to take a step back and get my bearings."

"Good." Tom patted her hand. He leaned around her, and asked Mary, "How about some breakfast?"

Mary folded her puzzle and moved to stand. "No, please," Ada pleaded. "You've both done enough. Besides, I'm still full from last night. I just want to go home."

Tom and Mary exchanged a glance. "Are you sure?" asked Mary. "I don't want to smother you, but what if..."

"I can't live with 'what ifs' hanging over my head, running my life." Ada turned away, gazing out at the lake, choosing her words. "I can't move in with you either."

"Then promise us you'll arrange for Jake and Marcy to check on you, or for you to check in so we'll know you're safe. They can do that, can't they?" She looked at Tom.

"We'll figure a way," he assured. "Maybe something will turn up today. Aside from one wild shot, it seems this character likes to do his dirt at night. Ada, just promise us you'll not stay there alone after dark until something breaks.

"That, I can do. I'm not stupid. Nor am I brave enough to spend nights alone in my house right now. I *do* have a business to run, though. If I don't repair the damage and move ahead, I'll never get caught up. Much as I hate the thought, I'm considering some kind of fencing, something to block off access from the road."

"That's good thinking, Ada. I'd be more than happy to help with the project." Tom held the door as they reentered the house. "Rich has all you'd need at the store."

"Good. I'll just stop by and take a look for myself."

Tom's mouth opened, but Mary laid a hand on his arm. "Good move," she said, "That's a good place to start."

Ada caught Mary's meaning. She gathered her things. "Thanks again, both of you, for being there last night." She tapped her handbag. "I've got a cell phone, and I'll check with Jake and Marcy this morning before I head home. Then I have some errands to run. I'll let you know what I decide about a fence and my plans for tonight."

Ada made her way into town. The rain had stopped before daybreak, yet trees still dripped, and wet leaves glistened in the sun. Her mind raced ahead, plotting the day.

She'd promised to be careful, and being no fool, she would honor her promise. Knowing Tom McGraw, he'd already called Pine Bluffs PD, alerting Jake and Marcy. She checked in with them first, and she'd been right. They'd already drawn up a plan to include house checks. Next in line, reassess the damage and order new berry bushes. Having a plan steadied her mind.

When she arrived at her cottage fifteen minutes later and stepped from the car, her stomach plunged. She took several deep breaths, a calming technique she'd learned in yoga.

She stared at thick clumps of earth covering the ground, and tears sprung to her eyes. Who was she kidding? Tilling wet mud would be hard, backbreaking work. The insurmountable task gave her a reality check smacking down all her high-minded plans.

She'd been able to handle the small tiller she'd used initially. What lay before her was more. More work, more time, more power needed to accomplish what must be done.

Dropping her handbag, she plopped down on the porch steps and, chin in hand, just stared. The heart and ambition she'd awoken with left her like a slowly deflating hot air balloon.

Chapter Twenty-Three

Rich scowled thoughtfully. Molly Hirtzel's gardens were the talk of Pine Bluffs, and she often stopped in to load up her small RV with flats of flowers. But when petite, five foot four Molly wheeled her brother's Silverado into the lumber barn with the skill of a semi driver, it caught Rich's attention.

Molly climbed out and tilted her head to one side, studying the stacks of lumber towering over her.

Rich left his post by the window and hurried down the back steps. "Hey, Molly," he called, as he came out the back door and crossed to her side.

Molly glanced up. "Mornin', Rich."

The sleeves of her plaid flannel shirt were rolled up, and her well-worn jeans were tucked into sturdy boots. "Got my order, right here." She handed him the pink copy used for loading and check-out.

He studied the order, flipping through several pages. "Why all the fencing, Molly? Deer getting to your flowerbeds?

Molly peered from beneath her floppy brimmed hat. Before she could reply, Hank Barnes approached. He paused, eyeing the papers clutched in his boss's hand. "Uh, problem, Mr. McConnell?"

"No problem," Molly declared, and before Rich could respond, she took her order back and read the material list aloud. "I need six eight foot fence panels and seven posts with caps. Make sure they're the rustic natural finish with matching hardware." She flipped the page. "Oh, and eight bags of ready mix cement."

"You load her up, Hank," Rich said, and plucked the order from Molly's hand. "I'll check the lady out."

With a brisk nod, his employee spun around and hurried away.

Rich was about to speak when a soulful rendition of Henry Mancini's 'Days of Wine and Roses' emitted from Molly's shirt pocket.

She cocked her head. "Oops, got a call." After retrieving a sleek cell phone, she checked its screen and raised the phone to her ear. "Hi, Mary." She glanced at Rich. "Excuse me," she said, and withdrew a short distance.

A blazing headache threatened as Rich rubbed the back of his neck and studied the receipt in his hand, struggling to calculate a descent discount. He'd been up half the night, alternately pacing and drinking weak decaf, waiting to hear from Gary. The call came shortly after dawn, and the news was not good

Will Steiner had relocated to Orchard Park, a suburb of Buffalo, New York. A hell of a lot closer than Rich liked.

Molly's laughter echoed in the big barn, and he remembered another early morning call. This one was from Tom McGraw and, recalling his conversation with Tom, things fell into place.

That *gang* of women, for want of a better word, including Tom's wife, Mary, were coming to Ada's rescue. Circling the wagons or, in this case, one big-assed truck, like a damn bunch of pioneers.

Rich had to grin. With all the shit going on, he gave them credit. Molly sent him a stiff smile when he glanced over at her. No doubt about it. He was on the equivalent of a female Pine Bluffs shit list.

*****

Ada studied her herbs, thankful the budding beds remained untouched in spite of the current damage. Several robins swooped down. They hopped about, tilting their heads, listening, and then plucking plump worms from clumps of ravaged, churned earth.

"Huh, at least someone's benefiting from this mess," she mumbled, tilting her head when she picked up the distant growl of an engine. The steady hum grew louder and she strained to pinpoint the source, scanning the road.

Mary's car came into view first. She shot around the bend and up Ada's driveway. Right behind her came Katy Kunzelman's flashy little compact. Ada got to her feet when a huge silver truck pulled in behind them. The truck's door opened and petite Molly Hirtzel hopped down.

"Morning, again," called Mary. Katy bailed out and gave a cheerful wave. She paused, pulling on a substantial looking pair of work gloves. It occurred to Ada all three looked like construction workers in drag, minus the hard bodies.

"Uh, good morning, ladies." Ada fell silent, gaping wide-eyed as a full size tractor chugged up her driveway. Well, that explained the noisy growl.

Molly's brother Ben drove the tractor. He came to a halt and shouted over the rumbling motor, "Molly, slow down, damn it! That's *my* truck you're drivin'."

Unperturbed, Molly shot him an annoyed look as she slammed the truck's door. Mary and Katy joined her and, working together, they unhooked and lowered the truck bed gate. Ben vaulted from the tractor and exchanged a few heated words with Molly.

Ada drew nearer to examine the contents in the truck bed. Mary reached out and wrapped her arm around Ada's shoulder. "We've come to help."

Ada's vision blurred, and she pressed both hands to her cheeks. Her friends gathered around, except Ben, who ducked his head and went to fiddle with the idling tractor.

"I can't... I don't believe this," Ada stammered, blinking rapidly. She vaguely recalled mentioning her need for a fence to Tom and Mary earlier. Could they have pulled this together so fast? "I'm, well I'm just amazed."

Hands on her hips, Katy challenged, "Think we can't put up a fence? Hah, piece of cake." She pushed up the sleeves of her Edinboro University sweatshirt. "We'll measure and line things up. Ben's buddy, Ed, from Corry, will be here shortly to help."

Katy pointed to Ben as he adjusted something attached to the tractor. "Did you see the neat drill thingy on the tractor? Looks like a giant corkscrew." She spun her hand wildly in the air. "Ben says it'll drill a two foot hole just like that," she declared, snapping her fingers.

Molly laughed. "The 'thingy' is a post-hole digger, Katy."

Mary gave Ada a squeeze. "Are you all right?"

Ada regarded her friends and drew in a deep breath. "God in heaven, if I'm not, there's something wrong with me. Before you arrived, I was sittin here alone, brooding, and feeling sorry for myself."

"Nothing wrong with a good brood," Molly pointed out. "Now time's up, we've got work to do."

All turned in unison as another truck arrived. A man as wide as he was tall emerged. Wiry hair streaked with grey stuck out from under his faded, orange cap. "I'm here," he shouted at Ben above the humming tractor, then turned to Ada and the others. He grinned and shifted a toothpick from one side of his mouth to the other. "Mornin', ladies." He gave a smart salute before ambling over to the truck and hauling one of the posts from the bed.

Without a word everyone stepped in to help. Ada lay her hand on Mary's arm. "Mary, I know you're behind this, and I thank you. But do they *know?*"

"Not personal details," Mary assured. "There were a couple of questions about Rich, more along the lines of 'why wasn't he there for you?'" She lifted her chin in Katy's direction. "Especially that one. Our Katy has a serious romantic fantasy going about you and the 'hotware' man. She's like a dog with a bone for details."

"What about Molly?"

"I think she's filled in the blanks herself."

"So, what do they think happened?"

"I skirted details, suggesting you and Rich had a disagreement, and for whatever reason, he'd pulled back for a while. Needless to say, when Rich left you to fend for yourself after you'd practically been *attacked* -- Katy's description -- it didn't put him up for man of the year."

"Attacked." Ada chuckled softly. Then she sobered. "If I wasn't so damned scared I'd find the whole situation funny. In some ways, Katy's right." She glanced over to where Ben and Molly waited. "I never dreamed I'd be putting up a barrier to thwart some kind of attack."

"Come on." Mary tugged her forward. "We need you to show us where you want your fence. Tom will be by to help shortly. Lois has to work at the Cow, but she promised to send over some box lunches and treats."

Ada hung back. "I assume Rich know's what's going on?"

"He helped load the truck, and discounted everything."

"I'll make sure whoever paid gets reimbursed. As for the labor, everyone gets free berries this summer."

"My, such a generous soul," Mary chided. "*I'll* be sure to take advantage. Rich wouldn't take payment from Molly. So, I guess you'll have to stop by and settle that yourself."

"Humph. I thought Katy was the one who harbored romantic fantasies."

Ben retrieved several wooden stakes from the truck, along with a heavy ball of twine. He handed a couple stakes to Ed, who shifted his toothpick from left to right and drawled, "Show us where to stretch the line, ladies."

Chapter Twenty-Four

Ada parked in front of Ace Hardware and took a deep breath. She didn't know whether to be grateful or angry, and now, glancing at Rich's store with its welcoming displays and comfy rockers out front, she added nervous to the litany of feelings making her insides pitch and roll.

She'd been forbidden to lift a finger to install her fence. In fact, Mary insisted she get out from under their feet. Once Ada pointed out where she wanted the fence located, her stubborn friend insisted she take the day off.

Unwind, relax, Mary advised.

Hah, fat chance of relaxing when stopping by Rich's store to pay for the fencing materials topped her *unwinding* list. Materials she'd never even gotten her hands on.

Wisely, she kept her planned detour to Ace Hardware to herself. As far as her well-meaning friends were concerned, sunshine and soaring temperature provided perfect conditions for Ada to relax and get away to Erie.

When she protested, pointing out that working in her gardens relaxed her, the protest fell on deaf ears. To tell the truth, they were right. Except for this necessary stop to pay her bill, Ada looked forward to a day in Erie.

As she entered the hardware store, the young girl running check-out called a cheerful greeting. Waiting patiently while the clerk rang up her customer, Ada perused the store. Several customers strolled up and down the aisles, and the distant sound of idling trucks filtered through double doors propped open at the rear of the store. Harley restocked shelves nearby. For a moment, the way he scowled thoughtfully at her made her uneasy. Then he gave a brief nod and turned back to his work.

No sign of Rich, though, and his office door was closed.

"Mrs. Blaine? Oh, I'm sorry!" the clerk said when Ada jumped. "I didn't mean to startle you."

"My mind was elsewhere," Ada replied with a smile, swinging around to face the young girl. "I'm playing hooky from work today, but I stopped to settle a bill before I left town. Is Rich McConnell around?"

"You just missed him." The girl leaned close and lowered her voice. "I think Mr. McConnell's playing hooky, too." A tiny smirk quirked her glossy pink lips. "I overheard him talking, and he's off to meet some old Marine buddy. Not that I eavesdrop," she declared when Ada lifted a questioning brow. "He was standing right over by the check out talking to Chief McGraw... er, I mean Mr. McGraw." She giggled and shook her head. "I can't get used to the new chief. Although, he's a McGraw, too, right?"

Ada nodded, struggling to keep up with the girl's ping pong rambling. "You mentioned an old friend?" she prodded, impatient to get the clerk back on track.

"Oh. Right. The Marine buddy. I got busy with customers and didn't hear *everything*. He's meeting this friend today, but I don't know where," she apologized.

"Mr. McConnell's plans are his business," Ada stated, softening her tone when the young clerk's brow furrowed. "This is about my account. Molly Hirtzel picked up supplies for me early today, and I want to settle the bill, that's all."

Ada rummaged in her handbag for her checkbook. "Can you bring up the invoice and give me an amount?"

"I'm afraid I can't do that, Mrs. Blaine." The clerk chewed on her lower lip, retreating behind the counter when Ada's head snapped up.

"Why is that?" Ada glanced at the tag on the girls red smock. "Mandy?"

"Before Mr. McConnell left, he took the invoice from the pending file into his office. I usually have a copy here," Mandy said, gesturing to a file drawer. "I don't have a copy of the one you want. Sorry," she said, hunching her shoulders.

Ada slipped her check book back into her bag, scowling at the closed office door.

"Is there anything else I can help you with?"

This wasn't Mandy's fault, so Ada smiled into the worried face. "It's not your problem, you've been helpful. When your boss returns, though, ask him to contact me concerning the charges."

She'd settle with Rich McConnell -- *the coward* -- later. "Have a good day, Mandy," she said, and strode out the door.

Harley happened to be leaving at the same time and held the door for her. "So, headin' to Erie for the day?"

Ada fumbled for her keys. "Ah, yes. Yes I am. A nice stroll along the bayfront sounds pretty good right now," she answered. She noticed he lingered on the steps of the hardware store, watching, as she drove away.

Driving north to Erie, the green haze of emerging foliage covered trees alongside the road. Subtle hints of color signaled spring in an otherwise bleak landscape. With each mile, Ada's tension slipped away, peeling off like layers of a sweet Vidalia onion. She laughed and lowered her window, letting a rush of air engulf her. Only a gardener would think in such terms.

Her relaxed state led to a more rational reflection of her current situation. Rich was up to something. He knew darned well she had feelings for him, for them, and what they'd briefly shared. Yet he'd deliberately avoided her, more than once in the past two days.

Why?

In the middle of all the upheaval, when did this reunion with his old service buddy, Gary Wilson, become so darned important? His avoidance miffed her. She'd bared her soul -- *and a lot more* -- to the man.

His actions didn't fit his ingrained protective persona. Also, Ada suspected he somehow knew, and paid attention to, every move she made.

Again, *why*?

Their relationship took a sharp turn after the near miss on her porch. Granted, she'd sensed a change in Rich's feelings toward her after the holidays this year. Then after the shooting incident, things moved forward in a rush.

Did the danger he perceived influence how he felt about her? Did she misread the closeness developing between them, spinning fantasies out of a male overprotective personality?

If so, she had no one to blame but herself if her feelings got crushed. On the other hand, what if his instincts were right? What if she *was* a target and in real danger?

Ada glanced in her rearview mirror.

The road behind her stretched long and straight. Not a car in sight. She breathed a deep sigh and smiled when she topped the ridge. Like a gorgeous mirage, Lake Erie glistened in the noonday sun, stretching as far as the eye could see.

She'd have a serious face to face talk with Rich as soon as she could track him down. Once they'd cleared the air, and she knew where she stood, then maybe she wouldn't be so miffed.

Hurt, yes, but she'd deal with that. If he had a good reason to believe she was in danger...well, fear trumped miffed.

*****

Gary looked the same. Maybe a little more flesh to bone -- the guy had been borderline skinny for a Marine -- but familiar tiny lines framing his dark eyes when he smiled remained.

Rich knew the exact moment the tall, lanky black man ambling along the sidewalk on Erie's bay front caught sight of him. "I can see the flash of those white teeth from a block away," he said, clamping firmly onto Gary's outstretched hand. "But, by God, it's good to see them."

"You got a problem with my teeth, cracker?" Gary Wilson shot back.

Rich returned Gary's wide smile. "It's good to see them and *you*. Damn, good. How was your flight?"

"Great. No problems. I rented a car in Buffalo and spent yesterday evening cruising bars near Orchard Park."

They settled at a table. When the waiter approached, Gary ordered two stouts on tap.

"Does Tish know what you're up to?" Rich asked.

"Oh, yeah. I'm not about to rock that boat. Damned if she didn't encourage me to make sure I checked any place deemed suspicious, which to my darlin' wife is every bar on the block. Thank you," Gary said when their waiter placed tall, foam-topped mugs on their table.

"I gather nothing turned up?" Rich sipped, eyeing his friend over the rim of his glass.

"As far as I could determine, no one's seen Steiner since he arrived in Buffalo."

"How'd you find out about that?"

Gary sipped his beer. A pair of screaming gulls overhead rode stiff lake breezes. "Delaney," he said. "Remember him?"

"Office of Naval Intel. A straight shooter, as I remember. How'd you hook up with Hank Delaney?"

"I freelance for ONI occasionally. We often cross paths, and I tapped him to see if he knew anything after Steiner was released."

Rich trailed one unsteady finger down his frosted glass. Memories from back then still shook him to the core, even good ones of Agent Henry Delaney. "Hank headed up the sting op that put Will Steiner away. We worked close, and I have the utmost respect for the man."

"No argument," Gary agreed. "He's kept tabs on our wayward ex-con. Apparently, Steiner has an aunt living in the Buffalo area. He's staying with her. Due to the proximity to Pine Bluffs, Delaney gave me a heads up."

"Hank knows I live in Pine Bluffs?"

Gary laughed. He drained the last of his stout and signaled for a refill. "There isn't much the man *doesn't* know. Any how," he continued, "Delaney faxed me a current picture of Steiner and, using my ONI ID, I flashed his picture around Orchard Park's finer establishments. Unfortunately, as per usual, nobody's seen nothin'."

"Of course." Rich gave a disgusted snort. "The bastard's up to no good. Most likely set on some kind of cockeyed revenge after all these years."

"Maybe. Let's get some lunch and I'll fill you in on what our boy's been up too while being *rehabilitated.*"

While discussing pros and cons of Will Steiner's agenda, tables around them emptied. A few patrons lingered, drawn by clear skies and unusual warmth so early in the season for Erie.

They'd switched to coffee after lunch, and Rich was about to take a sip of the steaming brew, when he caught sight of a familiar figure strolling down the sidewalk beside the lake. His hand froze midway to his lips.

"Shit."

Gary's brow wrinkled into a puzzled frown. "Beg your pardon, man. Did you say shit?"

"Oh, yeah. You're about to meet a real special lady. I just hope to hell she doesn't rip my hide to pieces in front of my best friend."

Gary sat his coffee down and swung around. "That's one foxy lady," he remarked, tossing a knowing smirk back at Rich.

Rich gulped down a fast slug of coffee. The hot brew burned a trail all the way to his churning gut as Ada Blaine locked onto his fixed gaze and stopped in her tracks.

*****

A sudden gust of wind off the lake plastered Ada's clothes to her body. She slapped her hand against soft denim, in an effort to keep her knee length skirt in place.

Her pulse jumped when Rich McConnell's bold gaze shot over her. He checked her out swiftly and, when his gaze locked on hers, everything inside her heated.

How could she be so mad at the man, yet want to tug his faded jeans right down those long, hard, endless legs?

Taking a deep breath, Ada shook off the unexpected spurt of lust and strode up to the table where Rich sat with his friend.

Rich shoved his chair back and, catching it before it crashed to the sidewalk, stood up. "Ada, what a nice surprise," he said, repositioning the chair. He ran a swift hand through his wind tossed hair.

Ada waited a beat, amused by his obvious discomfort, then responded, "Really? I'm rather surprised you didn't dive right into the bay when you recognized me heading your way."

The handsome black man disguised a chuckle with a fake cough. He cleared his throat, and stood. "You must be Ada Blaine," he said, extending his hand. "Gary Wilson. It's a pleasure to meet you."

Ada offered a genuine smile and took his hand.

"Rich said you were gorgeous," he said, gently squeezing her fingers before releasing them. "He underestimated."

An eye roll would be rude, so she said, "Why thank you, Gary." Then fixed her gaze on his face and without hesitation stated, "You're still covering his butt after all this time, aren't you."

Gary's full out laugh turned nearby heads. Rich regarded the interplay between Ada and his friend, then with a lopsided grin, he gestured to an empty chair. "Ada, please, join us. Can I order you something?"

Rich pulled out a chair and Ada sat down. He assisted as she scooted in close to the table.

"I had lunch earlier, but something cold would be nice. Hmmm... unsweetened iced tea."

Rich flagged the waiter and placed her order.

Ada contemplated both men. Different as night and day, she smiled at the comparison. Deciding she'd ignore Rich for the time being, she inquired, "Gary, what brings you to Erie?"

Gary and Rich exchanged a glance. She caught Rich's barely perceptible nod before Gary answered, "Someone my buddy cares about may be in danger. He asked for my help, so, here I am."

His straight forward manner caught Ada by surprise. Her gaze shot to Rich. Surely he'd be upset, or jump in to deny what Gary's statement implied.

The waiter chose that moment to deliver her drink. She selected a pink packet of artificial sweetener, dumped the contents into the tea, and stirred. She drank deeply, letting the cool liquid soothe her dry throat. Placing the glass on the table, she shifted her gaze to Rich.

His hand snaked across the table and closed over hers. "I owe you an explanation."

"You *owe* me nothing," Ada responded. "Except the truth. It's my mistake when I assume or misunderstand your actions and your intentions. When someone takes potshots at me, and then comes back and destroys my land, I deserve to know if you have some idea why it happened or suspect who did it."

She tore her gaze from his and faced the bay, blinking back unexpected and unwanted tears. A tangle of raw emotion jumped inside her like spring hoppers, threatening to snatch her control away.

"Excuse me a moment," Gary spoke softly. "I need to take a walk and call my wife."

"I'm sorry, I --"

"Not necessary," he said, placing a gentle hand on Ada's shoulder. "I'll not be long. Rich will explain some things to you. When I return we can talk about what has to be done."

Rich accepted Gary's comment with a silent nod, and, Ada noted, he kept his friend in sight until Gary turned the corner. Then he tightened his grip on her hand and pulled her to her feet. "Let's walk while we talk."

Chapter Twenty-Five

Erie's Bicentennial Tower loomed above them. Rich steered Ada beneath its shadow, holding her hand and toying with her fingers as they strolled.

At first, she resisted. She didn't yank her hand away, but she didn't respond, either. As he talked, laying his soul bare, straining to keep past bitterness at bay, the cold stiffness he sensed disappeared. By the time they reached the end of the long pier extending into Presque Isle Bay, her skin felt warm, and her grip tightened.

She turned to him, placed a hand on his forearm, and scrutinized his face. "I wish you'd told me sooner. Your marriage didn't just end, it blew up in your face. You wasted years, never letting anyone get close to you again."

He released her hand and, wrapping his arm around her, pulled her against his side. "I don't want your pity."

She drew back slightly, tilting her head to peer up at him. "You'll not get pity from me, Rich. In fact, anger you managed to tamp down could resurface. I *know* how tragedy can make us fold in on ourselves to survive," she spoke urgently, placing her hand over her heart. "Knowing that keeps me from landing all over you."

He wrapped her in his arms and delivered a bone-crushing squeeze. "Before your fuse reignites and you toss me in the bay, I need to explain why I kept away when you needed someone to stand beside you."

She untangled herself from his embrace.

A rag tag huddle of ducks swam noisily by, and Ada paused to watch them cruise past. They zigzagged and undulated cleverly through waves that slapped the side of the dock.

"I'm willing to listen," she began. "But understand, I determine what *my* needs are. I'm no stranger to things blowing up in my face. When I lost those I loved more than life, my whole world blew up." She turned away, facing into the bay and the wind swept spray lifting off the choppy water.

He stared at her ramrod stiff shoulders, then stepped forward and placed his hands on them. She folded her arms. "Now, tell me the rest."

*****

Rich talked and she listened. At times his voice grew coarse, rough with emotion. His hands remained on her shoulders, a silent connection, while his fingers flexed and gripped, loosened and stroked.

She took hold of those restless fingers when he relayed Will Steiner's history and how Gary pulled Rich back from a yawning, emotional abyss.

Hands clasped, they wended their way back to the hotel's patio restaurant. As they approached, Ada noticed Gary seated at a corner table studying a compact laptop. She admired Rich's friend. Despite the obvious -- one black man, one white -- they could have been brothers. In a manner of speaking, they were.

Ada checked the time. She'd arranged for a manicure and pedicure earlier. Calculating time and distance, she figured she had about a half hour before her appointment. Maybe she should cancel.

Gary glanced up. He shut down his laptop and slipped it into a case, smiling as they approached. "Feels like summer," he said, squinting at the mid afternoon sun. His eyes went to their joined hands. "You two have a nice walk?"

Ada returned his smile, and without invitation, disengaged her hand from Rich's and dropped into a chair. "I understand you two have decided for some reason this ex-con, this Steiner, has decided to enact some kind of revenge for something that occurred years ago?"

Gary glanced at Rich, who shrugged and sat down. "You are a direct kind of woman, Ada," Gary said. Lifting the case with his laptop, he tucked it against his chair. "I like that. So, right back at you. Will Steiner could be dangerous. He's a lethal combination of badass and trained marine who just might feel he has a long overdue score to settle with my buddy Rich."

Rich recaptured her hand, cupping it between his lean, strong fingers. "He's not the only one out there looking to settle a score."

Ada fixed her eyes on Rich and frowned. Not the *only* one?

Rich continued. "There's another possibility. Remember our night out with Tom and Mary, the night we went to North East for wings?"

Ada's head spun, night out with...."Oh, the bartender."

"Yeah, one surly bartender who caused a lot of trouble after his girlfriend got herself killed in your back yard. Never mind she set out to kill her sister, your niece Cassi, in cold blood. We have no idea what Sadie Mitchell told him about you. In her twisted mind, maybe you abandoned her, too. If she told him that, he might be looking to settle the score."

Ada clutched Rich's hand. Her sister had abandoned Sadie at birth, fleeing to Ada with Cassi, Sadie's twin. The discarded, mentally damaged child's life had been hell, through no fault of her own, and ended when she discovered Cassi years later and tried to kill her.

"Oh, Rich. Surely he doesn't blame me for Sadie Mitchell's miserable life?"

Rich raised her hand, pressing it to his warm cheek. He touched his lips to her fingers curled within his grip. "Who knows what goes on in a man's mind when he's hurting? By all accounts he cared for Sadie, and had lived with her for almost a year prior to her untimely death."

Gary's voice broke into her fragmented thoughts. "For some reason it appears you've become a target."

She flinched, and Rich's grip tightened.

A target? Icy fingers tiptoed up her spine.

"Rich tells me you're a very independent woman. An admirable quality," he added.

She straightened and warily withdrew her hands from Rich's. "Independent doesn't make me foolish."

"Good." Gary pushed his chair back and, as he rolled down the sleeves of his shirt and carefully buttoned them, he pursed his lips and nodded at Rich. "Then listen to what he says. I agree with his way of approaching this situation and, from the way your eyes are narrowing down on my sorry face, you might be a tad offended he shared certain aspects of it with me." He winked and stood up, slipping the strap of his laptop case onto his shoulder. "I'm nosy when it comes to my best friend, and what goes on in his life. So, if you need to be pissed at someone, I'm your man. But damn it, honey. Please be careful and take his advice."

He leaned down and placed a gentle kiss on her cheek.

Rich stood. "I'll be right back."

Ada stared after them, taking a moment to settle fragmented thoughts, as Rich and Gary walked to the entry of an adjacent parking garage.

With trembling fingers, she touched the spot where Gary's lips had brushed her cheek. Puffy clouds engulfed the sun, cutting the warmth as if a switch had been thrown, and the skin on Ada's arms and legs erupted in goose bumps. She rubbed her arms fiercely against the ominous chill.

Titling her wrist, she gaped at the time. Damn, she was going to be late. When she looked up, Gary was gone and Rich was striding toward her.

She jumped up, and hooked her purse over her shoulder. "Rich, I've got to go. I made an appointment for a manicure and I've got about ten minutes to make it."

Rich placed his hands on her arms. Frowning, he gave them a brisk rub. "Come back here when you're done. I'll wait."

Something in his eyes stopped her quick retort, and she took a deep assessing breath. "Okay. I'll be about an hour, maybe a little more."

When she started to move away he stopped her. "Gary had to leave. He'd planned to stay here," he said, motioning to the hotel complex behind them. "He's been summoned to a meeting in Buffalo, something he can't avoid."

Ada frowned, puzzled as to why he was telling her about Gary's plans.

"His room is paid for. Stay the night with me, Ada."

The simple request had Ada's blood pounding in her head, racing through her body and heating her chilled limbs to flash point. "Rich... I... I don't know..."

"Come back when you're done. I'll be waiting, we can at least have dinner and talk."

She agreed to the dinner, and then rushed away on trembling legs to where her car was parked along nearby State Street. She sped to the parkway and turned west, forcing her scrambling thoughts into submission while negotiating traffic.

With only minutes to spare she dashed into Sky Nails and an attendant directed her to a cushy massage chair. She stared blankly at the chair's control panel. This was only the second time she'd been there. On her first visit, Cassi had accompanied her. They'd enjoyed a spa day together as part of her niece's Christmas present last year.

A young Vietnamese girl smiled as she filled the footbath with warm water and poured something soft and fragrant over her feet. She took the control from Ada and deftly pressed a series of buttons. With a soft, rolling buzz the chair began to vibrate. Ada tilted back and closed her eyes.

She had an hour to decide if she'd be spending the night with Rich in a room overlooking Presque Isle Bay.

Chapter Twenty-Six

Rich had an hour to kill, maybe more, before Ada returned. He retrieved a thin briefcase from his truck. The case contained paperwork for the hardware store, enough to keep him busy while he waited. After moving inside, off the beaten path, he spread a variety of forms on the table before him. He ordered coffee, and a waiter placed a silver carafe on his table. Then after pouring himself a steaming cup, he settled in. No sense sitting here driving himself crazy wondering what lay ahead for the upcoming night. Might as well make use of the quiet pre-dinner atmosphere and line up orders for the coming week.

Yet, his mind drifted.

Would she say yes? *Hell, would she even come back?*

Before rushing away, she'd agreed to dinner. For now, that would have to do. As for the rest... who knew?

With rimless reading glasses in place, an irritating necessity of late, he was deep into calculating how many tons of bagged mulch had to be ordered for the upcoming season when a shadow fell across his table.

"You haven't changed, Rich. Beautiful setting in front of you, cold beer for the askin', and you have your nose buried in a fuckin' stack of paperwork."

A hard knot twisted in the pit of Rich's stomach.

He removed his glasses. Slowly, methodically, he tucked them into his pocket and laid down his pen. Inside he was quivering, but his hand was rock steady as he calmly poured a second cup of coffee.

Although bitter bile coated his throat, his voice came calm and strong. "Hello, Steiner."

The shadow shifted as the man took a seat across from him. Beneath the table, Rich's hands curled into tight fists.

After a long, steadying pause, Rich looked up and into Will Steiner's cold, gray eyes.

The years had been kind to Steiner, considering. A slightly receding hairline and a heavy sprinkling of gray throughout a close-cropped cap of thick hair indicated the passing of time. Lines cut deep, bracketing a long, lean face. His nose crooked to one side, as if broken at some point.

Cold gray eyes, guarded and devoid of emotion, observed Rich. The hint of a smile twisted his thin lips. "She's one hot woman, that Ada Blaine. I'll bet she's a hell of a handful."

Arm cocked ready to swing, Rich exploded from his chair. The waiter rushed forward. "Is there a problem, sir?" he asked, grasping the unsteady table, extending one arm between the two men.

Rich froze, then lowered his arm and sank back into his chair.

"Sorry," he muttered, inching back as the waiter whipped out a towel and blotted up coffee that spilled when Rich shot out of his chair.

"Can I be of assistance?" the young man asked, eyeing the two of them with apprehension.

Rich took a deep breath, and shook his head. "We're fine. Mr. Steiner took me by surprise, that's all. It's been a while." He gestured the waiter away. "If we need anything, I'll let you know."

"I'll have coffee, if ya don't mind." Steiner spoke out, resettled in his chair. "Black and strong."

Casting worried glances over his shoulder, the waiter hustled away. Once he was out of earshot, Rich took a moment to push down hot fury curling tight in his gut. "What the hell do you want, Steiner? If you so much as look at Ada Blaine, I'll beat you to a bloody pulp."

The man across from him shifted his gaze, staring out at the bay. "I guess that came out wrong," he mumbled. "Civil conversation ain't something I've been around for a while."

Though puzzled, Rich ignored the sage remark. He wasn't about to feel sorry for someone because they'd been rotting away in a cell for years. Especially when they'd managed to get there all by themselves. Yet, upon closer examination, the lines on Will Steiner's face suddenly appeared more weary than harsh.

He didn't comment while the waiter placed another cup on the table and filled both of them to the brim. After setting a newly filled carafe alongside the cups, he silently departed.

Rich took a fortifying sip, scowled over the rim of his cup, and demanded, "I'm going to ask you one more time. What are you doing here, and what the hell do you want?"

"I want you to understand."

"Understand?" Rich uttered through clenched teeth. He slid his coffee aside and leaned forward. He itched to drag the man outside and rearrange his face. Maybe flatten his crooked nose and blacken those stone cold eyes staring at him like a damn snake. "What I understand is someone took a shot at me a few days ago, and then ripped up some private property belonging to someone I care about a hellava lot. Then the same son-of-a-bitch who nearly wrecked my life a while back shows up like a damn bad penny. Do you understand *that*, Steiner?"

He slammed a fist on the table, causing Steiner's face to turn sheet white. "Now, you friggin' tell me why you're here and by God, you better include plans to leave, real soon."

Across the room, a lone man at the bar froze with his early bird cocktail halfway to his mouth. The bartender shook his head and went back to wiping the counter.

Will cleared his throat. He swallowed hard and wrapped both hands around his cup. There was silence, a long drawn out slice of nothing except for the distant clink of glasses being stacked somewhere. "Sometimes," he began softly, "sometimes we can't choose where we came from, but choices that determine where we end up are ours. I screwed up."

Those words, simple and direct, cut into Rich like a knife. *What the hell?* He didn't want to be an ex-con's therapist. Not when the man in question, to Rich's way of thinking, was a liar.

Steiner unconsciously rubbed his hand, then pushed up his sleeves and heaved a shaky sigh. Rich's anger wavered when his gaze centered on the Marine Corps emblem tattooed on the back of Will's hand.

"God, I could use a drink," Will muttered. His eyes met Rich's unyielding gaze. "Because I have no idea what you're talking about. If someone took a shot at me, I'd be pissed as hell, too. As for the other, the damage? I don't have a clue about that either."

Rich glanced at his watch. Shit, time was running out. Ada would be returning and he sure as hell didn't want her coming face to face with this particular piece of past history. "I don't know what your game is, and frankly, I don't give a shit. You had the world by the ass, and you screwed up. In retrospect, you took nothing of value from me. I made a promise when I married Dodie, and I kept it. She didn't. End of story. You just happened to be handy for her."

"I'm clean, Rich. I have been since the day I lost my freedom, along with everything else I'd busted my ass for. That's *my* problem. I regret it spilled over and became yours" He raised his hand, palm out. "Let me finish. I just want you to know, the Marine Corps gave me a chance and I blew it, but what I learned bustin' my butt at PI was also what kept me goin' all these years. I have no excuse for how I messed up both our lives."

Silence thick enough to cut with a knife descended like an invisible, ominous cloud. The strange admission, confession, whatever the hell it was, took Rich by surprise.

Will Steiner could be handing him a total load of bullshit. Yet, the man's haunted eyes said otherwise. Could all those years inside have changed someone so drastically?

Rich had to get a grip, take a step away. He wasn't one to believe being locked up and going through some canned rehab eventually turned a new man loose on society. Despite a lean, tough looking exterior, if he could believe the man before him, Steiner had undergone some serious soul searching. That is, *if* all he said was the honest to God's truth and not some well orchestrated scam.

Steiner pushed away from the table and got to his feet. He rolled his shoulders and scanned the area before meeting Rich's quiet gaze. "Sorry if I screwed up your day. I'll get out of your way. Looks like your lady friend is back," he said with a wry smile.

Rich's head whipped around, and sure enough, Ada's vehicle turned into the nearby parking garage. He shoved back and shot to his feet. *Now what?*

He stared at the hand Will extended. Caught off guard he hesitated, then, maybe because that USMC emblem on the extended hand somehow struck a chord, he shook the man's hand. Though he made sure his eyes revealed nothing.

Will gave a curt nod and walked away.

*****

The quiet, reflective hour getting pampered and soothed worked. Ada peered at her painted toes, exposed in newly purchased sandals, as she sauntered along the retaining wall by the bay. Late afternoon sun bounced off ripples on the water's surface, glinting beneath a sky where gulls screeched and soared.

She smiled, recognizing Rich the minute he stepped into view and moved toward her. His hands were shoved into the pockets of his jeans, and his dark green shirt hugged wide shoulders.

When had everything changed?

For years going to the hardware store was a necessity to replenish supplies for her gardens, or to simply replace a worn pair of work gloves. Rich became a friend, a consultant, always available, always there.

Oh, she'd been aware he was attractive. Hard to miss when Mary McGraw pointed out what a "handsome devil" he was. It was at Tom and Mary's Christmas Eve gathering things *really* began to change.

As he approached her now, his sheepish, almost boyish grin made her chuckle. How could she stay mad at him? He'd reacted in a manner he justified as necessary at the time.

She'd just have to set him straight about his cockeyed idea that staying away to protect her was in her best interest.

He shuffled to a stop and, tipping down her sunglasses, she lifted her gaze to meet his eyes. Sun slanted across the bay, washing his face with color, highlighting flecks of gold in his eyes. The rich color deepened as his lazy smile grew, and the thought of sharing a quiet dinner and good wine as the sun slipped into Lake Erie made her toes curl.

Her Mediterranean Moonlight tinted toes.

His gaze skimmed down, stopping when it reached those painted toes. "I don't recall seeing those shoes earlier," he mused, stroking his chin. "Had time for a little shopping side trip, didcha?"

"I did. Shopping relaxes me, and I wanted to be relaxed to enjoy our... dinner together."

"Good. Our reservation is for six, so we have time for a drink. Bayfront Grille has great appetizers, too."

He took her arm and steered her to a group of tables beneath wide umbrellas fluttering in the breeze. "Are you through being angry with me?"

"Working on it. Mediterranean Moonlight helped."

"Beg your pardon?"

"This," Ada said, gesturing to her polished fingers and toes. "Plus, what woman doesn't have a serious mood adjustment after indulging in new shoes?"

Choosing a table out of the brisk breeze, he slid her chair out and waited while she settled in. "Maybe a chilled Pinot will tip the scale. We have a ringside seat for one of Lake Erie's spectacular sunsets. Puts the odds in my favor you'll forget all about being upset with me."

Ada carefully removed and folded her sunglasses. She met his optimistic gaze straight on, quirked on eye brow and remarked, "You're a charming man, Rich, but you're not a stupid one. You have more explaining to do. I'm down to simmer right now. Doesn't mean I won't reignite under the right circumstances."

Rich chuckled, settling across from her as a young waiter wearing dark pressed slacks and a crisp white shirt approached. Before he could ask, Ada gave the waiter an easy smile and said, "A nice Pinot, thank you."

"Make that two," Rich added. "And an order of your sun dried tomato and porcini chicken bruschetta."

She took her time unfolding and placing a white napkin across her lap. How could she stay upset with him? For to many years she'd made safe, often lonely, choices. Despite the past few rocky days, there was something happening between them. If she'd miscalculated and all he felt was a need to protect her then she'd end it. Or, if the passion withered and died, the relationship would disintegrate.

Either way there would be pain.

But what if there was... *something?*

Chapter Twenty-Seven

Will Steiner's fingers drummed a rapid beat on his car's steering wheel. Late afternoon sun streamed through the windshield, making sweat pool at the base of his spine. He'd almost smacked into Ada Blaine as she exited the parking garage.

Frickin' fate, or just plain bad timin', she'd parked her snazzy, compact SUV almost beside the sorry piece of crap he used to get around these days.

Thinking fast, Will pasted on a wide smile and steadied her with one hand after almost knocking her off her feet. He apologized, claiming some dumb ass distraction.

His gut clenched when she studied him closely, then questioned knowing him. Much as he wished otherwise, she remembered their brief encounter on the lake. The lady was no dimwit. He'd rattled off some crap about how he was surprised she'd remembered and claimed to be late for some nonexistent meeting. Then he bolted.

He drove several blocks and pulled into a convenience store to use a phone. After a nerve wracking wait, the girl inside the Country Fair finally hung up the pay phone and departed.

Fuckin' aggravation.

Once he made enough to do more than put food in his gut, he'd have a cell phone. He glanced around, slid out of his car and entered the store, making a beeline for the phone.

"Hello." His Aunt Louise's voice sounded weak, and guilt crawled up his throat.

"It's me," Will responded. "I'm still in Erie. Just checkin' in like you asked me to."

"Is the car running all right?"

"What? Oh, yeah. Purrin' along like a big old cat." No sense telling her that every time he turned the key he held his breath. Though he suspected she made sure the car ran just fine before she handed him the keys.

"Will you be home for dinner?" she asked.

Will glanced at his watch. The Marine Corp emblem on the back of his hand taunted him. Why the hell couldn't Louise have been his mother instead of her piece of trash sister?

"Uh... I'll try. The job I heard about didn't pan out. Maybe I'll grab a local paper and see if there's anything else in the area." He shifted, switching the phone from one ear to the other, taking a swift survey of the store. Years inside made watchin' his back as natural as breathing.

"I'll make something you can warm up," she promised. "Drive carefully, Will."

The phone clicked and she was gone.

Will slowly replaced the receiver. He leaned his head against the wall by the phone and just breathed, in and out.

"Hey." The voice came from behind. He started, whirling around with one hand raised.

The woman who'd been using the phone when he first arrived took a step back. Placing her hands on ample hips, she tilted her head and snapped, "Are you done yet?"

Will stepped away from the phone. Hands spread he gave a short bow. "All yours, lady." Then he left the store. The tires on his piece of crap car squealed as he drove away.'

Chapter Twenty-Eight

"Nothing quite compares, does it?" Standing behind her, Rich settled his hands on Ada's shoulders and gave a gentle squeeze. "Once summer gets here, sunsets slide further west," he noted. "Sometimes I leave work early and drive to North East just to watch the day end, to watch the sun slide into Lake Erie."

"Hmmm." Ada softened beneath his touch. "You're right, Rich. Nothing compares."

Their room faced north. Five stories below, deep shadows stole across the bay and lights showcasing the Sheraton's exterior reflected on the water. Across the bay, trees on Presque Isle Peninsula fashioned a ragged outline, creating a stark contrast on the horizon against striking shades of blue and orange streaking across the sky.

Ada's mood turned reflective. The wine they'd shared over an absolutely decadent dinner smoothed out rough edges. Though she didn't totally agree with Rich's theory her misfortune coincided to his presence, she respected his point of view.

Upon close examination, all three incidents -- the shooting, the note, the vandalism to her property -- *did* occur either when she was with Rich, or shortly thereafter. She hadn't considered the pattern until Rich's calm, steady voice pointed out the obvious.

She leaned against his firm chest and smiled. It's a wonder she'd been able to grasp the meaning of what he said as they'd indulged in after dinner drinks, because while he talked, he'd touched her hand and twined those long, competent fingers through hers.

Warm hands. Chilled wine.

Very distracting.

Then he'd placed the room pass on the table and smiled that lazy smile. At which point, she figured her common sense took flight. Because here she was in a luxury suite, sipping *more* chilled wine, watching the sun set and letting those warm hands soothe away lingering tension.

He wrapped his arms around her, pulling her tighter against his solid heat. "Remind me to thank Gary for the room," he murmured.

"Gary, huh? The one who claimed he had a sudden business emergency? Was it business, Rich, or is Gary Wilson the consummate matchmaker?"

Chuckling, Rich reached out and retrieved the wine bottle from a classy, silver ice bucket. He topped off her glass. "I wouldn't put it past him. But, far as I know, it was business. Regardless, it was too late to cancel his reservation, so he made the offer."

"Oh, I see." She grinned, letting her fingers skim over the arms surrounding her. "Just a convenient turn of fate, then, and not some nefarious plan allowing you to seduce me with fine food and wine?"

"Just fate," Rich agreed solemnly. "However, *if* seduction *was* the plan, is it working?"

She turned into his arms, set her wine aside and slid her hands up, framing his face. Rising on tiptoe, she touched her lips to his. Her pulse jumped, and then raced, pounding in her ears as he pulled her in and changed the angle of the kiss.

She twined her arms around his neck and spoke softly against his lips, "I'm here because I want to be."

Pulling back, he fixed his gaze on her face. "Good to know, and I want *you*."

His simple admission made her insides quiver.

She touched her lips to his once more, and then rested her head on his chest. Skillfully, his hand glided down her back to the curve of her hip, and then slowly retraced the path. His touch soothed.

And aroused.

With some effort, she shifted back to admire the view. Only a slice of sun remained on the horizon, and as he held her close, she admitted softly, "I want you, too, Rich. And being *wanted* in return makes me feel..."

She trailed off as the sun slipped out of sight, and sighed when he nuzzled, pressing his lips to the side of her neck.

"You deserve to be wanted." His warm breath tickled her ear. "We joke about plans, about seduction. Having you here in my arms is no joke."

Ada turned into his embrace. "Then lets go with *my* plan," she suggested. Her hands slid down to boldly grip those lean, firm hips, and pulled him closer.

His lips curved slowly. "I think I'm going to like your plan." His amber eyes darkened in the fading light as his hands cruised over her. She fought to steady herself, to calm nerves bumping just under her skin. They'd made love before. The first time she'd taken the step with ease. She'd gone to his bed.

Clichéd as it sounded, this felt like the first time all over again. She quivered as he leisurely unbuttoned her top, then eased it off her shoulders and let it drop. He kissed a meandering trail, grazing over her heated skin and nipping at the ivory lace encasing her breasts.

"Touch me, Rich. Please, just touch me."

Faint light outlined the king size bed behind them, while outside the sky darkened. His trailing fingers, gentle strokes, and tender kisses roused and soothed. Anticipation sparked and flowed as he lingered, brushing his lips over the lace and skin. Her body reacted and a shuddering sigh escaped her in a rush when his mouth covered her breast.

She gasped when he swept her off her feet and wheeled around. Two giant strides brought them to the bed and, cradling her against him, he whipped the quilt aside and lowered her onto cool, satin smooth sheets.

When he reached for the bedside lamp, she laid her hand on his arm. "Don't," she murmured. "I want to make love in the twilight."

Clear, luminous eyes glittered down at her as he began to unbutton his shirt. "Then we will."

He stripped. Right down to bare skin and then turned to her. She reached for him. Her hands glided over his strong shoulders, roaming, feeling lean back muscles tense beneath her fingertips. He lifted her and unclasped her bra. Then he knelt on the bed, the outline of his naked body stark and exciting.

Tempting.

He unzipped the denim skirt and slid it down her legs. Then one by one, he slipped her new sandals from her pampered feet, lifting each in turn, to admire the color reflected in the fast fading light.

"Ah, Mediterranean Moonlight."

His tone, so pleased and smug, made her laugh, and the nerves dancing beneath her skin settled.

Lowering her leg, he traced a line up her body, gliding boldly over the single piece of clothing left covering her nakedness. He kissed the inside of her calf. His hair brushed her inner thigh, setting off waves of pulsing pleasure inside her. A tease, a lingering rub at the juncture of her thighs as he toyed with the slim band of elastic at her waist. Her heels pressed down, her hips lifted. Then he leaned in, touching his lips to the sensitive underside of her breast.

What a joy, a pleasure to have a man, *this man*, touch and explore her so intimately. For one brief second she remembered her John. Overwhelmed, tears sprang to her eyes. Not sad tears, for time erased sadness, but for years wasted mourning his death and never allowing another to touch her this way. She'd been wrong. Desiring another wouldn't diminish the love she'd had for the man she'd married all those years ago. She valued what they'd shared. What they'd shared was in the past, and this was *now*.

This was Rich, and oh, God she craved the newness and the thrill of *this* man's touch on her body.

With one swift move he stripped away the last barrier. She rose to meet him when he moved over her. His long, lean body covered her. So warm, so strong, he pressed her into softness. His heartbeat hammered against her breast.

She grasped his firm hips and thrust up, opening, meeting the searing heat, seeking, setting a rhythm until the world exploded and she cried out.

Again and again, he drove her up until her cries softened and he slipped inside her quaking body. "There's nothing left," she whimpered.

"Ah, I don't think so," Rich whispered against her ear, making her clutch around him. Making her spent body shudder. "Blame the Mediterranean Moonlight."

His grin flashed as he braced on strong, lean muscled arms above her. He gazed into her eyes, moving with purpose, sliding into her and reawakening needs until she cried out again.

This time he didn't stop. This time he gathered her close and held on while lusty madness drove them both.

*****

Moving quietly on bare feet, Rich crossed to the window overlooking Presque Isle Bay. Steam rose from the cup in his hand, along with the potent smell of fresh brewed coffee. He shoved one hand into the pocket of the jeans he'd pulled on after a fast shower and, lifting the other, sipped the dark liquid.

Far below, several early risers hustled along the bayfront. They wore jackets and vests, snapped and zipped up tight. Rich suspected a wind shift. A stiff breeze skimming over the still cold lake waters would make the air temperature plunge. Typical for Erie. Until the lake water reached a decent temperature, any change in wind direction could turn a spring day into a bitter reminder of months gone by.

Light filtered in, tracing a pattern across the floor to the bed where Ada still slept. She'd fallen asleep curled in his arms after their last bout between the sheets and he suspected last night had been the first sound sleep she'd had in days. To be realistic -- though his male ego begged to disagree -- the reason wasn't due to Rich's skills as a lover. The real reason fell somewhere along the lines of pure, nervous exhaustion.

Rustling sheets drew his attention back to the bed. Ada rolled over, squinted at the bedside clock, and then flopped onto her back. She blinked, turned her head toward him, and asked in a husky voice, "Is it morning, Rich?"

Before he could reply, she pushed to a sitting position, dragging the sheet up to cover her nakedness. Her eyes were wide open now. Light played across her features, highlighting color radiating from the very center of her eyes.

Rich paused, admiring her beauty. With vivid clarity, a past image of Ada wearing a mossy green sweater flashed through his mind. The rich fabric had enhanced her eyes, turning them deep green that night. Green and fathomless, like a deep spring fed pool. He recalled staring into them, much as he did now, and contemplating how he was diving in way over his head, much as he did now.

"Rich." Her voice came stronger. "You're staring at me. Do I look that bad?" She reached up and finger combed her tousled hair.

He detoured to a table bearing coffee and a carafe of hot water for tea. Pausing, he sat his coffee down and selected a tea bag from a sizable assortment. He dropped it into a cup, lifted the carafe, and poured. "Hope you like English Breakfast," he said, replacing the carafe.

He moved to the bed, leaned down, and gripped her chin. Tilting her face up, he placed a gentle kiss on her lips. "You look gorgeous."

She snorted. "I'll just bet I do." Then her eyes flew open wide. She grasped his hand. "Oh, Rich. I never told anyone I'd be gone overnight. Mary will be frantic. I've got to call and--"

"I called Tom and told him you were with me."

"Oh. Thank you, I guess." She heaved a sigh. "I don't suppose you mentioned we'd be sharing a room?"

"Certainly not." He returned to the table and retrieved his coffee. After taking a deep sip, he added, "Tom wasn't born yesterday."

Eyes closed, Ada shook her head. Rich chuckled and then gestured with the cup in his hand. "Are you going to lounge around in bed all day?"

She tugged and tucked the sheet beneath her arms, carefully covering what he considered an early morning feast for the eyes. Last night she'd curled against him, warm, soft... and naked. A pleasant memory. Yet here she was this morning, coy as a virgin, covering up assets he'd much rather enjoy along with his morning coffee.

"I need to shower," she declared. "Where are my clothes?"

Rich nodded to the neat stack of items on a nearby chair. "I took the liberty of gathering them up for you, and the bath is well stocked with personal stuff. So, go ahead and shower. I took one while you snoozed," he added, and drained his cup. He placed it on the table and gathered up his keys and wallet. "Why don't I slip out and head downstairs. I'll order some breakfast to be sent up to the room. Any requests?"

Ada slumped against the headboard, settling in and sending a warm smile his way. "You're a true gentleman, Rich McConnell. Scrambled eggs, wheat toast, and fruit should do it."

"You're a decisive lady, Ada Blaine. I'll take care of breakfast and be back shortly."

She was patiently waiting, still wrapped tight in the soft sheet, as he slipped out the door and, whistling softly, wandered down the hallway to the elevator.

*****

Gathering the sheet around her toga style, Ada rose and crossed to the window. Whitecaps covered the bay's surface. Summer-like temperatures they'd enjoyed the day before were unlikely today. She made a beeline for the shower, tossing the sheet onto the bed as she passed. At the bathroom door she paused, glancing over her shoulder at the rumpled bed.

Stepping into the bathing suite -- there was no calling this opulent luxury a bathroom -- she noted one large fluffy towel had been used. She selected an identical one, soft and luxurious to the touch, and leaned into the walk-in shower, adjusting the flow and temperature of water for a quick shower.

After showering and dressing, Ada located her handbag and used her cell phone to call Mary. She knew Rich had talked with Tom the night before, but thought it only right she follow up with a call to her friend.

"Good morning." Mary's voice sang out, brimming with warm humor.

"Good morning, back," Ada replied. She blushed, despite herself, realizing Mary identified her by checking her cell's display. "I assume you didn't worry about my absence last night?"

"Not at all." Her friend did nothing to disguise her laughter.

Ada remained silent. Still chuckling, Mary cleared her throat. "Are you on your way home? I thought I could come over and help catch up in the garden today."

"As a matter of fact," Ada drawled. "I'm in a very lovely suite overlooking Presque Isle Bay. I just indulged in an absolutely wonderful shower and I'm awaiting room service to bring my breakfast."

"Really?" Mary gasped, her voice raising several octaves. "Tom said you were staying in Erie, I didn't imagine you'd be wallowing in first class luxury. Good for you. You're long overdue for some pampering. Is Rich there right now?"

"What makes you think I shared these exquisite accommodations with Rich McConnell?"

"Oh, Ada. I wasn't born yesterday."

"Well, I'll be darned. That's exactly what Tom said when Rich spoke with him last night."

For the next few moments she talked with Mary, giving her a brief rundown of events leading up to her sleep over. They agreed to meet at Ada's cottage around noon, at which time she promised to fill in the blanks about her visit to Erie.

"I'll bring lunch and then help you catch up," Mary said before they disconnected.

Ada dressed, and was applying finishing touches to her hair when Rich tapped on the door and called out softly, "It's me." before entering.

He glanced around, smiling when he found her up and ready to face the day. Opening the door wider, he gestured and a waiter rolled a cart into the room.

When the waiter whipped off a silver domed cover, a sumptuous bowl of fresh strawberries, perfect scrambled eggs, and whole wheat toast appeared. Rich poured himself coffee and handed Ada a lovely china cup brimming with rich smelling tea.

They ate by the window, watching sail boats set out for the day. Sails billowed in the prevailing winds as the graceful boats cut through the choppy water.

"A perfect end to a perfect rendezvous," Rich declared, smiling warmly into her eyes.

Neither could afford to be away from their jobs another day. Her gardens needed attention, plus she was eager to see her new fence. While preparing to leave the room, she overheard Rich on the phone giving sharp instructions to someone at his store.

"Damn, Harley," he muttered, closing the door behind them. He took Ada's arm as they moved to the elevator. "Hank Barnes was to get off early yesterday. When five o'clock rolled around, Harley was nowhere to be found. They had to scramble to make sure there was someone there to close." He shrugged and grimaced. "I like Hank. He's reliable and I can count on him, but he had something important going on with his family last night and if someone else hadn't offered to step in and close up, he'd have missed out. I'm going to have a serious talk with Harley today."

Ada just smiled. Nothing was going to upset the state of bliss she all but wallowed in presently. She dug into her bag for the parking stub as they entered the multilevel garage next to the Sheridan.

"How do you like your CRV?" Rich asked, tilting his head to admire the sleek, compact SUV as Ada opened the door.

"I really like the way it handles. Cassi talked me into taking a test drive after I stuck my old reliable for the third time last winter. That did it. I just had it in for the first check up and oil change. It's running like a dream."

Rich ran his hand along the sturdy roof rack. "Did this come standard?"

"No, but I needed it for the kayak holder attachment I have on order."

He surveyed the sturdy rack. "A kayak will fit nicely up here. Maybe I'll dig mine out and we can bring them up to Erie sometime this summer and kayak around Presque Isle. I haven't done that in years. The waterways there are beautiful. Presque Isle's a gem we often overlook."

Ada agreed. The thought of kayaking appealed to her and also jogged her memory. "Oh, speaking of kayaking. Do you remember the man I ran into on Pine Shadow Lake not long ago?"

Absently Rich dug into his jeans pocket. "Yeah, I remember. What about him?"

"I saw him yesterday."

Rich's head snapped up. Ada jerked back, bumping into the door. His hard, direct gaze met hers. The keys gripped in his hand dug into her when he grasped her shoulder. "Where? Where did you see him, and when?"

Alarmed, Ada lifted her hand and touched the lean fingers digging into her soft skin. "It was right before I met you for dinner, after I had my nails done. I ran into him, literally, as I left the parking garage on my way to meet you. Why Rich? What's wrong?"

"You're sure it was the same man?" He asked, ignoring her question.

"Yes, though he's taller than I first thought," she mused, surprised when he turned her and eased her into her CRV.

"I want you to go to the exit and wait until I catch up with you. Then I'll follow you back to Pine Bluffs." His words snapped with authority.

Part of her wanted to snap back, to demand what just bit him in the butt. Yet the slight tremor she sensed as he guided her into the seat made her hesitate. He waited, glancing around the parking garage, as she fastened her seat belt. She turned to question him, but his warm lips met hers with a firm kiss. Then he straightened, closed her door, and strode towards his truck at the far end of the ramp.

Humph. Ada jammed her key into the ignition. Why should he be upset over something so trivial? If the kayak man had wanted to hurt her, he'd had ample opportunity.

With a shrug she turned the key, backed up and, pulling forward, followed the arrows as she wove her way to the exit. She paid the fee and rolled forward, noting Rich pulled in behind her before she turned onto the street.

As if glued to her bumper, Rich practically drove up the CRV's tailpipe. The move added to a budding irritation his 'man in charge' take over attitude provoked. Yet at the same time, a creepy sense of foreboding rolled through her. Instead of being provoked, should she pay more attention to his protective male instincts? She frowned and glanced in the rearview mirror. Rich waved. She waved back, relaxing and almost laughing.

Granted, the past few days *had* shaken her world, but, summoning new determination *not* to go looking for trouble, she'd not live her life jumping at every little coincidence.

Brilliant sun and a cloudless blue sky. Gifts to be wallowed in, used and enjoyed. The day stretched before her like a golden path. She itched to get her hands into the soil, surrounded by her fragrant herbs. Eager now to get on with the day, she checked both ways and then turned south onto State Street, heading for the parkway and home.

The first time she'd made love with Rich, savoring the experience got tainted when some idiot decided to trash her land. Her new fence guaranteed there'd be no repeat performance. A thick forest of trees and the lake bordered her land, making access impossible unless someone came on foot or by boat.

She'd share the day with her friend, Mary. Maybe she'd share the experience, the thrill of her night with a handsome, exciting man. She glanced in her rearview mirror. There he was, right behind her.

The day beckoned with blue skies and a golden promise.

Chapter Twenty-Nine

Rich hugged the sporty CRV's bumper as he trailed Ada up State Street to the Parkway. She caught the green light and turned east. Rich tucked right in behind her, but grinned and eased back when he noticed her frequent glances into her rearview mirror. No sense poking the hornets nest when things between them were back on track.

Yet he didn't feel comfortable letting her get out of his sight. Earlier, he'd been on top of the world. Relaxed, whistling as he rode the elevator down to the restaurant. He'd engaged in friendly chatter with the waitress after placing their breakfast order.

Now he felt as if he were going to explode. Will Steiner, the son-of-a-bitch, had come way too close to Ada. Not only once, but two friggin' times within the past week.

Without a doubt, the kayaker and the man Ada bumped into yesterday were one and the same. She was too sharp a woman to miss the obvious. Coincidence? He had too many friends in law enforcement who often pointed out coincidence doesn't exist in crime.

So, what is Steiner up to?

Driving along, he sorted through possibilities. None of them eased his mind. They reached the sharp turn onto the Bayfront Connector and Ada swung right, shooting up the incline toward the next major intersection. Rich slowed for the turn and followed, nudging his truck into the middle lane and picking up the pace. The light up ahead turned and Ada continued south without him. While waiting out the light, he rolled down the window and settled his arm within the opening, cursing his bad luck while drumming an impatient rhythm against the door.

The light flashed green and Rich hit the gas, weaving through traffic, keeping Ada's vehicle in sight. He grinned, catching another light while she breezed along toward Interstate 90. She *knew* he wanted to stick close, and he suspected she was pushing it, exerting that damn stubborn independence of hers.

Once they were on the thruway though, they faced construction and he'd easily catch up. Eastbound lanes over Wintergreen Gorge were fifty miles an hour. Replacing the outdated bridge caused a slow down every once in a while. By maintaining a steady pace, Rich closed the gap between them. Only a few cars separated them as they swept around the entry ramp, preparing to merge with eastbound traffic.

Shit. Wouldn't you know traffic would be bumper to bumper.

Several car lengths ahead, Ada moved along with the steady flow of traffic. In front of her, a pack of semis slowed as they rolled down the incline. Last in line, roughly ten car lengths in front of Ada, a flatbed carried a hefty load of pipes. Stacked one on top of another, long silver cylinders were lashed in place with wide strapping and extended several feet beyond the truck's bed. As the long, low hauler rolled into the construction zone, sun bounced off the precarious load.

*****

Once on the ramp, Ada applied the brakes to negotiate the sharp right hand curve and slow down in order to merge with traffic streaming eastbound on I-90. At first, the brakes didn't respond. Her insides tightened. The brake pedal caught, then released.

She wasn't slowing down.

Out of habit, Ada pumped the pedal. *Don't* pump disc brakes, she'd been warned. She had to do *something.* Fear grabbed hold, a twisting clutch inside her.

Even if she made the curve, she'd still enter fast moving traffic like a bat out of he-- Ah..., the pedal jerked, and then caught, slowing her approach.

Her hands trembled and she gripped the wheel, blowing out a long breath as she signaled and eased into traffic. Up ahead signs warned drivers to use caution and to be prepared to stop. Heart racing, she tested the brakes again, half expecting a repeat of that quick bump followed by a split second hesitation. As she applied slow pressure, her speed decreased. Though her nerves settled, she frowned. Something still didn't feel right.

Maybe her foot slipped? She readjusted and tested the response again. Pressing down gently she stole a glance in the rearview mirror. Several cars back, she spotted Rich's truck entering traffic.

She'd mention the little glitch, or whatever, to him when they got back into Pine Bluffs. Although strangely the pedal seemed to have reset. He'd probably laugh, and then explain away -- with great manly detail -- what caused the little spurt, or pulse or whatever it was giving her that scary sensation when she attempted to slow down on the ramp.

Traffic poured down the increasing grade onto the old section of bridge designated for eastbound vehicles. Bright orange signs warned of a 50 mile per hour speed limit through the construction site, and a digital sign advised drivers of their speed as they approached the zone.

Suddenly up ahead red tail lights blinked on, and the river of cars and trucks spewing across the bridge began to slow. Ada pressed her foot on the brake.

The pedal held, then gave a little hitch and plunged to the floor.

In the space of a heartbeat, a light on the dash flashed and the bottom dropped out of Ada's stomach. The CRV picked up speed.

Orange markers flashed by. She dared a glance left, glimpsing wide-eyed, startled faces as she sped by other cars. Her gaze snapped forward, and with icy clarity saw the distance between her Honda and a flatbed with a towering load of pipes closing fast.

Too fast!

Her heart pounded in her ears. Tears stung her eyes and, hard as she tried, *she couldn't get enough air!*

She was trapped.

Off to her right a culvert, several dump trucks, and a huge sign atop thick posts awaited her. Big ditch. Big trucks. Big sign. Bad odds, but she had to choose. Then panic skewed reasoning and, to her horror, the truck up ahead hauling pipe came to a dead stop.

In a split second decision, the sign won. Ada gritted her teeth, sent up a brief prayer and yanked on the wheel.

*****

Orange cones, typical for Pennsylvania's landscape during the summer, lined the berm as Rich headed into the construction zone. Frustrated and unable to pass, he struggled to keep Ada's Honda in sight and--

What the hell?

Up ahead traffic slowed. Semi's blocked both lanes and Rich stared, transfixed as the distance between Ada and the protruding pipes on the flatbed closed rapidly.

What is she doing?

Feeling frantic and helpless, he glanced around. A solid line of traffic blocked any chance to maneuver into the passing lane. His pulse skyrocketed and the metallic taste of fear filled his mouth. Ada's CRV shot forward, aiming straight for the huge truck.

He screamed, "Slow down, *damn it!*" Helplessness poured over him in waves as his useless warning ricocheted inside his truck. The squeal of tires split the air as he jammed on his brakes, stopping just short of slamming into the car in front of him. Cold sweat soaked his shirt.

Before his horrified eyes, the electronic mileage display blinked rapidly as Ada's vehicle approached... forty-six, forty-seven, and climbing.

For God's sake woman, stop! Panic welled like gorge in his throat when up ahead traffic slowed to a standstill.

Terrified, Rich looked on as she barreled down the slope straight toward the deadly pipes gleaming in the sun.

"No!"

Striped orange barrels flew and gravel sprayed up as the right front wheel of Ada's vehicle left the road. A cloud of dust enveloped the Honda as it snapped around and slid sideways. Then before his horrified, unbelieving eyes, it crashed into the protruding pipes.

Rich shoved his truck into park. He struggled with the latch, hands shaking, until with a vicious curse he flung open the door and leaped out.

Heart pumping madly, he raced down the middle of the road.

*****

Trooper TJ McGraw's radio crackled to life as he left route 531 and sped up the ramp toward I-90. Routine patrol, gorgeous day, he couldn't ask for more. He slowed to enter westbound traffic, listening to the succinct, controlled voice from headquarters and his upbeat mood plummeted.

Shit.

An accident. Some idiot had tail-ended a truck on the thruway in the middle of a friggin' construction zone. As TJ hit the siren and lights, he glanced at his watch. No way in hell he'd wrap this up before his shift ended, and if injuries went south and turned this into a fatality, he'd face a mountain of paper work.

Traffic parted in front of him and he sped across Wintergreen Gorge Bridge. He zeroed in on the accident at the far end of the bridge and, checking behind him, heaved a sigh of relief when he spotted a flashing blue light atop a truck less than a half mile back. He'd take all the help he could get, because up ahead lay a developing traffic nightmare.

Once past cement barriers dividing the lanes, TJ slowed and crossed the median in order to reach the accident scene. He cringed, bouncing over rough terrain and plowing through a small forest of tall, dry grass. Loose gravel pinged off the underside of his patrol car.

Why in hell wasn't there a descent crossover on this stretch of road? Penn Dot should have foreseen something like this, and he guaranteed someone's ass would get chewed.

He cut the siren, but left the lights flashing to alert oncoming traffic and blocked both lanes with the marked car. Within seconds, the truck he'd spotted behind him arrived. A young man hopped out. He flipped on a black cap bearing plain white letters. HCFD, Harborcreek Fire Department.

The volunteer rushed toward him. "Pop the trunk, Troop," the man called out. "I'll set up flares to stop traffic."

TJ flipped the release. "You burned up the road, thanks I appreciate it."

"Why we make the big bucks," the man shot back with a grin.

TJ chuckled, because firemen in the county were volunteers and didn't make a penny. Hustling toward the disabled vehicle, he glanced back when the man called out, "Here comes Johnson, he's an EMT."

TJ caught sight of another flashing blue light and acknowledged with a wave. Then he turned his attention to the scene, continuing across the road.

Crushed against the right rear corner of a flatbed truck was a Honda CRV. It appeared the vehicle spun sideways from the point of initial impact and pipes protruding from the truck's bed impaled the SUV through the driver's side window.

Holy crap.

The side air bag had deployed. Draped like an unholy shroud in the smashed window, it obscured the pipes and the driver. A sick feeling coiled in TJ's gut.

He immediately approached the rear of the vehicle, surprised when he spotted a man withdrawing from the passenger door of the wreck. The man turned, and TJ blinked, then he hastened forward.

A sheen of sweat coated Rich McConnell's anguished face.

"Rich? Are you all right?" Alarmed by his friend's violent trembling TJ gripped Rich's shoulder. "Here, let me help you."

Chest heaving, Rich gulped in air and shrugged off TJ's hand. "I'm fine." He bent over and took several deep breaths. "It's Ada, TJ," he said, straightening. "She's hurt pretty bad."

Rich's pained expression begged for help, and like a well-oiled gear, TJ's training kicked in. "Is she conscious?"

"She made brief eye contact before passing out. I got a pulse, but otherwise no response." Rich raked shaking fingers through his hair. His face was sheet white.

"That's good, Rich," TJ said. "You did exactly the right thing. The EMT's are here now. We need to move back so they can help Ada. There's none better," TJ assured, and together they stepped back, clearing a path.

Voices shouted out orders amidst an explosion of flashing lights and piercing noise as more firemen arrived, rushing to secure the scene.

As TJ talked to Rich, his voice sounded calm, in control, matter of fact, but the voice inside his head screamed, *Oh, God. Don't let her die.*

Footsteps crunched on loose gravel and both men swung around.

"What have we got trooper?" A ruddy faced, middle aged man approached, carting a medical bag. He paused, listening as TJ repeated Rich's findings. Then the EMT disappeared into the vehicle. Within moments, he withdrew and called out vitals to his backup. "Head trauma, weak pulse, minimal bleeding, no visible fractures." He scanned the thruway. "When the ambulance gets here, get it in close. I'll stabilize her neck and we'll slide her out through this door. No time for another angle, her head injury's top priority."

More bodies swarmed over the scene. Rich swiped his sweaty forehead with the back of his hand. "Something went wrong TJ," he said, shaking his head. "She drove straight into the pipe. What the hell happened to make her do that?"

Frowning, TJ stepped to the rear of the vehicle. He examined the pavement, calculating where Ada's vehicle left the road. Stooping down, he noted minor skid marks. An acrid smell enveloped him. He grimaced, maybe burnt oil?

As the EMT's climbed into the vehicle to work on Ada, TJ got to his feet. He rubbed at tension plaguing his neck. Ada wouldn't ram headlong into a truck for no good reason. Her CRV was practically new. So what the hell happened?

Something didn't fit.

TJ's hand held beeped. "McGraw, its Sanders. I'm going to reroute traffic around the scene but there's a truck sitting smack in the middle of the right hand lane with no driver."

TJ scanned the area, pinpointing the agitated trooper, and the abandoned truck. "Is it damaged?" While Sanders checked out the truck, eastbound traffic backed up. More emergency vehicles arrived, lining the berm, skidding into the median. Lights flashed, radios squawked and semis heading westbound rumbled past, adding to the noise and confusion.

He shook his head. *Looks like a damn carnival.*

Noonday sun beat down, wilting TJ's clean, pressed shirt as he waited, taking it all in through reflective, wrap around shades. "No damage." Sanders reported back. "Damn thing's just sitting here idling with the door hanging open."

TJ's eyes narrowed on the truck. "Rich," he yelled over his shoulder. "If that's your truck you have to move it."

After a quick glance up the road, Rich nodded and gestured impatiently. "The keys are in it. Just pull it off the road."

Once the truck was removed, traffic began to inch by in the left hand lane. Satisfied, TJ went to check on the truck driver involved in the accident. The man appeared shaken, but uninjured, and the sooner TJ interviewed him the better. He waited while an EMT checked the driver out, but before he could proceed the ambulance arrived, putting the interview on hold.

TJ shouted to a fireman directing traffic, instructing him to halt eastbound traffic while the big box ambulance swung into position. Emitting a piercing, steady, beep, it backed in close.

Moving with proficient speed, emergency personal placed Ada on a flat board and removed her from her vehicle. They lifted her into the ambulance, scrambled in behind, and closed the doors.

The driver involved in the accident paced, wringing his hands, sweating buckets, while TJ conducted his interview. He wanted to grab the guy and plant him in one spot, but took pity on the poor man and did the best he could. When they lifted Ada from the wreck she was unconscious and looked ghostly pale. She not only wore a neck brace, but a huge gauze pack covered the entire left side of her head and upper face.

The truck driver halted his nervous shuffle, watching as they hustled her into the ambulance. The blood drained from *his* face. Fearing the man would drop like a stone, TJ steered him to the side and made him sit on the bumper of his truck.

He continued with more questions, but the ambulance idling nearby seemed to distract the man. "Why aren't they getting her to a hospital?"

Patiently, TJ explained, "They'll stabilize patients before transport, making sure their vitals are under control." He wasn't sure his explanation sunk in, because the trucker just gave him a blank stare. When the siren kicked in and the ambulance took off, the man closed his eyes and slumped against his truck.

TJ concluded the interview. Then he made sure someone took charge of the man until a wrecker arrived to extricate the Honda from the flatbed. While waiting, he took measurements and jotted down notes. He'd compact the details into a concise report later. A two vehicle accident with injuries wasn't nearly as involved or time consuming as a fatal. He'd start by examining Ada's vehicle after it was towed to a garage, and to complete the report, he'd also need to talk with her.

As soon as the ambulance pulled away, Rich had dashed to his truck and followed it up the thruway. He'd want to question Rich, too. So many pieces to fit together.

He glanced at his watch. A wrecker should be close. Since Harborcreek FD responded, he guessed a service in the area would be tapped to haul away the vehicle. Though first available was the general rule, he hoped like hell he'd get someone who'd make his follow up go smooth.

Despite a brutal sun and choking dust, a big grin spread when he saw his buddy Tim's bright red wrecker heading down the thruway toward him.

With a jaunty wave, Tim Chasen wheeled the wrecker into position. He cut the engine and swung down from the cab.

"Hey, Tim. You're a welcome sight."

Tim ambled toward him. His trademark crooked smile and easy nature eased some of the knots in TJ's shoulders. Chasen's Towing had been around for years, and TJ learned early on it was one of the preferred wrecker services in the area. Tim treated the staties right, and many used his garage to service their personal vehicles.

"What ya got?" Tim hitched stained gray slacks up and strolled over to take a closer look at the damage. He listened, squinting as he studied the areas TJ pointed out. Tim's bushy brows spiked naturally over clear, brown eyes. Those eyebrows shot up when the acrid burnt smell TJ experienced was mentioned. "You'll want to take a look under this sucker, then," he remarked. "I'll make sure it's secured. Has everything belonging to the driver been removed? How about the keys?" He cupped his hand on the windshield and looked inside.

"Yeah, I sent her purse with a friend. Other than the owner's manual in the glove box, there's nothing of value to consider." As Tim straightened, TJ tossed him the keys.

"Then let's get this baby untangled here, and I'll take her in."

After some creative maneuvering, the pipes were moved and Tim hoisted the vehicle into the air. He winched it onto a long, low flatbed for transport and headed to his garage.

TJ stowed his gear, notebook, and measuring tools in the patrol car. By the time he wrote up and filed the initial, he'd be on overtime. Should he stop by Chasen's now, or hit there first thing tomorrow? Best to check with the shift supervisor on that one.

He unclipped his cell phone and dialed his mom. Ada was as close as family with his parents, and this call had to be made. He just hoped like hell his dad answered the phone.

Chapter Thirty

Ada remembered pain. It slammed through her, sudden and severe, and then someone spoke her name, touched her. Amidst the confusion, the contact calmed her and pushed down panic. There was noise and movement, voices overlapped against a roaring background. Sensations floated in and out of her head, vivid, scary.

Then... nothing.

By bits and pieces the awareness returned. Ada lay absolutely still, so afraid the pain would come back. Hushed silence wrapped around her like a soft peaceful blanket until...

"Can you hear me? Mrs. Blaine."

Ada turned her head toward the whisper of fabric. She tried to open her eyes. Upon succeeding, her vision was... Well, odd. A wispy fog framed the edges of everything around her.

Abruptly, a face appeared in front of her. A piercing light aimed into her eyes. She slammed them shut and turned away when pain speared through her head and nausea welled in her throat. She attempted to lift her hand, to push the pain inducing light away. The simple gesture took her breath away.

She tried to speak. "Where..." Words failed her, lodging in her parched throat. Frustrated, she swallowed and emitted a dry cough.

"Relax, Mrs. Blaine. We need to assess your injuries." The words filtered through the fog and the pain. "Try to relax, I'm going to check your pupils."

A firm, cool touch lifted first one eyelid, then the other. The light came again. Ada struggled to hold still. Hands touched her, and her muscles jumped.

"Her respiratory pattern is satisfactory, oculocephalic reflexes slow, but even. Deep tendon reflexes responding. I need to get her to open her eyes, to communicate. I don't want to order a CT scan unless absolutely necessary."

The words penetrated, and Ada fought to comprehend the man's voice drifting in and out of her throbbing brain. Another voice, softer, quieter, murmured responses. She sensed the difference in their touch -- his firm, slightly warm, hers, cool and gentle.

"Mrs. Blaine." His voice became louder, and he laid his hand on her arm.

The effort cost her, but she lifted her own hand and placed it over his. Then turning her head in the direction of his voice, Ada slowly opened her eyes.

"Ah, hello there." This time the face wasn't veiled in fog. Fine lines crinkled around clear blue eyes as he smiled. "Welcome back." He glanced at something above and to the left, then returned his gaze to study her face closely. "Can you see me clearly?"

She nodded, slitting her eyes against the pain. "Can I have a drink," she croaked.

He gestured behind him and a nurse appeared. She moved in and held a small cup to Ada's lips, "Its ice," the young woman cautioned. "Let it melt on your tongue, then swallow slowly."

Ada nodded, and careful hands lifted her head enough to take in a small amount of ice. The cold slivers melted quickly, bringing blessed relief to parched tissue and sliding down to bathe her aching throat. After she took a second mouthful, the nurse lowered her head. "The light hurts my eyes," she whispered, each word an effort, then responded to the doctor's question. "But, yes... I can see."

"Okay," he said, wheeling over a tall cart with a small laptop on board. "That's good news." While his fingers tapped the compact keyboard, he continued. "I'm Doctor Stormer. Just a few more questions. Think you can hang in there?"

"I'll try, but... where am I?"

"You're at Hamot in Erie."

Her chest tightened and, despite knife-like shots of pain, she opened her eyes wider. "What time is it?" she gasped.

Something beeped above her head, causing the doctor to step away from his note taking and adjust the tubes carrying oxygen to Ada. "Deep breaths, Mrs. Blaine," he instructed. After several moments the tightness dissipated, but she was fast becoming aware of discomfort throughout her entire body.

The pain engulfed her, and to her dismay, tears spilled and tracked down her cheeks. She pushed through the wall of it, shivering beneath a lightweight blanket which covered her head to toe. She had to know. How bad was she hurt?

She closed her eyes. Small pieces, bits of memory, filtered through her muzzy head. She'd been with Rich. The sun was out, a glorious day and then... and then...

She jerked, and the pain swallowed her whole.

Oh, God!

A truck. She'd hit a truck when her brakes failed. A helpless, out of control sensation barreled through her and, like a shard of ragged glass, the needle in her arm dug into her tender flesh when she seized Dr. Stormer's arm.

"Am I going to die?"

*****

Rich stared into the Styrofoam cup, as if the tasteless dredges clinging to the bottom held answers. Throughout the evening, time after time, he'd retrieved the watery brew from a nearby coffee machine. Going through the motions gave him something to do with his hands.

If he took one more sip of this shit, or paced to the window one more time to peer out into the dark moonless night, he was going to go friggin' mad. What the hell was happening behind those double doors marked with an ominous *Hospital Staff Only*?

He was sick and tired of doors shutting him out. The ambulance doors slammed shut as soon as the gurney carrying Ada slid inside. He'd raced to his truck, followed the screaming siren, and made it to Hamot minutes after they'd whisked Ada into Emergency. Another set of doors slammed in his face.

Not being family, details were not forthcoming. The staff kept him informed, generally, but their updates lacked facts. It wasn't until Tom and Mary McGraw arrived and it was determined they were listed as next of kin, along with Cassi McGraw, information regarding Ada's condition became available.

That was hours ago. Exhausted, Tom and Mary departed once they were assured the injuries Ada sustained were serious but not life threatening. There was nothing to be gained by them remaining at the hospital, so they returned to Pine Bluffs. A call to Cassi and Nick had to be made, and they agreed the call would be better coming from them.

Rich tossed the empty cup and stalked to the window. He winced at his reflection in the flat, black glass. Stubble scraped his palm when he rubbed his jaw, and his hair looked like a rat's nest. Maybe he should have gone home, too.

He spun around when the doors at the end of the hall whooshed open. A tall thin man in green scrubs ambled through the opening. Urgency displayed earlier no longer quickened Dr. Stormer's step. As he drew near, he rolled his shoulders as if relieving deep seated tension.

Not sure what to do with his hands, Rich shoved them into his pockets and waited.

"Mr. McConnell," Dr. Stormer addressed him. He gestured to the chairs in the alcove where Rich had been waiting. "Let's have a seat and I'll update you on Mrs. Blaine's condition."

A short time later, Rich left the hospital. He inhaled deeply as he walked outside. The cool night air cleared his head, something the murky liquid passing as coffee from hospital vending machines *hadn't* accomplished. His footsteps echoed in the parking garage next to the hospital. State Street was all but abandoned when he turned north toward the Bayfront Parkway.

Was it only this morning he'd shared breakfast with Ada in a room overlooking Presque Isle Bay? Tonight the bay looked dark and ominous. He wound down his window, there'd be rain by dawn, he'd bet on it.

Traveling along the same route they'd taken that morning, Rich experienced a stab of déjà vu. His insides rolled, emitting a hollow growl that reminded him he'd not eaten a thing since breakfast over twelve hours ago.

Hunger was the last thing on his mind before his spoke with Dr. Stormer. His report lowered Rich's anxiety level several notches. According to the good doctor, Ada was stable. They planned to monitor her closely overnight, and if she continued to improve, chances were he'd release her by late the next day.

That addressed the head trauma, but he planned to prescribe therapy once she could tolerate the pain, stressing torn tendons and damaged muscles had to heal before they could undergo the rigors of rehab. He assured Rich normal function would return, but the road back could be long and difficult.

Passing beneath circles of light on the Bayfront Connector, Rich smiled to himself. Dr. Stormer wasn't acquainted with the lady's iron clad will and fierce determination. Nor had he ever witnessed her ferocious anger which was sure to surface when she got a look at what remained of her brand new CRV.

Sure as hell, Rich assumed the 'long road' the doctor referred to would shorten considerably once his patient set her mind to recovering.

Slipping through the pitch black night, Rich focused on that assumption.

He made good time driving home to Pine Bluffs, though he slowed when he passed the accident site. Flattened grass in the median was the only sign an accident had occurred, easily missed by passing cars as they headed across the bridge.

Upon arriving, his converted carriage house appeared dark and deserted. To chase the gloom he hastened up the stairs and throughout several rooms, hitting switches as he went.

Calling the Wilson house would be a gamble. He didn't want to alarm Tish, but knew Gary was a late night TV junky, so after making a hasty sandwich and grabbing a chilled bottle of water, Rich dialed Gary's cell phone.

He answered on the first ring. Yes and yes. Tish was asleep and his friend was watching TV. Rich unloaded the day's events, starting with Ada's surprise meeting with their old friend Will Steiner in the parking garage.

Doggedly, Gary pried for details. He asked questions, a lot of *lousy* questions, irritating questions. Gradually though, Rich's exasperation subsided and the knot in his belly unfurled.

"You're sure it was Steiner she saw in the garage?"

"He walked away from me, heading in that direction, and two minutes later Ada's walking along the retaining wall toward me. It had to have been him."

"*She* was sure the man she saw kayaking a few days ago was the same one she talked to in the garage?"

"No question. At the time I didn't push for details, or an explanation. I was more interested in getting her the hell out of Erie. Fifteen minutes later it hit the fan."

"Let's take a closer look at the accident. Is it possible she was distracted? You said she kept watching you behind her, maybe she didn't realize how close she was to the truck?"

Rich chewed the bite of sandwich he'd taken while Gary talked. "I don't buy that," he mumbled and washed down the food with a hefty gulp of water. "When we came off the ramp and merged onto 90, her attention was on the road in front of her. Traffic was heavy. She signaled to merge and didn't look back. Next thing I knew she was flying like hell at a flatbed full of pipes. Christ in heaven, Gary." His voice cracked. "I've never felt so helpless!"

Shaking, he gulped down more water.

"But last time you talked with the doctor things looked good?"

Rich heaved a deep sigh. "Yeah, thank God. For now she's stable."

After a long pause, Gary asked, "You said TJ McGraw is the trooper investigating?"

"Yeah. When I backed out of her mangled CRV and saw TJ, my knees almost gave out. What a freakin' relief. He held it together like a pro and did what had to be done. Later, I talked to him from the hospital. He's going to start by going over the Honda first thing in the morning."

"Good. That's good. Now, I have something not so good to tell you."

Rich set his water down and switched ears. "Regarding?"

"I talked to Delaney before I left Buffalo. Remember I told you Steiner has an aunt in the Buffalo area? Well, it appears she's taken our bad boy under her wing."

"What is she, stupid?"

"No. Neither is Hank Delaney. He's concerned about our boy relocating so close to you, but apparently Will had a clean slate for good behavior when released. The aunt stepped up to the plate, even going so far as to keep Hank informed about all she's doing to help her nephew get a fresh start."

"How is she going to manage that?" Rich said, sarcasm dripping from each word.

Gary chuckled. "Still have that 'trust no one and walk damn careful around the dead' outlook, Bunkie. Just listen to me a minute. The aunt assured Delaney Steiner's looking for work, and he was aware her nephew was checking out the Erie area. It's possible, bumping into you was pure accident and not Steiner's plan at all."

"Could be you're right. Hank Delaney doesn't make many mistakes. So, I'll give him that one. However, Steiner sure as hell wasn't looking for a job in a kayak on Pine Shadow Lake last week, and if bumping into Ada was an accident today..." Rich glanced at his watch. "Or yesterday. That doesn't mean he didn't get a bug up his ass to pull something after he talked to me and then ran smack into her."

"You're thinking he messed with her car."

"Damn straight."

"Then give Trooper McGraw your views and let him do his job."

"I have no problem with TJ doing his job. I'm going to make sure all the cards are on the table when it comes to Steiner's involvement.

"Aunt *Tillie*, or whoever, in Buffalo be damned."

Chapter Thirty-One

Remnants of an all night rain dripped from the eaves as Nan Chasen handed TJ a steaming cup of coffee. He smiled and inhaled the rich aroma. She might as well have given him a hundred bucks. That's the price any policeman worth his salt put on a superb cup of brew. "Thanks, Nan." TJ took a sip. The taste measured up to the tantalizing smell.

"You're welcome, TJ."

He'd met Nan shortly after being transferred to Troop E. The guys all liked and respected the wrecker driver's wife, agreeing her quick mind and organizing skills were behind Tim's quick response time. Plus, she had a knack for appearing with fresh brewed coffee just when a harried trooper needed the boost.

This morning TJ needed the boost.

He'd put in overtime yesterday, organizing and filing. Then gone home, grabbed a quick meal, and spent several more hours working on his own time. The nursing staff at Hamot was vague during discussions by phone, and stressed any interviews must wait for the doctor's approval. His mom and dad reported in after they returned from the hospital. Hearing Ada's status directly from his parents helped. Their update on her condition and prognosis for recovery eased his mind and he slept like a brick. At least until his friggin' alarm buzzed him awake at dawn.

"He's on his way." Nan slipped her cell phone into the pocket of neat tan utility pants. "He should be here in about ten minutes." She shook her head, sending her dark brown pony tail dancing. "Go figure," she remarked with a laugh. "A dead battery this time of year."

TJ sipped coffee, raised his brows. "Let me guess, some little old lady."

Nan laughed. "He's such a softy." She gestured toward the fenced yard behind the garage. "How about I let you get started? The CRV's right up near the gate. Tim said you'd want to look underneath. Once he gets here, it won't take much to pull it out and put it on the lift."

TJ started to hand her the half finished coffee.

"Take that with you, TJ," she said. "I'll get the cup later."

"Thanks, Nan. I'll make sure you get it back." He followed her to the enclosure and waited while she unlocked the gate.

First, he took a slow stroll around the Honda. Other than the left side, the vehicle looked untouched. Using the heel of his hand, he gave the frame above the driver side door a solid nudge. Then hunkered down to peer inside. Both airbags had deployed. Along with the sturdy frame, they probably kept Ada from being seriously injured.

Probably saved her life.

He bent lower, balancing the cup and gripping the bumper to look beneath the vehicle. No luck. He'd have to wait for Tim.

He shoved to his feet. Thankful he at least had some decent coffee in his gut. Breakfast had consisted of a fast bagel and a glass of juice. Being dead on his feet last night, he'd forgotten to grind fresh beans for his morning coffee. Pissed him off when he did that.

He heard the rumble of Tim's wrecker as he tipped the cup and drained the last of Nan's coffee. He'd make a point to thank her before he left.

Tim swung his truck around and backed through the open gate. He stopped just short of the Honda's bumper and slipped the wrecker into park. "Suckin' up Nan's coffee, I see." He grinned, yanking the hook and chain into position.

"Only hospitality we get around here," TJ shot back, then laughed when he realized that he'd addressed his snarky comment to Tim's butt as he knelt down and reached under to fasten the tow hook.

Tim hauled the car out and hoisted it on the lift. Together, they stood beneath the mangled vehicle and studied the underside intently. Tim ran his hand along the lines leading to both front and rear wheels. He stepped closer, poking them one at a time, then pulled a stained red utility rag from his rear pocket and wiped away debris on one line. "Take a look," he told TJ, moving aside to make room.

Using the flashlight he'd retrieved from his car, TJ directed the beam where Tim indicated. "Brake lines, right?"

"Damn straight. There wasn't a drop of brake fluid in the reservoir under the hood," Tim added. "Look at these black streaks on the manifold. That's brake fluid. Burns like a son of a bitch when it hits that hot underside."

"Could be what I smelled at the scene." TJ scoped out the entire underside. "The lines are intact, though. Isn't that kind of cockeyed?"

Tim just grinned. "Look closer, son," he said, lifting those all knowing brows.

TJ did, taking his time, retracing lines. At first, all he saw was dirt and dark blotchy stains. Then he zeroed in on what looked like a blowout on the rear line. He switched to the front and, after a careful search, spotted an almost identical spot. "There *are* holes in the lines." His gaze shifted from one to the other. "I could see where hitting a stone or something could punch through one line. But two holes, one front, one rear? I don't buy that."

He turned to Tim.

"Me neither. See the pattern?" Tim said, indicating the area in front and behind the holes. "Whoever did this was one clever bastard."

"No accident, huh?" TJ aimed the light directly on the front hole and scanned either side.

Tim's hand entered the flashlight beam. "See those little dots, kinda like specks of grease?"

It took him a moment. "These?" TJ ran his finger over several rough spots.

"Yep. Must have used something like a fine point nail. Look, they're spaced out all along the line. Then about half way back, right before the hole, they're closer together. Whoever did this didn't want the fluid to leak out until the vehicle was moving. Pressure built, then force from a slow down or sudden stop triggered the blowout. Crafty son-of-a-bitch. He knew she'd only have minutes, maybe seconds, to get off the road once the sensors detected fluid loss and triggered the alarm."

"When that happened, Ada had nowhere to go."

"Looks like," Tim agreed.

"And when the second line blew she lost her brakes entirely."

Tim eyed the damaged lines. "In my opinion, whoever did this gambled. They took a calculated risk. When the first line went, I'll bet her dash lit up like Christmas. Depending on speed and location, reacting and stopping before the other line blew would be a bitch. This joker bet on the second going within minutes, maybe less, leaving *no* reaction time."

"Son-of-a-bitch." TJ raked his fingers through his hair. She must have been terrified. If Tim's theory proved true, whoever tampered with those lines knew damn well chances of her being able to react before the second one blew were next to none.

Tim followed him out from underneath the vehicle. They brought in work lights to illuminate the underside and TJ took a series of pictures.

"Tim," he asked, tucking the camera away. "Could you write me up a description of what you discovered? Date and sign it, too.

Tim shrugged. "No problem."

Being an inspection mechanic, Tim's statement would carry weight. Every bit of information he included in his report could prove valuable, and at this point, there was no telling where this investigation would end up.

He noted the time. He'd grab some lunch, and then call Hamot for an update. If the doctor cleared Ada for an interview, he'd head into Erie and get her statement. If she could pinpoint exactly when she began to have brake problems, then he could backtrack.

It all had to fit. Every piece. From where she parked prior to the accident, to who may have had access to that location. He'd follow up with interviews. A lot of legwork.

Depending on what he turned up, he may have to involve the crime unit.

Because if Tim Chasen's theory was right, someone had tried to murder Ada Blaine.

*****

Slate colored clouds hung low over Presque Isle Bay, and rivulets of rain coated the window. Restless and uncomfortable, Ada resisted the urge to slide down and pull the covers over her head. She'd catnapped off and on throughout the night, and at frequent intervals the doctor's face hovered as he shined that irritating light in her eyes.

Did the man ever sleep?

Around daybreak she awoke feeling muzzy headed and uncomfortable. Shortly thereafter, they exchanged ice chips for real fluids. A welcome relief. Chomping on ice just didn't get it. She asked for tea and forced down two cups of the watery brew, after which her weary brain finally kicked in, and her head began to clear.

Depending on how she looked at it, remembering was both good *and* bad. Vague images lulled her along. As the mental fog lifted, a clear vision of careening toward disaster brought numbing, ice cold fear.

She shifted, seeking a position to relieve the ever present pain. Craving uninterrupted sleep, she closed her eyes... and drifted.

"Looking better, lady."

Her eyes popped open to find Rich's tall, lanky form framed in the doorway of her hospital room. Clean shaven, he wore a crisp blue shirt and khaki slacks and clutched a bouquet of flowers in his hand. Despite dark circles beneath his tawny eyes, the sight of him took her breath away.

Ada closed her eyes again and heaved a deep sigh, imagining how she must look.

His footsteps drew near and he touched her arm. "Are you okay?"

Without opening her eyes, she managed a smile. "You've caught me looking like something the cat dragged in," she complained, making Rich chuckle.

She gingerly touched the bandage on the left side of her head. "This must look lovely, along with an assortment of multicolored bruises. Oh, yeah. I'm just great," she replied with sarcasm, and opened her eyes.

Rich leaned in and his lips touched hers. When the kiss ended she lifted her hand and cupped his smooth cheek. While gazing into his eyes, heat pooled inside her like warm honey and she murmured, "Hi, handsome. Are those flowers for me?"

"Absolutely," Rich said, his voice a bit husky. "I'll just put them here where you can see them." He placed them on the bedside stand, then pulled a chair in close. "Has the doctor been in today?"

"I don't think he left the hospital all night. Every time I drifted off he woke me to check my eyes. Around dawn he quit bothering me, but by then I was starving and couldn't sleep anyway."

"So they fed you?"

"Not much. Tea and toast." She squirmed, pulling the blanket higher. "I want real food, some of my homemade muffins. I want a comb, and some makeup."

"Ada, considering you were in a serious accident, you look pretty good." He touched a purplish bruise on her forearm.

Her humor faltered, and she placed her hand over his. "I'm told I'll need physical therapy. The doctor said my being in good shape helps, but it still won't be easy."

At that moment, Dr. Stormer strode into the room.

"Good Morning, Mr. McConnell, how're you this morning?"

"I'm dealing," Rich replied as they shook hands.

"Let's take a look," the doctor said, using the dreaded light to check her eyes. He turned her head left to right, examining several bruises, and then tucked the tiny light into his shirt pocket. "You gave us a scare, young lady, but I like what I see this morning. How do you feel?"

"Like I ran into a truck."

He chuckled, rechecking her chart. After speaking briefly with a nurse, he had Ada move her legs, which hurt like the devil. Then he stepped back and crossed his arms. "I'll let you go home on one condition."

Ada raised her brow, wincing when the bandage caught and tugged. "Which is?"

"You need someone with you for a few days. I don't want you sitting around, but," he cautioned with a raised finger, "I don't want you overdoing either."

"I won't be sitting around. Not if I want to eat next winter. Customers depend on my herbs and berries. Plants don't weed themselves. The next few weeks are crucial and if not cared for my harvest will be down. That's unacceptable."

"Get some help. Doctor's orders," he insisted when Ada's chin lifted. "I want to see you in one week. If I'm satisfied with your condition you can start rehab. Until then, I'll provide instructions to keep you moving so you won't stiffen. Follow them. If you do too much you'll damage those injured muscles. That *will* set you back. Pay attention. Do what you're told, Ada."

She shot a swift look at Rich and caught his smug look. "Damn peas in a pod," she muttered.

"I'll give you something for pain and the instructions I mentioned." The doctor continued, ignoring her sass. As he turned to leave, the sound of hurried footsteps approached and Cassi McGraw burst into the room.

"Oh, Aunt Ada."

The next thing Ada knew, she was wrapped in the arms of her sweet smelling niece. Tom and Mary slipped into the room, followed by Nick, Cassi's husband.

Well, well. The gangs all here.

Cassi loosened her grip. Her deep brown eyes filled as she skimmed a hand over Ada's bandage and gently cupped her cheek. "I thought we'd never get here." Her words came in a rush, and a single tear trailed down her cheek. "Are you all right? Oh, God, Aunt Ada, you're all bruised and you look so pale."

Ada wiped the tear from Cassi's face. "Why thank you, honey. I was getting all full of myself thinking I looked just gorgeous this morning."

Cassi choked out a laugh and gave her another hug. Ada winced and Cassi gasped, "Oh, I'm sorry." She released her hold and settled on the edge of the hospital bed.

Ada's gaze swept the room and settled on Nick. Though handsome as ever, his face looked carved in stone.

Uh-oh.

She took in his stance, his attitude. He knew, she concluded. He knew about everything, and the man was not pleased. How much he'd shared with Cassi remained to be seen.

She summoned a smile. "Hello, Nicholas."

Nick nodded, his expression unchanged.

"You've got your 'chief of police' face on, Nick," she teased.

Though it didn't reach his eyes, a smile curved his lips. "Hmmm. Maybe the chief of police should have been notified when his wife's aunt needed help."

Before Ada could respond, TJ walked into the room. In full state police mode, his uniform crisp and spotless, he stopped dead just inside the door. He greeted everyone, and broke into a wide grin when he spotted Nick. "Hey, cousin."

Cassi crossed the room and planted a kiss on TJ's cheek. He wrapped one arm around her, and his gaze flicked from her to Nick. "You both look great. How was the honeymoon?"

"Perfect," Cassi replied. "We're home a few days early, but that's okay," she promptly amended, and returned to Ada's bedside. "Family is important."

Her gaze locked with Ada's.

Ada's chest tightened and she swallowed, blinking unexpected tears into submission. This upheaval in *her* life interrupted happiness in Cassi's. That upset her. But the word 'family' yanked at her heart. Speechless, she bit her lip and took the hand Cassi offered.

"Well." TJ cleared his throat and glanced around the room. "I'm going to interview Ada. I need you all to leave us alone." He focused on Ada. "Are you up to talking about the accident?"

"I'll try my best, TJ." She patted Cassi's hand. "Go, get settled in. I bet you haven't even unpacked yet. Your Rufus is with Marcy's family. I should be home later today, then you can come see me and we'll catch up."

Everyone moved toward the door. Mary circled and placed a kiss on Ada's brow. "We'll be back to take you home later today."

Rich kept to the background. Hands shoved into his pockets, he lingered as Tom and Mary departed. Ada caught his eye. "Rich thank you for the lovely flowers."

When he approached her, Cassi shot them a puzzled look.

"Looks like you don't need a ride home," he said. "I'll head back and line up some help with your gardens."

Ada recognized the tone. No nonsense. He gave her a stern look then said, "We'll talk later."

She reached for his hand. "We will," she agreed.

His hand closed over hers, then released. He turned to TJ. "I have information for you, TJ, you too, Nick," he added, casting a glance at Nick. "When can we get together?"

"I'll give you a call this afternoon, we'll set something up," TJ responded.

"I'm stopping by the station later today," Nick said "Will you be at the store?"

Rich nodded. Then he said good-bye to the others, gave Ada a long, considering look, and left the room.

Cassi canted her head, appearing bewildered and bemused as she observed Rich's departure.

"Cass," Nick touched her shoulder. "Why don't you catch a ride with Aunt Mary and Uncle Tom? I've some things to take care of," he said, and pulled her in for a kiss. "Go get your wayward dog. I'll be home soon."

Cassi hesitated, and then crossed to Ada. "I'll see you later," she promised. "*We* have a great deal to talk about."

*****

TJ organized his thoughts. The accident was his primary concern since any connection to the shooting, the note, and the vandalism involving Ada had yet to be established.

If and when that happened, he'd be working with Nick.

He liked the idea. Better to work with him as opposed to butting heads, which is exactly what happened when, as a Pine Bluffs officer, TJ'd hauled Cassi in for questioning. At the time, Nick was in town on vacation and discovered Cassi standing over a dead body.

Complicated, but to make matters worse, Nick fell for Cassi just as a twin sister -- who Cassi didn't know existed -- began to stalk her. Then all hell broke loose, and a hair-raising race through a foggy night ended in death.

A lot had happened since then.

Nick approached. "TJ, do you mind if I sit in on this?"

TJ set out a compact hand held recorder. "I don't mind. Ada?" He cast a glance at Ada.

"No, that's fine."

She looked tired. Just plain tired, and beat up. He'd much rather put this off until she was stronger. Unfortunately, that wasn't an option. The quicker he followed up, the fresher her memory would be.

"It helps if I record everything, if that's okay?"

"I'm fine with that, too." She refilled a large tumbler with ice water and settled in.

"For starters, I want you to back up the clock. Take me to where you were yesterday morning. What were you doing, and with whom?"

TJ repositioned the recorder, waiting for Ada's response. A long stretch of silence followed. "Ada? Do you understand what I want?"

"I'm not sure. You're investigating my accident, right?"

"Yes, initially, but there's more." Reaching out, he switched off the recorder. "Let me explain what Tim Chasen and I found this morning. It'll help you understand where I'm going with my questions."

Ada's brow wrinkled. "Tim Chasen?"

"Chasen's Towing. He hauled your vehicle from the crash site, and this morning we went over your Honda. Right off we discovered there wasn't a drop of brake fluid left," he explained. "Once we had it up on the rack, we figured out why."

Before he could continue, Ada's eyes flew wide open. "Oh, my, God. Something *did* happen to my brakes, then. It wasn't my imagination."

Nick turned and stared hard at TJ. "Did you know this at the scene?"

"I felt something was off. Rich was driving behind her and his description made no sense. I'll talk to Rich later. He's got a good head for details but at the accident scene he was distracted. To be honest, I don't think I've ever seen Rich McConnell so rattled."

Nick shook his head. "I've seen seasoned officers freak out at a bad one."

"Could be," TJ speculated. "When I got there, he'd just crawled out of Ada's vehicle and damn near collapsed when he saw me. The man was white as a sheet. He'd been inside taking Ada's pulse, and checking her breathing."

"I remember," Ada mused. A tiny smile curved her lips. "He talked to me, laid his hand on my arm." She blinked several times. "Then everything went black. When I woke up, I was in the emergency room and had a blazing headache.

She rubbed two fingers alongside the cumbersome bandage and fixed her gaze on TJ. "Before the headache returns, tell me what you found wrong with my Honda."

"I'll forego details, but someone tampered with your vehicle, Ada. That's why I need to know where you were prior to the accident. Where was your CRV parked unattended?"

TJ started the recorder again. Ada shot a look at Nick, then met TJ's steady gaze head on, and took a deep breath. "I spent the night in Erie. Stayed at the new Sheraton on the bay. I'd been on the west side getting my nails done, and when I returned there were no parking spaces along State Street so I pulled into the parking garage."

"Returned? Where you there earlier in the day?"

Ada nodded. "Yes."

"By yourself?"

"No, I'd run into someone I knew."

TJ rubbed the back of his neck. Then he reached over and flipped off the recorder. "Ada, I'm no dentist, but I feel like I'm yanking them out one by one. Are you sure you're up to this? I can come back later and--"

"No, no." She waved away his concern. "I'm not one hundred percent, but that's not the reason I'm dragging my feet. This is... awkward." She took a long sip of water. Indicating the recorder with a tilt of her head, she instructed, "I have a few things to say, then you can resume recording and we'll start from the beginning."

*****

With Nick, TJ studied the gray overcast sky as they paused outside Hamot. Tires hissed on wet pavement as cars sped by on State Street, but it appeared the sun would win the battle and end the day rain free.

"I assume you've talked to Montroy and Marcy?" TJ slipped his PSP hat into place.

"Reamed Montroy's ass," replied Nick. "I'll do the same to Marcy Williams when I see her." He slipped on wrap-around shades. "Someone should have called me, TJ."

"I understand your feelings. In their defense, maybe they figured the situation didn't justify ruining your honeymoon," he pointed out, and then added, "Until the accident."

"I consider a round almost taking out my wife's aunt justification."

"You're beatin' a dead horse," TJ said. "What's done is done." He unlocked his car and opened the door. Propping his elbow on the door frame, he grinned. "Though I can't say I disagree with a good ass-reaming for the officer you left in charge."

With a wry smile, Nick fished his car keys from his pocket. "Where're you headed?"

TJ glanced at the time. "I've got about an hour. Since I'm here, I'm going to check out the parking garage where Ada left her car overnight."

Nick gave his keys a little toss. "Damn, I missed that one entirely."

"Ada and Rich?" TJ slid into his car. "Personally, I like the idea."

"Yeah. Me, too, I guess." He tilted his shades down. "Love's in the air, cousin. How about that sexy green-eyed friend of Cass's? Any luck there?"

"Not my cup of tea." TJ shook his head. "Too damn much attitude."

He did *not* want to discuss Elaine Delacor. The woman wrote the book on attitude. Too bad, because Lanie Delacor had a curvy, drool worthy body and eyes green as Irish shamrocks.

"Hey." Nick's amused voice broke in. "Did mentioning Lanie shut that sorry brain of yours down?"

TJ narrowed his eyes at his cousin and changed the subject. "You want to check out the garage? Then follow me," he retorted, and closed the door on Nick's irritating smirk.

Nick followed TJ's patrol car to the bayside parking garage next to the Sheraton. While waiting for Nick to join him, TJ rechecked his notes. Ada's directions were clear. He'd have no trouble locating where she'd parked, and, being new, the inside pavement was relatively clean. If Tim was right, there'd be no brake fluid left behind. As planned, pressure on the line hadn't done damage until she'd made it to the thruway.

He might get lucky with interviews. If someone identified Will Steiner and placed him near Ada's car it would be a start. He'd only learned about Will Steiner while interviewing Ada, which ticked him off. But since he'd not been officially involved until the accident, there was no one to blame. He'd get details from Rich, and hoped Rich's connections at ONI would net him a recent photo of Steiner.

As far as he knew, the only person who actually saw Steiner entering the garage was Ada. That was something, but not enough. Her car had been parked there overnight. Free access for a lot of people.

Steiner's presence made him a suspect, but TJ knew better than to eliminate other possibilities. He'd look closer at Rick Andrews, the disgruntled bartender from North East.

The night PSP stopped Andrews in Pine Bluffs he took off. They nailed him with several charges, none tied him to Ada's damaged land. Further investigation wasn't warranted. What happened that night may have nothing to do with a threat to Ada's life, but TJ couldn't ignore a possible link, a connection to that threat.

Ignoring *any* link was foolish.

They were the ones that tended to sneak up and bite a man on the ass.

Chapter Thirty-Two

Ada ran into a truck. Rich felt as if he'd been run *over* by one.

He drove straight from Hamot to work and holed up in his office, forcing himself to tackle a backlog of messages and to return phone calls. Simple mechanical tasks. Anything more demanding would be a disaster.

After a near sleepless night, since daybreak he'd ingested enough caffeine to float a damn boat, and the nameless sandwich he'd bolted down for lunch sat in his gut like a brick. Or maybe it floated in that sea of coffee causing his recurring waves of indigestion.

He got a bottle of water from his compact fridge and settled at his desk. "Come on in," he invited when someone tapped on the door.

He glanced up, hoping to see TJ, Nick, or both. The brick sandwich in his gut rolled over when Harley Phillips stuck his head in the door. "Hey, boss."

"What do you need, Harley?" He shot him a swift look, then did a double take. A jagged gash cut across his employee's forehead, and the man looked like hell. Rich took a swig of water and leaned back in his chair. "Are you all right?"

Harley grimaced. He shifted from one foot to the other and tugged on the bill of his cap. "Yeah, yeah. I'm okay." His scowl said otherwise. "I heard you were back and, I wondered... uh, how's Mrs. Blaine?"

Ordinary question, Harley knew Ada. Yet something in his stance, or the way he didn't quite meet Rich's eyes, struck him as strange. He seemed detached, like he was just being nosy and really didn't give a damn about Ada's condition.

"She's fine," Rich responded. "Should be home later today."

Harley shifted *again*, lingering.

"I've work to do, Harley." Rich flung up one hand impatiently, then glanced at his watch. "I'm expecting someone, so if there's nothing more..."

He had enough to deal with, and Harley's being there grated like nails on a chalkboard. He didn't want to deal with whatever was buggin' the man, not today. With a disgusted huff, Rich slapped his water bottle down and pushed out of his chair just as Nick and TJ stepped up behind Harley.

"Hello, Harley." TJ said.

Harley started, then wheeled around and almost crashed into the two men. TJ's gaze skimmed over him, and then moved to Rich. "Problem, Rich?"

"Harley, what the hell?" Rich growled. "Watch where you're going."

Harley raised his hand, palm out and stammered, "Sorry, I... I was ah, just leaving." He backed up several steps.

"Run into something?" TJ asked.

Harley's hand shot to his head. "Somethin' like that," he muttered. "Nothing big, just rapped my head." He broke eye contact with TJ and looked at Rich. "I'll get on back to work now." Then he turned and hurried away.

TJ fell silent, watching Harley until he disappeared.

"Strange little guy," remarked Nick.

"Come on in. Don't let Harley bother you, he's a weird duck, always has been. Today he's just weirder than usual." Rich sunk back into his chair. "My sorry ass is draggin'," he admitted, and gestured to a couple of chairs. "Pull those over."

TJ stood there frowning and continuing to watch Harley's departure as if he didn't hear Rich.

Nick nudged him. "Your sorry ass draggin', too?"

"What?" TJ glanced at Nick. He scratched his head and gave it a shake. "No, I'm fine, just thought of something I want to recheck."

Nick and TJ stepped inside and closed the door.

Rich gulped down more water. "Help yourselves," he said, pointing with the container of Deer Park. "I'm fresh out of coffee, but there's plenty of water."

TJ got a bottle and handed one to Nick. He twisted the cap off, dropped down on a chair, and took a long swig. Nick strolled to the window and propped one hip on the wide sill.

Rich caught Nick's lazy half smile and pointed out, "We're here to exchange information. Not examine my personal life."

"Not long ago in this very room you told me spending time with Cassi Burke was *only* a date," Nick drawled. He tipped the bottle and took a drink. "She's Mrs. Nick McGraw now, and I'm still not sure how the hell that happened."

TJ burst out laughing. With an ironic smile, Rich raked a hand through his hair. He regarded both young men shrewdly. "I care about Ada. That's all I know for sure right now. We've grown close, and *that's all* the details you two are getting."

He leaned forward, resting both elbows on his desk. "Now, let's start from the beginning. Nick, I assume you've talked to Marcy and Jake?"

TJ chuckled. "Bet Jake's ass is still smartin'."

"You can bet yours," Nick responded. "Not calling sooner pissed me off. I've gone over their file on Ada and they did a decent job. Sounds like your fast reaction saved Ada's life, Rich. Now I'd like *your* version of what happened that morning."

Rich sobered. He lined up his thoughts and began with his arrival at Ada's the morning someone shot at them. He covered each incident, the wild shot, the night Rufus freaked out, the note, and the vandalism. He'd only actually been *with* Ada when someone fired the shot. But they'd been together either before or after the others occurred. Significant, in his mind.

Nick looked up from his notes. "You were with her the night her gardens got trashed?"

"We had dinner at my place and I followed her home. When we got there, I checked inside her cottage. No problems, nothing out of place. Outside, fog. From her porch all the way to the lake you couldn't see crap."

Rich gritted his teeth, gave his head a shake. He pushed out of his chair and paced, thinking back. He stopped by the window. "I remember smelling fresh turned earth that night, and didn't give it a thought, damn it."

"Ada's a gardener," Nick scoffed. "You knew she'd recently used a tiller. Christ, Rich, don't be so hard on yourself."

He resumed pacing. "Nick, this whole damn mess has me tied in knots. Especially after talking with Gary."

Nick flipped open a small notepad. "Sit down. I want to hear all about that."

As Nick scribbled notes, Rich explained why he called Gary Wilson. He laid out details from the beginning, and tearing the scab off his personal life again wrung him out.

"Will Steiner and Rick Andrews," Nick muttered. He glanced up from his notes. "TJ, who followed up with Rick Andrews?"

"Trooper Adamski. I'll get you a copy of the report," he added. "There was no reason at the time to follow up. Maybe now they'll take a closer look."

*****

Late afternoon sun slanted across her gardens and a light breeze rippled the lake's surface. Ada opened the door of Tom's car and inhaled the heady aroma of rain soaked herbs. She slid her legs out. Frustrated by her helpless state, she frowned and waited for Mary's help.

"Are you getting out, or are you just going to sit there scowling at your feet?" Mary said.

"I'm mad," she blurted. "I don't want to wait a week to start therapy." Her head throbbed and her knees threatened to fold when she stood.

"You'll be fine," Mary said, yet her hands hovered, ready to assist. "Let's get you inside and into bed."

Ada shook her head stubbornly. "No. Not yet. I need fresh air. I want to look at my gardens and just... *breathe*."

Tom got out and strode around the car. "Are you going to be difficult?"

Ada shot him a swift accusing look. "Only if I don't get my way. I've been lying in bed for almost two days. So if you'll help me up the steps, I can make it around front to a chair. Please." She softened her tone, glancing from one to the other. "I need to unwind."

Tom studied her, then nodded to Mary and gently took Ada's arm. Moving slowly between them, Ada managed to climb the steps. The short distance winded her, each step a jarring reminder of her sorry state. She made it to her favorite rocking chair and gingerly eased her tender body onto the cushioned seat.

She sighed softly, closing her eyes. "Ah, heaven."

Mary went to make tea, Tom settled on the porch steps, and Ada set the rocker in motion. She wished they wouldn't fuss, though she didn't know what she'd do without them. She took a moment to let the gentle rocking soothe her nerves.

After several moments, she opened her eyes and scanned her gardens. Her gaze came to rest on the new fence. She'd had serious doubts about the project, but what she observed now pleased her. Six foot vertical sections created a natural looking secure barrier. The sturdy gate would allow access to the new berry patch, yet prevent anything bigger than a wheelbarrow from entering.

Planting new bushes would be a challenge, for she faced weeks, maybe months, of therapy. She wasn't a foolish woman. There was no magic healing, no easy way to get her strength back without hard work. She'd take the time and do what had to be done.

She sensed Tom contemplating her as she rocked and planned. "I know someone's been taking care of my gardens," she mused. "I appreciate that."

"Thank Molly's green thumb," he said. "Everyone's pitching in. You're going to have to let go, Ada, and accept help." He focused his full attention on her. "Mary and I are stayin' the night. You shouldn't be alone until you're stronger."

Ada stilled the rocker. "Then what?"

"Whatever it takes." He spied Mary at the door and got to his feet to slide it open. "Someone tampered with you car," he said, as Mary emerged and handed a steaming cup of tea to Ada. "That's fact. TJ's investigation confirmed it. He and Nick have leads to follow, a lot of legwork to do. In the meantime, *you* only have to concentrate on getting better."

Smiling, Mary moved to his side and he looped his arm around her shoulder.

Ada sipped her tea, eyeing her two determined caretakers.

*****

She awoke the next morning to sun pouring in her window. Having fallen asleep early, Ada missed dinner and slept right through the night. She stretched her arms up slowly, testing her muscles. Not too bad. Actually, better than she imagined. Though stiff and a little sore, her muscles gave inch by inch. She chuckled. Like stretching a taut rubber band. Deciding not to push the issue, she relaxed, savoring the feel of soft cotton against her skin.

A seductive fragrance filled the air and her belly emitted an unladylike growl. She pulled herself up and eased her legs over the side of the bed. Sitting there, debating what to do next, she caught the sound of quick footsteps, accompanied by the familiar clicking of nails on wood. Both stopped outside the door to her room and, after a timid knock, her bedroom door opened a crack.

"You're awake." Cassi's smiling face peeked in. The door swung wide, and Rufus made a beeline for her bed. Laughing, Cassi halted his mad dash. "No, you don't," she exclaimed. "Now, sit." Rufus' rump smacked down. He whined, loud and long, while his tail thumped a happy beat.

Cassi stepped closer, scrutinizing her. "I was beginning to worry. Mary said you went to bed early. When I arrived this morning, she told me you hadn't stirred all night."

"Other than being ravenous, I'm fine. I needed a night of uninterrupted sleep." She fingered her forehead. No longer bandaged, though tender to touch, the swelling seemed to have gone down.

"Does it hurt?"

"Just a little if I poke at it."

"Then don't poke at it," Cassi admonished. She placed a hand on one hip "Are you going to be difficult?"

Ada laughed. "Yesterday Tom asked me the same thing. No, I hope not, but I may get a little testy if I'm not fed soon."

Cassi sat on the bed beside her, and Rufus slipped forward, resting his head on Ada's knee. His eyes begged for attention and narrowed to mere slits when Ada rubbed his soft ears.

"How does French toast sound this morning?"

"Wonderful," Ada replied. "I'd like to shower first."

Cassi's brow wrinkled. "Can you manage?"

"I took one before I left the hospital. Since I was still a bit unsteady, a nurse hovered outside the bathroom. This morning I feel much better, no dizziness."

"How about pain?"

"More stiffness than pain." She rolled her shoulders. "Maybe you can help me with some stretching after I shower and eat."

"You can't do much until next week after you see the doctor," Cassi pointed out. "However," she continued, grinning. "I spoke with the therapist who'll be working with you, and she agreed to let you begin *gently* working your muscles. Under my supervision," she added.

Ada couldn't stop the smile. "Breakfast, then a shower. After that, I'm all yours."

A short time later she made her way to the kitchen and settled at the table, angling her chair to look at the lake. Rufus stretched out in a pool of sunlight, and Cassi began making French toast.

"Mary will be by later," Cassi said, tipping vanilla into the batter. She lifted the bowl and, whisking the mixture, faced Ada. "You had a caller early this morning. He left flowers."

Ada glanced around.

"Over there." Cassi indicated the bookcase across the room.

A simple glass vase overflowing with daffodils sat on the top shelf. Ada rose and approached the bright arrangement. She lifted a card resting against the vase and read the inscription inside. *Sorry I missed you, hope you're having sweet dreams.* He'd signed it simply, *Rich.*

She fingered feathery baby's breath surrounding the trumpet-shaped blooms.

Throughout everything, even when he'd pulled back fearing for her safety, she'd known he'd be there. Where did they go from here? Things were bound to get complicated. Pine Bluffs was a small town, prone to small town gossip. Although so far they'd been discreet, she'd bet these flowers came from Molly's greenhouse. Molly was no gossip, but how long before word spread Ada Blaine and Rich McConnell were having an affair?

"So." Cassi's voice interrupted her thoughts. Carrying the bowl of batter, the young woman strolled closer. "Been kissed 'blind, deaf, and dumb' by the sexy hardware guy yet?"

"Cassandra." Ada admonished.

"Ah, ah. You used that very quaint expression the first time I spent the night with Nick. Back at ya' lady."

Ada hesitated. The flowers and Cassi's astute conclusion caught her unprepared. Buying time, she tucked the note in her pocket and admired her daffodils. "He's a thoughtful, considerate man with excellent taste."

Cassi returned to the heated griddle. She tapped the whisk on the bowl, removing excess batter, and began to coat slices of bread with the mixture. "Thoughtful and considerate," she mused, sliding two prepared slices onto the hot surface. They sizzled, and a sweet, cinnamon aroma filled the air.

"I'm sure Rich is thoughtful and considerate. Tasteful words," she reflected. "Nick shared wine and chocolate before a roaring fire before he kissed me for the first time. Thoughtful and considerate? Of course."

She flipped the toast.

"Except his *thoughtful* kiss before that roaring fire almost melted the chocolate."

Ada took a careful sip of tea.

Cassi tilted her head and crossed her arms, still gripping the spatula. Her brows rose and a smile tugged at her lips. "How's the tea?"

"Hot," Ada declared. "Very hot."

Their laughter startled Rufus. He sat up, but got distracted when the door opened and Nick strode into the cottage.

"Mornin' ladies." He paused to briskly rub an enthusiastic Rufus.

"Well, hello Chief McGraw," Cassi drawled. "Is this official business?" She crossed the kitchen and wrapped her arms around his neck. She kissed him soundly, then leaned back and peered up at him. "Or are you just wearing that uniform because you know I can't keep my hands off you when you do?"

With one brow arched sharply, his expression dead serious, Nick contemplated his wife. "I'm on duty, Mrs. McGraw."

Cassi grinned. Using one hand she straightened his collar and smoothed the front of his crisp, pleated shirt. "According to my calculations, we have two days and nights of honeymoon coming to us."

Nick's stern look softened. He glanced over Cassi's shoulder. "Excuse us, Ada." He winked, and laid a blistering kiss on his wife.

Ada rescued the unattended French toast, and Cassi, laughing when she pulled away from Nick, rushed to help.

"Almost melted the butter," Ada remarked dryly, handing over the spatula.

Nick agreed to join them for breakfast and coaxed Cassi into brewing coffee for him.

Coated with maple syrup, the sweet, spicy bites melted in Ada's mouth. She glanced up when Cassi slid another serving onto her plate. Best medicine in the world. Good food, laughter and family. Even Rufus, begging silently with soulful eyes netted a few handouts

So far there'd been no mention of her accident, or her condition. Other than a casual 'how ya feelin' this morning?' Nick didn't bring the subject up. His sharp gaze didn't miss a thing though. He observed her without comment. She refrained from asking questions. Why spoil a perfect morning? But after she'd eaten and poured a second cup of tea, her energy level plummeted.

She hated to admit it, but she feared the shower and her stretching session would have to wait until later. "I can't eat another bite," she declared, pushing her plate away. Give the next one to Nick, Cassi."

The words barely left her mouth when Rufus went on alert. Cassi glanced out the window, broke into a grin, and slid another piece of toast onto the griddle just as TJ tapped on the screen door and entered.

"Hey." He grinned, slipping his gray campaign hat off and snagging it on a hook by the door. "I smelled cinnamon French toast from three miles down the road." He helped himself to Nick's coffee, adding half and half before sliding into a chair across from Ada. "You're looking better today." He took a sip. "I talked to Mom this morning. She said you didn't stir all night."

"Nothing like your own bed. I didn't even hear your parents leave this morning, Cassi and Rufus were here when I woke up." She folded both hands around her cup and leaned back. "How long am I going to have this round-the-clock baby sitting service?"

"As long as it takes."

Ada rolled her eyes. "You and your dad."

"I take it he told you much the same thing. Thanks," he said, shooting a fast grin at Cassi when she placed a heaping plate of French toast in front of him.

"My pleasure," she said, and bent down to give him a kiss on the cheek.

"Hey." Nick scowled when his cousin caught her hand and gave it a squeeze.

Cassi shrugged. "Uniform," she quipped.

TJ shoveled two quick bites into his mouth. He eyed Nick. "Uniform?"

Laughing, Nick rose and went to rinse his plate. "Yours is dull gray, so you only get a friendly kiss on the cheek." He grabbed Cassi's wrist and yanked her into his arms. "She really digs the way I look in navy blue. Can't keep her hands off me," he teased. "In fact, if I--"

"Well, well. Special on donuts today?" Lanie Delocor strolled into the kitchen, and Ada handed TJ a napkin when he gulped down a slug of hot coffee and choked.

*****

The pullover Lanie wore clung to her lush curves. Like a friggin' vine. TJ tried another sip of coffee, this time letting it slide down as he observed a petite, well rounded backside hugged in a pair of brown cropped pants.

There wasn't much to the woman. She barely reached Cassi's shoulder as the two friends hugged. But what there was sure curved in all the right places.

"Hi, Lanie. What's up?" Nick helped himself to another coffee.

Lanie's attention swung to Ada. "Why am I always the last to know? I hear you tried to pull an Evil Knievel over Winter Green Gorge," she accused, pulling up a chair and plopping down eye level with Ada. Yet her voice cracked, and those big green eyes went damp "How are you, Aunt Ada?"

TJ took another bite of toast, chewing thoughtfully. So, the lady with attitude *did* have a soft side.

"TJ."

He lowered his fork and focused on Nick. "What?" The smirk on Nick's face set his teeth on edge.

"Sorry to interrupt, but are you still heading up to North East this morning?"

They'd agreed to meet in Pine Bluffs and then proceed to North East. Rick Andrews worked nights at the Corner Bar, and TJ figured he'd chance catching him at home during the day. Nick wanted to follow up on Ada's vandalism case, so having him along when TJ talked to Andrews made sense.

"I'm ready when you are," TJ responded. He finished the last bite. Gathering up his plate, he headed for the sink.

"Why, hello there *Trooper* McGraw." Lanie's green-eyed gaze flitted over him. "I'm sorry. I didn't mean to ignore you when I arrived."

"Not a problem, *Miss* Delacor. I'm sure you had other things on your mind."

Cassi stepped in and relieved him of his plate and cup. "TJ's the officer investigating Ada's accident," she informed Lanie.

TJ paused by Lanie's chair. She arched one dark brow and angled her head to gaze up at him. "Don't you think it's time you called me 'Lanie'?"

He met her dark fringed, intense green eyes. His pulse spiked and he itched to rub his sweaty palms on his trousers. "I'll keep that in mind. *Lanie*," he murmured, and moved out of the danger zone to retrieve his hat. He turned to Nick. "Ready to go?"

Nick nodded and pulled his wife in for a good-bye kiss. TJ approached Ada. "I'm following up some leads today. If there's anything new, I'll make sure you're told. Mom and Dad insist on sticking close for the time being. I agree," he said firmly when Ada heaved a deep sigh. "I don't want to scare you. But facts don't lie, and what I've uncovered so far scares *me*."

"I understand, TJ. I'll be careful. I do appreciate being kept informed."

He thanked Cassi for the breakfast and followed Nick outside.

Nick picked a few stray dog hairs from his trousers. "You got kinda quiet in there, *Trooper* McGraw. Those eyes seem to get you every time, cousin."

TJ tossed his hat into his patrol unit, not taking the bait. His cousin liked nothing better than to yank his chain about the way Lanie Delacor affected him. From their very first encounter, back when the lushly curved lady was Cassi's manager, he'd had a problem dealing with her. His dilemma never escaped Nick, and TJ refused to discuss the matter. To admit she not only set his teeth on edge, but turned him on like hell would be a big mistake.

So he pasted a smile on and drew out his notebook. "Can we get back to the business at hand?" he said, and couldn't help adding, "And wipe that shit-eatin' grin off your face. Yea, I noticed her eyes. Along with the outfit she poured herself into. Doesn't change the fact she's trouble with a capitol 'T'."

TJ drummed his pen on the notepad. "You want to hear what I've got, or do you want to waste more time bustin' my chops?"

Chuckling, Nick reached into his car and pulled out his own notepad. "You're too easy." He flipped his pad open. "Let's compare what we've got. First, I talked to Rich this morning and he's going to put me in touch with his friend, Gary Wilson. This guy was in the Corp with Rich. He knows the background and what went down with Steiner."

TJ nodded, and made a note. "Okay. I managed to get a fairly recent photo of Steiner. Came by fax late yesterday. Here's one for you." He handed Nick a copy.

"What's wrong?" Nick asked when TJ muttered a soft curse.

"I meant to show this to Ada. To verify this really was the guy she saw on the lake and in Erie." He glanced back at the cottage, considering.

"She looked beat, TJ. Wait until later, or better yet, stop back tomorrow. We'll deal with Andrews today and get that out of the way. Hopefully our interview with him will give us more to go on."

"Agreed." TJ tucked his pen and notes away. "Let's go find Andrews."

He had an address on Andrews, verified by Rob Adamski. If they were lucky, he and Nick would catch the guy at home. He'd read him his rights and hope like hell Andrews didn't balk and make a big deal out of a few questions. Right now, the only connection they had was the night he'd been stopped near Pine Bluffs. Not much.

On the other hand, Steiner popped up on the radar several times. Once on Pine Shadow Lake, once in Erie when he approached Rich and later that same day he'd encountered Ada.

Motives? Neither man had what he'd call a solid motive. Rich's suspicions could be considered a bit far-fetched. Or not. Rich wasn't a man to jump at shadows. He had good instincts, to bad he wasn't a cop.

Now, Andrews. The tie there was Cassi's dead sister. He'd been involved with Sadie Mitchell, and went berserk when he found out she'd been killed. TJ's dad had a serious run-in with the guy. Maybe he'd stop by his parents' place after work and find out exactly what happened that night. Worth the time.

He crested the ridge. I -90 lay directly in front of him. Once he'd passed beneath the thruway, miles of grape vineyards surrounded him, and Lake Erie spread endlessly in the distance. Andrews lived on the outskirts of North East. Adamski said his apartment was over the garage where he housed his truck. He also said the man kept his truck spotless, seemed to dote on the classic Ford.

TJ signaled and turned onto a street just south of town. He glanced back, making sure Nick followed. Up ahead he spotted the garage apartment, and...

Well, well, would you look at that. He'd bet the man beneath the hood of the shiny Ford truck was their Mr. Andrews.

"Interesting," he mused as he rolled up the short drive and stopped. A dolly alongside the truck caught TJ's eye. Seems Rick Andrews knows his way around under the hood *and* under the vehicle.

Andrews jerked his head out from beneath the hood. He straightened, staring hard eyed at TJ as he alighted from his patrol car. His gaze shifted when Nick's Pine Bluffs PD unit pulled in behind TJ's.

Rick Andrews' expression revealed nothing, but his grip on a large wrench tightened visibly as TJ and Nick approached.

"Rick Andrews?" TJ inquired.

The man gave a brief nod and placed the wrench on the protective cloth draped over the fender of the truck. Squinting at TJ and Nick, he pulled a cloth from his back pocket and wiped his hands. "What's this about?"

"I'm Trooper McGraw," TJ said. "This is Chief McGraw from Pine Bluffs. I need to question you regarding a case I'm working on. The chief has a vested interest in the case, so he'll remain while I speak with you."

He narrowed his gaze on Nick. "I know you." He shot a swift look at TJ. "Is this about Sadie? Cause if it is, I ain't got nothing to say," he snapped, and started to turn away.

"You have the right to remain silent," TJ began.

"What the hell's goin' on?" Andrews spun around so fast TJ stopped mid sentence and placed his hand on his weapon.

Nick eased up beside TJ. "I think it'd be to your advantage to let the trooper finish reading you your rights and get this over with."

Andrews raked shaky fingers through his hair. Sweat glistened on his brow and he used the grubby cloth to swipe at it, leaving a smudge of grease. "All right. I'll talk to you." He looked around. "Give me a minute," he asked, reaching for a large take out cup. Ice rattled in the cup as he tipped it up and swallowed rapidly. Using the back of his hand, he wiped his mouth then tossed the cup aside.

TJ read him his rights. "Do you understand, Mr. Andrews?"

"Yeah. Now, what do you want to know?"

"Can you tell me where you were from approximately 6pm this past Friday until 8am the next day?"

"This past Friday? Hell, I worked until damn near one in the morning. Then went home and slept till noon the next day."

"Can anyone verify you went straight home after work that night?"

The bartender's face scrunched into a puzzled frown. "This has nothing to do with the night I took off from that trooper, does it?"

"We'll get to that," TJ stated. "I want you to answer this question first. Where were you after work that night?" He watched carefully for telling signs. The man was sweating, big time, but seemed confused about the question. "Do you understand what I'm asking?"

"I understand what. I just don't know *why* the hell you want to know."

"Just answer the question, Mr. Andrews."

He threw up both hands and dropped them, shaking his head. "Like I said. I worked, went home, went to bed. End of story. Unless my nosy neighbors keep track of when I come and go," he said, waving one hand at the thick forest of trees on each side of the garage. "Guess you'll have to take my word for it."

TJ glanced around. Shit. Unless someone happened to be driving by, the man could dance naked in his driveway. He looked back at the street. Since they'd been there maybe one car had passed. "All right. I'll need the name of your boss to verify you worked that night."

Andrews rattled off the name. TJ read it back, making sure he had it right then continued. "The night Trooper Adamski pulled you over near Pine Bluffs, why did you run?"

He shuffled his feet and huffed out a breath. "I may have had a bit too much to drink. Maybe," he added quickly. "Not sayin' I did."

"When you were questioned the next day, you'd washed you truck, inside and out. Why?"

"Why?" Again, the puzzled frown. "I guess it was dirty." He pointed to his truck. "Take a look. I live in a rat trap," he said, jerking his head to the building behind him. "This here truck is the only decent thing I own. I'll wash it every day if I want. Sometimes I do."

The second story apartment needed a paint job and the roof sagged, TJ observed. His eyes briefly met Nick's before he turned to study the truck. The silver paint sparkled. Even the tires gleamed black and shiny. "I see what you mean," he addressed Andrews with a wry smile.

He scribbled a few more notes, ignoring the man fidgeting and shuffling nearby. "That's all for now, Mr. Andrews."

Andrews turned from rubbing a smudge from the door of his truck.

"I see you have a nice selection of tools, even a dolly for getting underneath." TJ slid his pen away and closed his notebook. A half smile crossed his face. "Bet you're a good mechanic. Probably do your own brakes and everything," he added. "I envy you there, cost me an arm and a leg to get my car worked on."

Andrews shrugged. "I had a brother who knew his way around a car. He was a good teacher." He paused, staring reflectively at his truck. When he looked back at TJ, his posture seemed more relaxed. "Any more questions?"

"Not at this time, Mr. Andrews. I'll double check your hours with your boss, but unless I think of something else, we're done here. Chief, any questions?"

"I think we have all we need for now."

TJ followed Nick to his car and Rick Andrews began to gather up his tools, casting curious glances at them.

"Nice," Nick said after they were out of earshot. "You can't put him at the scene, but you found out the guys a half decent mechanic. Sneaky. I like that." He smiled and slid into his car.

"My shift is about up," TJ said, glancing at his watch. "I'll run by the Corner Bar and then head in. We'll catch up later."

"Sounds good. I'm going back to the station and try to reach Gary Wilson. I'll keep you posted."

As TJ backed down the rutted driveway, he caught a brief glimpse of Rick Andrews sliding beneath his big, silver truck. "Bet you know exactly how brakes function," he muttered, punching the gas and heading into North East.

Chapter Thirty-Three

Rich helped load several bags of pine mulch for a customer. It was a toss up. Should he go home and get some rest, or stop by Ada's? She'd called that afternoon and thanked him for the flowers. Under Cassi's supervision, she'd managed to stretch her muscles, but admitted the effort wore her out and she'd slept several hours afterwards. He'd detected impatience in her tone. No surprise there.

He checked the time. The store didn't close till eight, but he *owned* the damn store, so why not take off, grab a bite to eat, and make a quick stop at Ada's. He left his office and stopped at checkout to let them know he was leaving.

"Leavin' early, boss?" Placing two gallons of paint on the check-out counter, Harley glanced at the keys in Rich's hand. "There you go, Mrs. Sherman," he said as the customer added brushes to the paint order.

"Maybe," Rich responded, and then turned to greet Lillian Sherman.

Lillian frowned with concern. "How's Ada, Rich?" I heard about her accident. What a shame."

"She's home, and doing well last I heard."

"Bet she liked the lovely bouquet of flowers you sent over."

Caught off guard, Rich just smiled. Then it hit him. Lillian's husband delivered flowers for Hirtzel's Greenhouse. He politely excused himself when another customer called his name, stepping aside to advise a young contractor. By then, Lillian had departed and Harley, after blatantly eavesdropping, had disappeared. He should track Harley down and chew the man's ass about calling him boss and advise him what time *he* left the store was none of Harley's business. Dealing with Harley was bound to put him in a shitty mood, so Rich followed his earlier plan and drove over to The Pines Diner for a quick meal.

He consumed a small filet, grilled asparagus, and hot rolls, shoveling the food in like a starving man. Being tired and preoccupied, he'd skipped lunch. Something he seldom did. The waitress topped off his coffee, then tempted him with fresh berry pie. Hard to resist, knowing their homemade, melt-in-your-mouth, pies contained berries from Ada's gardens.

He'd lost count of how many times the waitress replenished his supply of hot rolls, so by adding pie to the list, he slid a little further down a slippery slope of sinful indulgence.

"There you go, Mr. McConnell." Rich stared down at the generous slice of pie. "Will there be anything else?"

"I'll have more coffee in a few minutes, Sal. Thanks."

The first bite melted in his mouth. He broke off a second, savoring as he chewed, and his thoughts turned to another 'sinful indulgence.'

What the hell was he going to do about Ada?

Until recently, he'd considered himself past a certain stage. Older, wiser. Not over the hill, damn it, but he figured he'd closed the door long ago on any lasting relationships. Now he wasn't so sure. He wasn't sure about loving again. *Making love,* he knew, yet even that was different with Ada. Incredible came to mind.

Gazing out the window, he thought back to the last time they'd been together. A steady stream of traffic flowed past. More than likely heading home from work to share their day with someone, and maybe share a glass of wine.

To share their life.

No, loving wasn't just about losing the battle with hormones, but about losing his heart. Did he have that kind of love left to share, to give?

The waitress refilled his cup, and Rich finished every bite of the tart berry pie.

Now wasn't the time to think about *his* future. Not when danger threatened Ada. Nothing specific, and that in itself made him crazy. The case remained unresolved, yet his gut told him that *something* was linked to his past.

Rich wasn't so naïve as to think TJ and Nick didn't doubt his suspicions. Nick talked to Gary today. 'Leave no stone unturned' he'd told Rich, even though the call apparently hadn't shed much light on the case.

Keep turning those stones, buddy, there's a snake hidden under one somewhere.

He left a generous tip for Sal and paid his bill at the counter. Outside, the cool air revived him. Though several cups of coffee probably had something to do with his renewed energy.

He slid into his truck and headed to Ada's. He'd like time alone with her, but until she was stronger and this low life was caught that wasn't going to happen. Probably for the best, because he needed time. Time, and distance, to figure out if he had anything left inside *to* share.

*****

Changing of the guard, Ada thought when Tom and Mary arrived. She waved to Cassi as she drove off with Nick. What a pleasure to see her niece and Nick so in love, so attuned to one another. She'd had that once, long ago with John. Could she reclaim the feeling? Did she dare plan a future with Rich?

She pulled the throw around her shoulders tighter and slid the glass door closed. As a young woman, falling in love just *happened.* Now, there'd be so much to overcome, so many differences. Independent careers and deeply ingrained habits, to name a few.

"Are you all right?" Mary touched her arm.

She covered Mary's hand with hers, gave a little pat. "I'm fine. I wish I could tell you and Tom to go home and that I didn't need you tonight."

"Oh, Ada," Mary began. "I don't think--"

"I won't," she interrupted. "I thought I'd bounce back after a good night's sleep. But after I spent fifteen, maybe twenty minutes, stretching and moving around, I feel like I've worked a ten hour day." She cupped Mary's face between both hands. "I love you, dear friend, and right now I *need* you. That's tough to admit."

"You're going to beat this, honey." Mary wrapped her arm around Ada's waist, steering her to a chair. "I shouldn't tell you this, but Cassi was surprised, and pleased, at the way your body responded today."

"I'm going to surprise all of you," Ada declared as Mary plopped down in another chair.

They turned to look as the door opened and Tom entered. "Look who I found lurking outside," he called out, grinning.

Rich sauntered in the door. His hands were shoved deep in his pockets and he'd draped a jacket over his shoulders, tying the sleeves together in front. He needed a shave, but when he met her gaze across the room and he broke into a lazy smile, something tugged at her heart.

"Rich, what a nice surprise." Mary rose and crossed the room. "Can I get you something?"

"Not a thing. I stuffed myself at the diner, complete with a hefty slice of pie, and I've had enough coffee to float a barge."

"Could I talk you into a glass of wine?" Tom asked, placing a bottle on the counter. "Mary and I just got here, and to celebrate Ada's first day home we brought one of her favorites."

"Cab or merlot?" Rich asked, shooting a grin at Ada.

Tom laughed. "Actually, a blend. You know the lady's tastes pretty well."

Ada rose to join them and Rich reached out and grasped her outstretched hand. "Thanks, my workout today left me a bit shaky."

Tom paused, ready to pop the cork. "Maybe this isn't such a good idea."

"If you don't hurry and open that," Ada threatened. "I'll do it myself. As long as I'm not taking the pain killers, a glass of wine won't hurt."

Tom and Mary carried the wine, and Rich steadied Ada, wrapping his arm around her as they moved to the porch overlooking the lake. Settled in comfortable chairs, they sipped wine and watched evening fall, catching up and dissecting the past few days.

Spring peepers chorused as the sun sank low, and Mary lit the tiny lamp on the table between them. Wine spread through Ada like smooth honey, and cool air skittered over her as she enjoyed the nighttime serenade.

She listened closely as Tom and Rich discussed the case. Aggravated assault, a felony of the first degree, all serious charges according to Tom, just legal terms to her. How much was edited for her benefit?

Tom said Nick talked to Gary Wilson and learned that, so far, Steiner was keeping his nose clean. Aside from being in Erie, they had nothing to tie him to her accident. According to Tom, Steiner's presence was circumstantial unless tangible evidence turned up.

So far, none had.

Mary rose and stretched. "Tom, come help me in the kitchen. We'll leave these two alone for a while. I'm sure Rich didn't come over here just to talk law enforcement with you." With her back to the men, Mary winked, and went into the cottage. Tom followed.

"More wine?" Rich asked, as the door slid closed, leaving them alone.

"Not for me." She lifted her glass. "I think one is enough, considering."

"How *are* you feeling?"

"Better," she said. "Or, better than I thought I would after tail-ending a truck."

She turned her head, meeting Rich's calm gaze. "I liked your friend Gary. Did you talk to him after he spoke with Nick?"

"Briefly. He confirmed what Nick said. Will Steiner's turned into a model citizen, and, Hank Delaney stands behind the man."

"Delaney, that's the man you worked with in New Jersey?"

"Yes, he's still active at ONI." Rich fell silent. He reached over and took Ada's hand. "I'm not convinced Steiner is so damned innocent, but I respect Hank. So I've got no choice at the moment but to step back and see where the investigation goes."

The warmth of his hand comforted her, and sitting there, alone amongst the sounds of the night, he soothed away the rough edges. Not entirely though, she couldn't forget that beyond that shifting circle of light encroaching darkness could mask unknown danger.

"By the way, Gary liked you, too," Rich said. "Once you're feeling better, he'd like to bring Latisha, his wife, for a visit."

"I'd like that. Right now I'd like anything normal. Having two of my friends leave their own home, their own bed, night after night to keep me safe isn't normal. Necessary," she added. "But sooner or later it has to end."

Rich lifted her hand and touched his lips to her fingers. "Sooner or later, it will."

She pulled their clasped hands close, rubbing the roughness of his against her cheek. "I love the flowers. It was a thoughtful gesture."

"I wanted to brighten your day, welcome you home," Rich said, then he chuckled and asked, "Do you know Lillian Sherman?"

"Yes, not well, but I know her."

"Well, seems her husband delivered those lovely flowers."

"And?" It took a moment, but suddenly light dawned. "Oh. *Oh,* I see."

He leaned in and gently pressed his warm lips to hers. "By this time tomorrow, all of Pine Bluffs will be aware I sent those flowers. Our lives just got even more complicated," he said, and came back for another kiss. This time he lingered, sending a flash of heat through her body.

When he pulled back, his grip tightened on her hand. He stood, pulling her to her feet. "I have to go, and you need your rest."

Reaching up, she smoothed her hand over his beard roughened face. "Thanks for stopping by. Once I'm stronger, we'll plan a special dinner with Tom and Mary. Maybe even go out somewhere extra nice. I enjoyed dinner in Erie at the Sheraton."

"I enjoyed more than dinner at the Sheraton." Rich clicked off the light and his lips brushed hers in the darkness. Her heart raced as he wrapped her in his arms. Drawn by his body heat she pressed against him, trembling.

"I think we'd better go in," Rich murmured, his voice raspy as he gently eased her away. He paused before sliding the door open to readjust his clothes. "You make me feel like a darn teenager."

Ada pursed her lips, stifling a grin. Then something she'd thought about earlier popped into her head. She laid her hand on Rich's arm as he reached for the door. "Rich, I need to tell you something."

"Okay."

"Do you recall when we talked about guns and I asked you if I should get one?"

He didn't say anything, just looked at her with those tawny eyes.

Beneath her hand his arm turned rigid. "Please, hear me out," she pleaded. "I'm almost completely healed, yet day after day, friends work in my gardens and watch over me at night. I appreciate it, but I don't *like* it. I don't like having to depend on others. Right now, I have no choice but to accept the situation."

"Accepting help is smart, Ada." Rich ran his hand down her arm, catching and holding her hand.

"It is," she agreed. "But I have a plan. By the end of the month I'm taking my life back. I refuse to jump at shadows, to be afraid to work in my gardens, and to have someone sleeping over night after night to protect me." She squeezed his hand. "Unless invited."

"I'll volunteer." He grinned. "Now tell me your plan."

"I'll have an alarm system installed."

Rich tilted his head thoughtfully. "Reasonable, and smart."

"Necessary," she added. "I don't *like* the idea, but it's unavoidable." She let go of his hand, turned toward the door. "I've decided to purchase a gun and learn how to use it."

Rich caught her arm and swung her around to face him. "Ada, I--"

She pressed her fingers to his lips. "I need your help with the gun, Rich. Please think about it, because my decision is nonnegotiable."

She brushed a quick kiss over his lips, slid the door open, and slipped inside.

Chapter Thirty-Four

Ada sat back, removed her wide-brimmed hat, and took a break. Memorial Day loomed on the horizon. After three weeks of therapy her muscles still protested. She'd surprised them though, and wiped the condescending smirk right off the face of the young therapist by surpassing every level on his *expected progress chart* the first week.

"Come have some iced tea," Called Cassi from the porch. Ada waved toward her and pushed to her feet, just in time to see a Pine Bluffs patrol car cruise past.

Pocketing her trimming shears, she joined Cassi on the porch. She welcomed the soaring temperature. New shoots could succumb to a cold night, so in western Pennsylvania farmers often held their breath until early June.

"Thank you, honey." Ada plopped down and took the frosty glass Cassi handed her.

"You're pushing it," Cassi scolded. "You've another week of therapy and one final check-up before you're ready to put in a full day."

"I'm fine. By this time next week everything should be back to normal." Her definition of *normal* was having her house to herself and getting on with her life.

She tossed her hat aside and relaxed, enjoying the fresh brewed, cold tea. "How much longer is Nick going to make officers cruise up and down the road in front of my house? It's a waste of their time. And don't give me that innocent look, Cassi McGraw. You were on the phone to chief hubby before I even got my hands in the dirt." To stress her point, Ada tipped her glass toward her niece. "You should be home, working in *your* gardens, helping Nick with all those renovations he's got going."

"We've got contractors doing the work, and I'd only be in the way. I'm managing to teach my fitness classes and I'm home every night."

"I've got Molly, Lois, or scatterbrained Katy hovering over me while the Pine Bluffs Police ignore crime all over town to drive up and down the lake shore all day. And night," she added. "Come to think of it, who's in your class when half your students are hanging out here?"

Cassi's voice took on an edge. "Crime? What crime? *Hello*, this is Pine Bluffs, remember?" she snapped. "My classes have grown to near capacity, regardless of whether you and your friends attend."

"The problem *is*," Ada shot back. "They should be attending your classes, taking care of their own gardens, and selling milkshakes, for God's sake!"

Cassi fell silent, and Ada took a deep, calming breath.

"Have some more," Cassi said, reaching for the pitcher. Avoiding eye contact, they focused on the amber liquid filling the glass as if watching the first moon launch.

When Cassi's cell phone chirped, she pulled it out, checked the display and snapped, "What?" She listened, and then retorted, "I'm fine." Her stern look softened, and she slowly turned her head, meeting Ada's gaze. "Actually," she said, humor creeping into her voice, "My aunt and I were having a rather *heated* discussion. Sorry I reacted that way," she added. "No, I doubt that would settle me down." She laughed aloud. "Or settle my aunt. Though you could pose the question to Rich."

Ada's jaw dropped. "Cassandra!"

"Just a moment," Cassi said, taking the phone from her ear. "I need to talk with Nick a moment, okay?"

"Go." Ada chuckled. "Maybe he'll leave work early and you can go home and *settle down.*"

Blushing, Cassi mouthed, "I'm sorry."

"Me, too," Ada whispered, and waved her away with one hand.

Cassi strolled to the far end of the porch, and Ada took their empty glasses inside.

They'd never argued so fiercely. Disagreed? Sure, plenty of times, but this was the closest they'd come to an all out shouting match.

Physically and mentally exhausted, she showered, slipped into soft sweats, and stretched out on her bed, but sleep wouldn't come. She tossed and turned, and ended up staring wide-eyed at the ceiling.

Things had to change.

Although TJ and Nick put in long hours, the investigation was going nowhere. She just wanted the ongoing nightmare to end.

For three weeks now she'd been driven to therapy, to the doctors, to the damn store, for Pete's sake. Partly because she didn't have anything to drive. Even if she had, someone would have been glued to her side. She loved these people, but, truth be told, she was getting tired of their faces.

Except for Rich. Now there's a face, and *body*, she'd like to see more of... alone. This time of year was busy at Ace, requiring his presence there. Even so, he'd stopped to see her almost daily, or at least called. When he came by, they often sat on her porch until dark or took walks at dusk. Even then, they were never completely alone.

She swung her legs over the edge of the bed and stood. She hadn't slept, but the down time restored her energy. A low murmur of voices echoed down the hallway. Her nighttime sitters had arrived.

After freshening and changing, she joined her friends in the kitchen. Something bubbled on the range and Tom relaxed on the porch having a beer. Cassi was nowhere in sight.

Mary looked up from stirring the bubbling pot. "Hey, lady," she said, tapping the spoon on the pan. "Have a nice nap?"

"I rested, and I feel better. Did Cassi leave?"

"Uh huh. She said you were grumpy and needed a nap."

Ada filled her teapot and put it on. "I yelled at her today, Mary. After all she's done the past few weeks, putting her life on hold to take care of me. You all have," she added. "Now, it's going to stop."

Tom stepped through the door. "What's going to stop?"

"I've contacted a company to have a security system installed. They'll be here after the holiday weekend. What's going to stop," she continued, "is round the clock live-in body guards. I want my friends to visit. *Normal visits*," she emphasized. "Not guard duty. After my alarm is installed, I'll be staying here alone. If Nick insists on patrols checking on me, well, I can understand that and accept it. But enough is enough. I've got to get on with my life."

Tom and Mary exchanged a fast look.

"That's less than a week. You don't have any way to get around," Mary objected.

"The insurance is settled and my new CRV will be delivered before the weekend. I can pick it up Friday."

Mary looked helplessly at Tom.

"Let's sit down," Tom suggested. He finished off his beer, pulled out a chair for Mary, and sat down beside her.

Ada slid into a chair across the table from them. She reached over and took Mary's hand. "I can't live like this any longer. I promise you both I'll be careful. I'm not so naïve to think it will all go away." she admitted. "But if I give in and let this creep run my life, I might as well just let him shoot me."

The teapot shrilled its high pitched whistle, cutting through heavy silence.

Ada jumped to her feet. "See." She glanced around, hoping to lighten the impact, "I can even make tea myself."

Mary pushed away from the table. "I'm not worried about you making tea," she shot back. "What I'm worried about is the person out there who wants to shoot you."

*****

Rich stepped inside Ada's cottage. It was a toss up who looked more distressed. Mary gripped a spoon like a weapon. Tom looked ready to bolt.

Ada calmly sipped tea.

He plastered on a smile and closed the door. "Evening, everyone."

A long moment passed. "Did something happen?" His gaze shot from one tense face to another, stopping on Ada. She looked fine, but that didn't mean there hadn't been another attempt on her life. Goose bumps dotted his skin.

He jumped when Mary rapped her spoon on the pan. "No. Everything's not all right. We're being replaced by an alarm."

A flood of relief washed over him. Oh, Lord. Wait until Ada told her plan B. The gun. When he didn't react, she narrowed her eyes and pointed the dripping spoon at him. "You knew," she accused.

"Mary, an alarm system's not a bad idea," Tom pointed out.

"I agree," Rich said, earning a relieved smile from Ada. "Yes, Mary. I knew she was considering a system. Among other things." He gave Ada a pointed look. Her smile faded, but Mary didn't catch the inference, so Rich let it go. He accepted a cold beer from Tom and they adjourned to the porch.

"Let her get used to the idea," Tom said once they'd closed the door. "This has been hard on Mary. All those years I was on the job she was rock steady. Since this started with Ada, she's been a nervous wreck. I just don't get it."

Rich propped his hip on the railing. "Think about it a minute. You were trained to take care of yourself. It was your job to be able to do that. I'm sure Mary had her moments, but this is different, Tom." The cold beer slid down and curled around the knot in Rich's belly. One that hadn't quite dissolved since Ada's accident. In some ways he understood perfectly what Mary was going through.

He gave Tom a minute, and then said, "Did Ada mention she wants to get a gun?"

Tom took a long sip of beer, and said, "Shit."

Chapter Thirty-Five

Friday brought a brand new Honda CRV. Tom and Mary gave Ada a lift to the dealer and, though they now followed her back to Pine Bluffs, she indulged them knowing a weekend of freedom lay ahead.

Alert Security inspected her cottage and suggested several options an hour later. All done under the watchful eye of Tom and TJ. After learning more about the system, it turned out less intrusive than expected. Now if she could only remember the codes they'd told her she'd need and not set the darn thing off every day, she'd feel better about having it installed.

After intense discussions, and a few tears, she and Mary were back on solid ground. With input from TJ, Tom, Nick, *and* Rich, Mary reluctantly agreed to the top notch alarm system.

The gun. Another matter entirely.

To keep the peace, and Mary's peace of mind, she'd drawn Rich into her scheme. She agreed to hold off purchasing a gun until she'd learned how to handle one. And who better to teach her than a former Marine?

She dubbed the upcoming weekend the 'learn to shoot' caper, knowing full well Mary approved because while learning to shoot, Ada would spend the weekend with Rich. A big fat pacifier for Mary the matchmaker.

At first, she'd worried how Cassi would respond. Then Cassi and Nick were invited out of town to visit friends overnight Friday. Problem solved. Cassi wasn't naïve. She'd been included in the 'gun' discussions, along with Nick *and* TJ. Ada and Rich weren't fooling anyone. Least of all Cassi, who popped in on their way out of town. With a wink, she handed over a beautifully wrapped box before scooting out the door.

Later, in private, Ada lifted the lid to discover a soft, green negligee. Not Victoria's Secret style, but classy, clingy and semi-transparent. The card inside read; 'Warning! May interrupt target practice.'

The negligee was tucked in her overnight bag in the back seat.

She reached the outskirts of Pine Bluffs and turned onto the road leading to Rich's place. When his renovated carriage house came into view, Tom beeped and Ada waved as her friends continued past. She turned into his driveway and immediately spotted Rich, lounging on a glider beneath a large maple beside the house.

Pine Shadow Lake's surface shimmered in the background, and at the edge of Rich's property several deer fed in the early twilight. A breeze rippled young maple leaves overhead, and when Ada parked and swung open the door she detected the sweet aroma of lilacs. Though past their peak, fading purple clumps still covered the thick stand of bushes alongside the carriage house.

Rich rose and, shoving his hands into his pockets, ambled toward her.

She opened the rear door and pulled out her overnight bag. "I wasn't sure I'd like this color, but I do," she said, running her hand over the new Honda's shiny finish.

"I like you in green," he remarked. He looked her up and down

"Yes, I... Green? This isn't really green. It's called Opal Sage Metallic and..." She turned and their eyes met. "We're not talking about my new Honda, are we?"

He smiled that lazy smile and shook his head.

Her heart leaped into her throat. His eyes darkened as he cupped her arm and ran his hand from shoulder to wrist then back. Well aware he meant her green pullover and matching crop pants, she tilted her head provocatively. "Then you're going to love what I have in this bag," she teased, and handed him her overnight case.

"Is this all?" Rich held up the bag. "You only brought one bag for three days?"

She laughed at his wide-eyed expression. "Who said I'd be here three days?"

"You're going to be here three days and *four* nights. That's the deal. Learning to use a firearm takes time. I have a plan for the weekend. It's on my list."

"You have a plan?" They began walking side by side toward the door.

Inside, Rich closed the door behind them. "I do," he said, flipping a switch to light the stairway. He motioned her ahead and traipsed up the stairs behind her. "Dinner is marinating."

"Rich," she admonished, stepping into the warmth and light of his home. "Are you trying to seduce me with marinating shrimp, again?"

"You're too smart for that darlin'." He winked. "This time I'm marinating steaks. I'll put this in my room," he said, holding her bag up. "The wine's breathing on the counter. Help yourself."

Ada moved into Rich's kitchen where granite counters gleamed. Like a still life, a bottle of cabernet and two generous wine glasses sat alongside a chef's block upon which a wedge of brie and a large, golden apple waited.

She poured the wine, breathing in the classic red's intense aroma. Wine in hand, she strolled to the windows facing the lake.

"Our friends are going for a drink, too." Rich's voice came from close behind her. He wrapped his arms around her, and they watched the deer from earlier meander toward the water.

"They're beautiful," she murmured."

His lips brushed the back of her neck. "Wanna hear my plan?"

She laughed, and he nipped her ear. "Why don't I guess?"

"Be my guest," he invited.

She stepped from his embrace, and passed him a glass of wine.

Taking a knife, she cut apple wedges and, placing a piece of the soft cheese on top, she held it to his lips. "We've about two hours of daylight left," she began. Pausing, she popped a slice of apple into her mouth, chewed, and swallowed. "Before dark, you'll ask for the keys to my new toy and tuck it safely away in your garage."

"Good guess," Rich said around the cheese and apple treat. "It doesn't count, though."

"Why not?" Ada frowned over the rim of her glass.

"Because you saw my truck parked outside."

"True. I know you, Rich. Besides the fact you wouldn't leave your classic Volvo outside, you're still in 'body guard' mode."

He sipped, studying her closely.

Guilt made her to turn away. She'd ruined the mood. "I'm sorry. I wanted tonight to be ours. It's been over three weeks and I've missed being with you." Rich remained silent, prompting her to defend her words. "God, Rich, I'm struggling to overcome this pressing fear and put what happened behind me. It haunts me, and I can't shake the sheer panic I felt when I couldn't stop and knew I might die." Her voice hitched. She sat her glass down and gripped the counter edge with both hands.

He reached around her and gently pried her hands free. Then he pulled her into his arms.

Ragged sobs shook her, head to toe. She'd held back for weeks, tossed and turned when nightmares brought the terror back. Now it poured out, raw and ugly.

His arms tightened, and she laid her face against the soft cotton of his shirt. She inhaled the clean scent of it, and his heart thudded in her ear. His hands moved gently over her rigid back, comforting, stroking.

"Let it out." His warm breath brushed her ear. "You're safe now. I won't let anything happen to you. I promise."

When she gained control, she wiped her eyes and met his tender gaze. "I didn't hear the rest of your plan."

He retrieved her wine. "Here, take a sip."

She complied, then fiercely swiped lingering tears away. "I feel like an idiot," she complained, taking a deeper sip.

"Not even close, and don't gulp. Wine's to be savored." He brushed a kiss across her forehead.

She set her glass aside and her lips sought his. The wine softened the rough edges, his lingering, gentle kisses melted her and tension slipped away. Then, tilting her head back, he demanded more.

Only the present mattered. The feel of him, the warmth, the thrill of his hands gliding over her. She wanted to stay there forever, safe and protected in his arms. "You make it all go away," she whispered, and he pushed her collar aside and pressed his lips to skin. "Here with you... like this, I feel safe, and..."

"Shh." He took her hand, pressed it to his heart. "Feel *wanted*. Don't think, just know you *are* safe, and I want you."

After dining on tender steaks and polishing off a bottle of classic red wine, in silence, he led her down the dimly lit hallway. The scent of lilacs drifted through his bedroom window as he lowered her to his bed. Her fingers tightened on his shoulders and she pulled him to her. There was no talk, only the rustle of fabric as she unbuttoned his shirt and pulled it away, running her hands over him. His intense gaze held hers and his muscles bunched and tightened, warm and taunt beneath her fingertips.

He shifted above her and she arched up when he drew her top away. She sighed when his lips lingered, teasing the exposed flesh. His warm hands brushed her skin as he slid her crop pants down, and she shuddered when he caressed her.

How many times had she dreamed of this? Vivid dreams chasing nightmares. She reached for him and his body, hot and urgent, pressed against her. Rising to meet him, she thrust against the heat, seeking release until she cried out his name and he held her through the storm.

Shadows deepened into twilight and a soft breeze from the open window cooled her heated skin. He rose above her, his eyes piercing and dark in the softening light. He guided himself to her. More than ready again, she lifted her hips and took him in. He began to move and his mouth found her breast.

Her breath caught and her body met his thrust for thrust. They made love, slow and easy, caressed by the evening breeze and surrounded by the scent of lilacs. She wrapped her arms, her legs around him, pulling him deep. His kisses became frantic, demanding as he possessed her and drove himself harder.

Pleasure exploded, over and over and her cries mingled with his deep satisfied moan. His body shuddered when he released, and he pounded into her.

Her heart still raced when he rolled aside, drawing her against him. She pressed her face to his neck, inhaling the lingering scent of his aftershave and of *him*.

He ran his hand down her side and caressed her bare hip. "You're still bruised. Did I hurt you?"

She smiled, nuzzling the soft spot beneath his jaw. "Didn't you hear me scream?"

"I did," he said, pulling her full against him again. "Several times, in fact."

She slid her hand down, pinched his bare butt. "Smug, aren't you?"

He pulled back, turning serious as he studied her face in the twilight. "They remind you every time you undress, don't they? The bruises."

She touched his cheek. "They'll eventually fade. I hardly know they're there until I look in the mirror. It's what's inside that hurts."

"With time that will go away, too."

She raised her eyes to his. "I'm not so sure, Rich. I've come through so much over the years, and managed all by myself. I left the pain behind and kept the good stuff. Memories saw me through the tough times." She looked away, blinking back a fresh threat of tears. "I can't seem to leave *this* threat, this monster who wants to deliberately hurt me, behind. For the first time in my life, I'm scared.

"You're not alone this time. You've got close friends, and you've got family now, too." He tipped her chin up and brushed away a stray tear. "And, you've got me."

*****

Rich slipped out of bed, careful not to disturb her, and pulled a light sheet over Ada's naked body. He tugged on a pair of sweatpants before stooping to retrieve the seductive little number he'd tossed carelessly aside earlier. He draped it over a chair, letting the soft fabric slide through his fingers. She *did* look good in green, and he *had* liked it, as she'd promised.

He quietly closed the door and made his way into the kitchen. Grabbing the empty wine bottle and keys she'd left for him on a stand by the door, he slipped on a pair of shoes and jogged down the stairs. After tossing the bottle into the recycle bin, he flipped on the outside light and went out the door.

Rich circled her new CRV, checking it over before securing it in his garage. He admired her taste. Soft leather seats and every gadget imaginable had him lingering, inhaling the classic new car smell.

After closing the garage door and making sure his truck was locked, he returned to her, undressed, and crawled between the sheets. In her sleep she reached for him. He pulled her close, cradling her head on his shoulder. She'd showered and smelled of vanilla, and her hair felt like silk when he smoothed it away from her face.

The rare, disembodied call of a Whip-poor-will drifted through the open window as he stared at the ceiling. Beside him, the rhythm of her breathing, deep and slow, told him she'd finally found peace from the haunting dreams.

Tomorrow she'd learn to use a gun. Would learning give her peace of mind, or create another kind of nightmare? He'd insist she try his M14 so she'd understand the weapon's destructive power.

Locked away with his M14 was a .45. He'd had them since he was in the Corps. More recently, after firing Nick's Walther PPK, he'd searched and finally found a used one made in Germany. A Walther fired a .380 round, perfect for what Ada needed. He'd hunt for another brand of the same caliber once she got the feel of the gun. Walther's were expensive, and the German made original like his and Nick's model was no longer made. He'd ask around and find a compact weapon similar, yet suitable.

Rich was on his second cup of coffee, watching the sun rise over the lake, when Ada joined him. "Water's on for tea," he said, and then grinned. "Though my selection lacks imagination. I've got Lipton or Lipton Green Tea. Take your pick."

On her way to the cupboard, she ran her hand over his back. "Lipton's fine."

"How'd you sleep?"

A tiny smile curved her lips. "Like a rock." She turned, leaning against the counter with her tea. "It sounds like a cliché, but good sex tops any sleep remedy on the market."

Rich strolled her way, grinning when she blushed. "Then my work is done, at least for one night. There are six nights in a week, though."

She held her cup aside as he bent and kissed her. "Good morning, handsome."

"Mornin' beautiful." He leaned close and sniffed. "You smell good, kinda like vanilla. Kept me awake a while," he added with a wink.

She laughed, smiling up at him as she lifted her cup to drink. Her hand froze inches from her lips, and the laughter died. Rich knew without looking she'd spotted his Walther and a box of ammo on the table behind him.

Chapter Thirty-Six

Upon arrival, TJ spotted his dad's truck outside Ace Hardware. He wondered what project his mom had lined up for him since now Ada wouldn't need them as much. Ada's decision to install an alarm made sense. He'd encouraged the idea from the start. Response time to her cottage would be minutes from Pine Bluffs PD.

Though on the night he'd raced like hell through rain and fog to get to Cassi, the drive seemed endless.

He entered the store and spied his dad halfway down the second aisle. Moving in that direction, he glanced around hoping to see Harley. His dad looked up as he approached.

"Hey, Dad. What cha' doin'? Let me guess," he said, lifting his hand palm out. "Now you and Mom have been replaced by an alarm, you're playing catch up with house projects."

"You know," his dad said, turning his attention back to the paint. "Sometimes you're a pain in the ass." Frowning, he stared at shelves of paint cans. "What the hell color is 'desert breeze'?"

"Why don't we track down Harley? He'll know."

Tom tucked a crumpled paint chart into his pocket. "I saw him when I came in, he's around." He paused and took a long look at TJ. "You've got something on your mind, son."

How did he do that? As far back as TJ remembered, his dad could read him like a book. The brief time they'd worked together at Pine Bluffs PD there'd been several times this strange connection had paid off.

On his mind was a return trip to the parking garage in Erie. A long shot, but like a bug buzzin' in his friggin' ear, he wouldn't rest until he followed through. He crossed his arms and shrugged. "We've hit a wall with Ada's case," he explained. "The bartender in North East looked good for a while. Seems he's a half decent mechanic, and whoever tampered with Ada's vehicle knew what he was doing. We've got nothing solid. Nothing to put him in Erie the night we suspect the brake lines got punched, and nothing to tie his truck to the damage done to her property."

"Wasn't he stopped near Pine Bluffs that night?"

"Yeah, but took off like a damn rabbit when the trooper left his unit and approached, left Adamski in the dust. Shit like that happens. He suspected Andrews had been drinking and opted not to pursue him. He had Andrews's license number, so he let it go."

Tom shook his head. "Then the son-of-a-bitch went home and washed his truck."

"From what I saw when we interviewed him a few days ago, he's a bit tight assed about a clean truck. So..." He spread his hands and shrugged again.

"How about Will Steiner? What did Nick find out?"

"Same damn brick wall. Nobody saw anything and, according to Rich's friend at ONI, the man's been next to a saint since he got out of jail. They're keeping an eye on him. Meanwhile, I need to recheck something in light of new findings."

"Well, son, good luck with whatever you're chasing down. You're not on the state's dime, are you?"

"Ada's like family, Dad. Plus, for some reason the state gods smiled on me and I've got the holiday weekend off. Since you and Mom aren't having the picnic till Monday, I might as well do something useful."

"Humph. You could come by and help me paint the bathroom."

TJ laughed. "Let me guess, desert breeze?"

"Well, well. The McGraw men," Harley strolled up to Tom and TJ. He wiped his hands on a cloth and tucked it into his back pocket.

"Just the man I'm looking for," Tom said. "I need two gallons of... Ah, shit." He pulled the chart from his pocket. "Desert breeze. Latex semi gloss."

"Not a problem." Harley perused the cans and quickly pulled two from the bottom shelf. "Anything else?"

"I can handle the rest, thanks."

"You paintin' something for Mrs. Blaine?" Harley asked.

"No," Tom shook his head. "Mary's decided *our* guest bathroom needs repainted.

"So, you're not stayin' with Mrs. Blaine now?"

TJ looked at Harley. "What makes you think they were staying with Mrs. Blaine?"

Harley gave him a cold stare. "People talk, *Trooper* McGraw."

TJ met the look with one of his own. "By the way, Harley, how's your head?"

The little shit all but sneered, but his cheeks flushed and he rubbed the band-aide on his forehead. "I ran into a fuckin' door, okay?"

Tom's head shot up and he glanced sharply from Rich's employee to TJ.

Harley grabbed the paint. "I'll take this up front for you," he said to Tom, and escaped down the aisle.

"What the hell was that all about?" Tom asked. He thoughtfully tapped a paint brush against his palm. "Harley's been a good employee but, according to Rich, lately he's been a pain in the ass." He grabbed another brush. "Guess I'm ready. Where are you heading?"

"I'm on my way to Erie, but I need batteries and swung by to get some. I'll see you up front."

TJ grabbed two packs of batteries and caught up with his dad at check out.

Harley packed Tom's paint into a box, keeping his head averted as TJ approached.

"Wow, both handsome McGraw men at the same time. Hi TJ," Mandy remarked, flashing a wide grin as she rung up Tom's sale. "We've been *so* busy today," she gushed. "Mr. McConnell took the *whole* weekend off. I sure miss him when it gets crazy like this." She tilted her head at the line behind TJ.

To speed things along, TJ paid cash and hurried out the door. "I'll see you on Monday, Dad," he said, tossing the batteries in his car. "Is there anything I can bring?"

"Just your appetite. We're grilling, first time this season." He hesitated, poised to get into his truck. "Good luck today."

As his dad drove away, TJ considered going back into the store. Then more cars arrived. A busy Saturday was not the time to bug Harley with questions. Could be why the man was in such a piss poor mood.

TJ understood the pressures of a busy day. "Count your blessings, McGraw," he mumbled as he drove north toward Erie.

Maybe he'd get lucky, find something they'd all overlooked, and solve the damn case.

*****

"You're awful quiet," Rich said, his eyes on the compact Walther PPK in Ada's hands.

"I've been listening," she declared, examining the weapon she held. "You told me if I like this gun, the feel and... What was it... the grip?" Rich nodded. "Then we could check around to find one similar, a .380 caliber?"

"Right" He turned, unlocked a built in cabinet and pulled out his M14. "I want you to fire this today, too." She laid the handgun down carefully on Rich's workbench. He handed her the rifle. She took her time, cradling the larger weapon. If he didn't know better, from the way she handled it, he'd have assumed this wasn't the first time she'd held an M14. She presented a natural acceptance, a control, which eased his mind. She'd do all right.

"You take good care of your guns. This looks like new," she said, examining the shiny barrel and running her hand over the polished wood stock curving nicely against the barrel.

"See this?" Rich held up a rectangular thin metal case. "It's the ammo clip. This one holds twenty rounds and fits right here." He tilted the stock and showed her where it slipped in a few inches in front of the trigger.

"This is what he used, isn't it?"

"The round we dug out of your wall was from an M14. So yeah, I'd say this is the kind of gun he used."

Ada passed the rifle back to Rich. "Why do you want me to fire one? I'm only interested in the handgun."

"Because I want you to see, to feel, the power of this weapon. This isn't a game. If you're going to own a firearm, you're damn well going to know about them and what they can do."

172

She looked him straight in the eye for a very long moment. "Okay. Let's get started."

Setting the rifle aside, he placed both hands on her shoulders. "Maybe this isn't the time, or the place." He pushed her slightly away from him. "But you mean a lot to me, Ada. I'll ask a lot of you today. I'll push, hard. Just know it's because I don't want *anything* to happen to you."

"I understand, and I'll pay attention," she said.

He couldn't miss the subtle gleam in her eye, so he gave her a little shake and grinned at her. "Don't be a smart ass."

She reached up and twined her arms around his neck. Then she rose on her toes and kissed him. "I understand, and I'll pay attention, *Sir*."

Rich threw his head back and laughed before he yanked her tight against him and kissed her. He broke away and looked down at her. "I... God, Ada." His throat tightened and he pulled her in for another kiss.

He drew back slowly until his eyes met hers. His heart lurched. "I can't get enough of you lady. Guess we'll have to talk about that. Soon."

She cupped his face between her hands and kissed him gently. "I guess we will."

He tucked the Walther into a holster on his belt and picked up the rifle and ammo. "Let's get going before I forget my plan for today. The range we're using isn't far," he said, as they moved into the lower foyer.

Suddenly, the distinct chimes of his doorbell rang. Annoyed with the interruption, he placed the rifle and ammo on a bench just inside the door. "Wait here," he told Ada. "I'll see who that is at the door."

He turned ice cold and instinctively put his hand on the gun at his waist when he opened the door and came face to face with Will Steiner.

*****

TJ had a rough idea where Ada parked the night she stayed at the Sheraton. At least within the general area. He wandered along, the beam of his flashlight scanning the sloped floor slowly, left to right, back and forth over the dusty cement.

He stopped beside a light colored, fairly new Toyota Corolla and knelt down. His light caught dark splotches beneath the vehicle, but in order to get a closer look, he'd either have to crawl under the damn thing or wait till the owner showed up and moved it.

Careful not to damage the door, he grasped the car's handle and hung there while he aimed the light and peered underneath.

"Hey! What the hell are you doing?"

TJ turned his head and stared at boney knees above big feet in thick-soled flip flops. He pulled himself up and faced an indignant young man.

"I asked what you're doing," the man repeated.

The guy looked up, because TJ stood several inches taller. He took a cautious step back, and the scowl on his face deepened. "That's my car, fella," he declared. "Who are you?"

TJ pulled his ID out and flipped it open. "I'm Trooper McGraw with the state police," he said evenly, and held up his badge. "What's your name?"

The guy's eyes widened. He studied the badge then looked TJ up and down. "You're a cop?"

"A Pennsylvania State Trooper," TJ corrected. "An incident occurred at this location a few weeks ago and I'm chasing down leads." He put his badge away. "I need to get a better look at something beneath your vehicle. Could you move it for me... uh, what'd you say your name was?"

"Tony, sir. I'm Tony Villa. I'm a waiter at the Cove."

TJ held out his hand. "Nice to meet you, Tony."

They shook hands and Tony dug into the pocket of his baggy shorts and pulled out a set of keys. "I'll move my car, no problem, Officer."

He moved the Toyota a couple of spaces away and returned to watch with interest as TJ searched the garage floor. Tony dropped down beside him when he squatted and brushed some loose dirt from a splotch on the floor. "Whadda' you see? Did somebody get shot, or... or, maybe stabbed?"

TJ smiled and pointed to several dark spots. "Nothing so exciting, Tony. These spots could be blood, but it's been so long it's hard to tell."

Tony scrambled to his feet when TJ stood. "How about luminol?"

TJ's brow lifted. He turned and looked at Tony. "Luminol? What do you know about luminol?"

"I watch CSI." A smug smile split Tony's face. "You can spray it on and it glows, shows up blood stains."

While staring at the young waiter it occurred to him Tony paid attention to details, and he worked nearby. "Do you often work late, Tony?"

Tony shrugged. "Most of the time."

"What time do you get off work?"

"Most nights around 1am," he said, and then asked, "Not goin' to check out the blood, huh?"

"Sorry, fresh out of luminal. I do have a couple pictures I'd like to show you, though. Do you have a minute?"

"Sure." He nodded vigorously. "Mug shots, huh?"

"You might say that. I'll be right back," TJ said, chuckling as he jogged down the row to his car. He grabbed the file folder containing pictures of Will Steiner and Rick Andrews and returned to where an eager Tony waited.

He handed over the picture of Andrews first, and wasn't surprised when, obviously disappointed, the kid shook his head. Tony studied the picture of Steiner a bit longer, chewing his lip and tugging one ear thoughtfully. "Sorry," he said, finally. "I don't recognize him either."

TJ thanked him and tucked the photos away. He took a last look at the spots and turned to leave. Suddenly Tony lit up like Christmas and grabbed TJ's arm. "Wait, wait. I know where those spots came from, and they *are* blood!

Something on the kid's face had TJ's instincts humming. He'd seen something. "How do you know that?

"Shit I should have remembered. Sorry," Tony said, hunching his shoulders. He grimaced. "Though I'm afraid the blood is just from a stupid accident."

"Tell me anyway, about the accident," TJ said.

"I worked late," Tony began. "It was one-thirty when I left work that night, a little later than usual. I parked... there, on the end," he said, turning and pointing several spaces to the left. "The garage was deserted, so when I hear someone swearing a blue streak I kinda stopped and looked around. This older guy slides out from underneath an SUV parked right here," he said, pointing to the space with the spots. "The guy was bleeding like a son-of -a bitch. I asked him what the hell happened and he almost jumped a foot. He kind of looked around, you know, like he expected something to happen?"

"Wait, hold it." TJ dug into his pocket for a pen. It was oddly exciting, knowing he might be close to breaking the wall they'd been banging their heads against. While at the same time, a cold feeling stole over him. "Okay. The guy was bleeding and he'd been under an SUV. Can you describe him?"

"He wasn't a big guy, kinda average, but nervous. Jumpy. Dark hair, thin face. When I tried to see if I could help... you know, with the bleeding and all, he got kind of nasty. Told me he just rapped his head lookin' for something."

"So you didn't get that close?"

"Not really. By then I was kinda' pissed. I'd worked late. So I figured, 'then go to hell buddy', I'm goin' home."

"Was he still there when you left?"

"He picked something up, still holding his head, and headed the other way. Musta' taken the stairs down."

TJ gauged the distance and scribbled on the back of Steiner's picture. "Can you remember anything else, Tony?"

"Sorry, that's all I got."

"Thanks, you've been very helpful. I'd like your address and a number where I can reach you." TJ jotted down the information Tony rattled off and handed him one of his cards. "If you think of anything else, contact me."

He shook Tony's hand and started to walk away. Shit, he almost forgot to ask. "Tony," he called out. "Do you remember what kind of SUV the man was under?"

Tony grinned. "I sure do, Trooper McGraw. It was a really nice Honda CRV."

TJ speed dialed Nick on his cell phone as he dashed toward his car.

*****

175

Ada waited while Rich went to answer the door. She picked up the rifle's ammo clip and studied it, mentally sorting through all he'd gone over about handling guns.

Her attention shifted when Rich opened the door. His body filled the narrow opening, blocking the entrance and hiding whoever rang the doorbell from view. At first, she figured Rich was protecting her. Or rather, her reputation.

Very few were aware of her relationship with him. Of course there was the flower delivery guy's wife, Lillian, which made Ada wonder if the person at the door was on a fishing expedition into their private lives.

"What do you want?"

Ada stiffened, and hastily put down the ammo clip. Rich sounded cold, angry. With his legs spread and his back ramrod stiff, he faced the unknown visitor. Her breath caught when she noticed his hand resting on the Walther at his waist.

"Rich?" Her voice wavered.

His other hand shot out, blocking her from the opening. "Go upstairs, Ada."

Heart pounding, Ada moved to the stairs. With one foot on the first step, she glanced over her shoulder and froze.

Oh, God!

Sweat slicked her skin. Twice before she'd come face to face with Will Steiner, but having seen his picture, this time she knew who he was, knew the threat. She shivered, rubbing her arms when air streaming through the open door swept over her moist skin.

"Ada, please." Rich shot her a fast look. He expressed no emotion, no hint of what lay beneath his calm, cool outward appearance before he tuned back to the man at the door.

Steiner shifted his gaze to her. His eyes were dark gray, almost black. Yet she sensed no anger, no threat. Will Steiner looked beaten, almost sad. He had on a dark tee shirt and green khaki's. His shoulders slumped and his arms hung loosely at his sides.

She didn't know how, or why, but something about the downtrodden figure shook her to the core. Not panic, and strangely, not fear. More pity or compassion. At that moment, she doubted he meant to harm either of them.

She went to Rich and laid her hand on his arm, facing the man in the doorway. "Hello Mr. Steiner."

Rich stretched his arm out in front of her, nudging her behind him.

Steiner's gaze flitted nervously to Rich's hand still poised on his Walther. He spread his arms, palm up. "This is the last time I'll bother you Rich. I promise."

"I don't trust you or your promises, Steiner. What do you want?"

Steiner ran a hand over his face. He hooked his thumbs in the front pockets of his pressed green slacks. "I want you to know." He fell silent, staring at the ground. "I want you to know," he began again, lifting his eyes to meet Rich's unflinching look. "I'm sorry. Wait, wait," he pleaded when Rich gave a harsh laugh. "Just hear me out. Then I'm out of your life for good."

"Rich," Ada pleaded. "Let him talk."

Steiner nodded his thanks and continued, "I had one good thing in my life, one chance, and I screwed it up." He rubbed the Marine Corps tattoo on the back of his hand. "If there was any way I could go back, to undo the damage, I'd do it in a heartbeat."

Lines bracketed Steiner's face, and gray threaded through his hair. The day Ada first met him while kayaking, he'd seemed younger, stronger. Now, he just looked... tired.

"That's all I have to say." Steiner pulled a cap from his pocket. He put it on and turned to leave. He'd only gone a few steps before he turned and looked back at them. "I know you don't believe me, but coming here, facing you..." He shook his head. "It was something I had to do, Rich."

Ada stepped up beside him and Rich wrapped his arm around her. He waited until Steiner reached the end of the driveway, then he pulled her inside, closed the door, and enveloped her in his arms. He held her tight, shaking.

"Rich," she murmured. "Are you all right?"

"I will be, just give me a moment. That little encounter just brought the past I've worked years to put behind me front and center."

He held her, rocking in place.

As she rubbed her hands gently over his back, tension dissolved beneath her fingertips. "Rich, let's forget the shooting lesson today. Let's just be together."

He drew away and gave her a crooked smile. "You're screwin' up my plan."

She laughed. "Well, we could--" and the doorbell's insistent chime sounded.

Rich dropped his chin to his chest. "Shit," he muttered. "Now who?"

Ada went with him this time, and heaved a big sigh when they discovered Harley Phillips fidgeting nervously on the doorstep.

"What are you doing here, Harley?" Rich glowered at his employee.

"I have something for Mrs. Blaine. Can I come in?"

Rich opened the door and stepped back. "Why not. Just make if fast, we have plans," he stated, and turned to Ada. "I want to check on something. I'll be right back."

She knew without asking where he was going. He jogged down the walk and stopped to peer in the direction Will Steiner had disappeared.

Harley slipped past her and into the foyer. She turned and followed him inside. He had his back to her, fussing with something in his hand.

"What is it you have for me, Harley?"

"Oh, just this." He spun around. His hand shot out and clamped on her wrist, jerking her toward him.

"Harley, what..." She gaped at the curved edge of a very large knife. He yanked her closer and pressed the cold blade against her cheek.

"I've waited a long time for this." His voice shook, high pitched with excitement. "You're a nice lady, Ada, and I'm sorry you had to be the one. I have no choice. It's Rich McConnell's fault, and today... today I'll finally get my revenge."

Chapter Thirty-Seven

"Come on, come on." TJ muttered impatiently, waiting for Nick to answer. When Nick's voice mail picked up, he broke the connection. He raced to the ground level, burst through the door of the parking garage, and sprinted to his car.

Pausing to catch his breath he speed dialed the barracks, only to be told the patrol in the Pine Bluffs area was tied up with an accident. "Then transfer me to the shift supervisor," he demanded, and waited for the corporal on duty to pick up.

Corporal Pearce's gruff voice came on the line. "You have the weekend off McGraw, what's up?"

"I have a situation," said TJ, and relayed what he'd found. To his advantage, Corporal Pearce knew the case and had been involved from the time of Ada's accident. He advised TJ to pick up Harley and promised he'd get a car to the hardware store ASAP.

"In the meantime, how about I call Pine Bluffs and have someone meet me there to assist?" TJ responded. "We can take Phillips to Pine Bluffs PD until a patrol's free to transfer him to headquarters."

"Sounds, good. You're on the clock McGraw."

"Yes, sir."

TJ dialed Pine Bluffs PD. "Marce, let me talk to Nick." he instructed briskly, grappling for his keys when Marcy picked up. He shifted the phone to his other ear and shoved the key into the ignition.

"TJ? What's wrong?"

"I need to talk to Nick. *Now.*"

"Did you try his cell?"

"Got his voice mail. Where is he?"

"He and Cassi are on their way home. He's due here in about half an hour. TJ, what's happened?"

"I don't have time to explain." He hesitated, not wanting to create panic. "Just listen, okay?"

"Go ahead," Marcy's calm control checked his speeding pulse.

"Is Jake there?"

"Yes."

"Have him go to Ace Hardware and meet me. I'll be there as soon as I can, I'm in Erie. Tell him to wait outside. If he sees Harley Phillips try to leave, he's to pick him up and hold him until I get there. Got that?"

After a beat of silence, Marcy stated, "I'm going to repeat your request so I understand."

"Go"

"You want Jake to meet you at Ace and detain Harley Phillips if he tries to leave?"

"Yes. Don't ask, Marce, not now. Just do it."

He shot up the parkway toward I-90. Common sense dictated caution. Just follow up what he'd discovered and see where it led. Yet urgency drove him as Harley's behavior earlier kept replaying in his head.

A disturbing pattern came to light as he shot across the thruway. At the time of the shooting, he recalled Jake mentioning how Rich blew up when he couldn't locate Harley. Then this morning, his dad brought up Rich's complaints about several changes in Phillips' attitude.

The events in themselves were insignificant. But when he linked them to the vague offhand remark Harley made about the gash on his head, and how he got so friggin' defensive when TJ asked about the injury... a new picture emerged.

Throw in what he'd learned from good ole' 'detective' Tony this morning, and the picture turned nasty.

He glanced at the time. If Jake left right away, he should be at Rich's store. Once he joined Jake, they'd grab Harley. Doing so without creating a scene would be tricky, and made him wish Nick was around to assist. He tried Nick once more. This time he left a message, and then decided to call Rich and Ada.

He hated to bother them, but their connection to what he'd uncovered couldn't be ignored. They should be warned. Up till now there'd been nothing solid to tie the shooting, the vandalism, and the accident together. Now there was, and if the ticking bomb inside Harley Phillips exploded and drove him to act, TJ feared they could be his prime targets.

*****

Ada gasped, surprised and in pain when the tip of the knife pierced the tender skin of her face. Blood, warm and wet, trickled down.

"Move!" Harley's voice grated close to her ear. "Or I'll carve up that pretty face of yours."

His hot breath fanned her cheek and she clutched at his hand. He removed the knife and twisted her arm behind her, making her cry out. "Shut the hell up and get moving."

Keeping the knife in sight, he gripped her wrist tighter and pushed her toward the stairs. "I'm right behind you so don't try anything or the next time I won't just *nick* you with this," he said, brandishing the knife. The shiny blade flashed in the dimly lit hallway.

"Harley," she gasped, stumbling up the first few steps. "You're hurting me."

He ignored her and increased the pressure. She had no choice but to climb the stairs, burning pain shot down her arm from her twisted shoulder. Unhealed muscles and tendons screamed until he shoved her forward into a room at the top of the stairs and closed the door behind them.

She rubbed her throbbing muscles and touched her face where the point of the knife had pricked her skin. Her hand came away bloody. The tiny slice burned like a paper cut, bringing tears to her eyes. She blinked to clear her vision. "What do you want?"

He threw back his head and laughed, then broke off abruptly and once more brought the knife within inches of her face. "I want *revenge* for the one decent thing in my life Rich McConnell destroyed. He took her and he put her on a pedestal, even married her. Then he tossed her like *garbage!*"

Ada backed away, cringing when his voice rose to a screech. A vein throbbed on his furrowed brow and sweat glistened on his face. He beckoned with the knife. "Come here. Now." His eyes narrowed when she failed to obey, and with deadly calm he told her, "If you try to get away, I'll kill you. I don't want to, *yet.* But make no mistake pretty lady, I'll cut your heart out here and now if you ruin my plan."

Crossing her arms to keep them from trembling, Ada took shallow breaths and kept her gaze fixed on the madman before her. Her eyes darted to the closed door.

Where was Rich?

"He'll come after you." Harley grinned, as if reading her thoughts, and his eyes turned hard. "He'll want to be a hero. Just like when he turned in Steiner, a fellow Marine, for a fuckin' pat on the back."

He moved toward her and Ada retreated. She bumped a small table and a pottery vase crashed to the floor. With a sweeping kick, Harley sent the shattered pieces flying. Then he grabbed her arm and dragged her into the kitchen. Keeping a firm hold with one hand, he tucked the knife in his waistband, slid the door to the second story deck open and stepped outside, pulling her along.

It hurt to look at the sun in the bright blue sky overhead. The crisp, cool air carried the distant sound of ducks on the lake, splashing and muttering. Normal sights. Normal sounds. Ada gulped in air. The contrast -- normal to madness -- made her head spin.

She glanced over the railing, calculating. One story up, at least fifteen feet to the ground below. She'd be foolish to jump, but if it proved to be the only escape she'd take the risk.

"Don't try."

Her head snapped around, meeting his cold stare. Stretching her arms out, she gripped the railing on either side of her. Talk to him, distract him. "Why do you care that Rich turned in Will Steiner?" Her voice shook and she bit her lip to keep it from trembling.

"I don't. Steiner's a bastard, too. Another one who wanted to have her."

"Who?" Curiosity burned inside her. What was the connection to Rich's ex and Harley?

"Dodie. My little sister."

He started to pace, always between her and freedom. Unless she jumped, there was no way to escape. If she kept him talking, help would come. Rich wasn't far away, he'd only gone to make sure Steiner left. It angered her to be so helpless, but Harley had re-injured her, and words were her only defense. "Rich's ex was your sister?"

He stopped in front of her and his expression changed. "I took care of her," he said, his voice cracking. "She was a baby, damn it, a kid. My stupid mother hooked up with Dodie's dad. They didn't care, neither of them." He retrieved the knife, waving it dangerously close. "He was scum and my mom..." He ran a shaking hand through his hair, wiped it across his mouth. "She was a bitch."

Like a caged animal, he paced, but a clearer picture began to form in Ada's head. "Mom wouldn't listen," he whined, his face twisting as if in pain. "She had to have the bastard."

Ada cleared her throat. "Was he your Dad?"

He gave a harsh laugh. "No. My dad was dead." he said, then shrugged and looked away. "Dodie and I might as well have been dead, too.

His gaze followed a small bird overhead, and a glazed, far away look came into his eyes. "She depended on me, Dodie did. I was all she had back then. Don't you see?" He frowned as if confused. "I was all Dodie had, she *needed* me. No one ever needed me or cared until Dodie."

Switching tactics, Ada softened her voice. "You must have been a good brother. I understand," she said. "What does this have to do with me? What changed, Harley?"

Something evil flashed in his eyes. "I took jobs, lousy jobs, to buy things for her. I tried, damn it. I worked my ass off for her. And what does she do?" He brought a clenched fist to his chest. "She leaves me."

His hand fell to his side and he jerked one shoulder, a brief dismissing shrug. "So I figured what the hell, and went on with my life. Then years later I run into her, and she's not only married to one son-of-a-bitch, she's screwing another one."

He moved directly in front of Ada and she recoiled from the foul odor of his breath. "What does all this have to do with you?" he whispered, low and evil. "You're the payment. *They* took and used what I saved from hell. First Rich, then Steiner, and she had to settle for me." His eyes bore into Ada's, and the railing cut into her back. Nausea rose in her throat. "I lost her because of men like Rich McConnell. Now he'll see how it hurts to lose something *he* cares about."

"But you were there for her. That's good, Harley. She turned to you and--"

He slapped the knife against her neck. "They spoiled her. She came to me because she had nowhere else to go and--"

"Ada?"

Harley froze at the sound of Rich's muffled call from below. He wrenched Ada away from the railing and spun her around. Wrapping his arm around her waist, he pulled her back against him and held the knife to her throat. "Be quiet," he ordered. "Don't make a sound."

*****

TJ's Camaro kicked up a cloud of dust when he swung into the parking lot at Ace Hardware. He spotted the Pine Bluffs Patrol car and pulled alongside. Jake got out and waited until TJ joined him.

"What's up TJ?"

"I'll explain once we've contained Harley Phillips. Just follow my lead."

Jake frowned, glancing at TJ's jeans and shirt.

"I'm on the clock, in case you're wondering. This could be big, Jake. Let's go."

Together they entered the hardware store. Behind the checkout Mandy glanced up and smiled. "Hi, guys," she said, closing the drawer with a snap. "How can I help you two?"

TJ's gaze searched the store. "We'd like to speak with Harley," he said. "Can you tell us where to find him?"

"Oh, he's gone." She shuffled a pile of receipts, a definite pout forming on her young face. "The busiest day of the year and he *has* to take something to Mr. McConnell."

TJ smacked both hands down on the counter. "What did you say?"

Mandy shrank back, dropping the neat stack she'd collected. Her eyes widened and, casting nervous glances at both men, she hustled to gather up the scattered pile of receipts. "I... I'm sorry," she said, her face as white as the papers she clutched.

"Mandy, *I'm* sorry," TJ apologized. He rubbed a hand over his face and his eyes met Jake's, which were almost as big as Mandy's. "How long ago did he leave?"

Mandy scrunched her face in concentration. "Ah... ah, maybe a half hour?"

TJ tore out of the store, pounded down the steps, and raced across the lot. Close on his heels, Jake shouted. "We'll take my car."

With a curt nod, TJ yanked open the passenger door. He dropped into the seat and Jake slid in and started the engine. "Rich's place, right?" Jake said. His tires dug in, squealing as they hit the pavement. "For God's sake, TJ. What the hell's going on?"

"I'll brief you after you call in for backup. Lights and siren, buddy. *Hit it!*"

*****

Puzzled, Rich stood in the empty foyer listening for Ada's answer. He glanced nervously through the open door at his back. He'd left her right here with Harley when he stepped out. Where in the hell were they?

He called her name again. Ominous answering silence made the hair

183

on the back of his neck stand up. Something wasn't right. He moved quietly to the stairs, noting the door at the top remained closed, just as they'd left it earlier. Silent as a cat, he mounted the stairs, pausing on the top step with one hand on the door knob. Then Ada's muffled cry came from within and he shoved open the door and rushed into the room. Something crunched beneath his feet and he slid to a stop. He smacked his hand against the wall for support, and shot a swift look around for the source of the cry.

"We're out here, boss."

He followed Harley's voice, and several strides brought him to the patio door. Like frigid chards of ice, chills shot straight to his heart when he saw stark terror in Ada's eyes.

Harley stood behind her with one arm around her waist. Her head tilted unnaturally, almost resting on his shoulder, and he held a knife against her throat.

"Harley, what the hell..." Rich swallowed hard. Instinctively his hand went to the Walther at his waist.

"Uh, uh, boss," Harley warned. He inhaled, rubbing his cheek against Ada's hair. "Your lady friend smells sweet. Sweet as honey." Rich fell silent. He wanted to spring across the room and rip her from Harley's grasp.

Harley straightened and edged further behind Ada. His mouth curved into a sly smile as if he sensed Rich's seething anger. His eyes narrowed. "The way I see it, you don't want to make a move or try and shoot me. Not with your lady love in the way."

Ada leaned to one side, as if to move away. He gave a quick jerk, and she froze, quivering visibly in his grasp. No way could Rich get a clear shot, not when her body created a near perfect shield.

"Put the gun on the table, then I want to see both hands at your side," Harley ordered. He waited, not flinching, his eyes flat as a hunting shark. "One cut," he said through clenched teeth. "Just one swipe and she bleeds out in seconds."

"You're a dead man if you draw another drop of blood." Rich's hand tightened on the gun.

"She'll die while you play hero and shoot me," Harley replied. "No way in hell can you get help in time to save her if I slit her ear to ear. Before you get a clean shot, she'll be half dead."

A single tear traced down Ada's pale cheek. Her voice came weak and strained, "He's Dodie's brother. He thinks you hurt her and he wants revenge."

Rich gaped at the monster holding a knife to the woman he loved. He spoke soft and slow. "You're wrong, Harley. Dodie landed on her feet, just like an alley cat, and she--"

"She's *dead*." Harley screamed. "You were so wrapped up in your fuckin' career you couldn't see she needed you. When she turned to Steiner, you made damn sure he went away, too. I couldn't help her anymore, and she just gave up." Moisture glistened in his eyes and he murmured, "The only good thing she got from Steiner, the son-of-a-bitch, was a way to end it without pain."

Rich's mind raced, trying to wrap around Harley's words. He'd lost track of Dodie after the divorce, struggling in his own hell. If what Harley said was true, it meant she'd used drugs and ended it all.

He pushed the thought aside and, moving with caution, slid his handgun from its holster and laid it on the table. His hands curled into fists when he dropped them to his sides. The man was mad. Rich had to focus, to somehow get Ada away from the monster threatening to kill her for some kind of sick revenge.

Suddenly Harley stiffened, and his eyes narrowed. The sound of a distant siren's high pitched wailing grew louder, *closer.*

Ada slowly reached up and wrapped her hands around the hand at her throat.

Harley ignored her touch. He lifted his head away from Ada's, listening. Then he looked to the side, over and down toward the ground.

Rich inched forward, dropping instinctively when the crack of a rifle split the air.

A fine spray of blood rose like a cloud as Harley's head exploded and he toppled over the railing and disappeared. Rich leaped up and sprang forward. As if in slow motion, Ada's legs folded beneath her and she collapsed face down on the deck.

Rich's heart hammered against his ribs, and his hands shook as he gently turned her over. Blood and gore covered her entire back. He searched for the knife, and bile rose in his throat when he spotted it several feet away in a pool of blood. Had Harley kept his promise and plunged it into her before he died?

Suddenly, her body began to shake. He dropped down and pulled her against him. His fingers skimmed over her face, her throat, and he brushed the hair from her eyes. They fluttered open and he choked on a sob as he pulled her against him.

Footsteps thundered up the stairs and TJ, followed by Jake, burst through the open door and raced toward them. "Do we need an ambulance?" gasped TJ, dropping down beside them.

"I don't think so," murmured Rich. Against his chest, Ada's heart beat strong and steady. He eased her onto the deck and began a methodical check of her crumpled body. Blood still oozed from the small slit on her face, but he soon discovered most of the blood covering her belonged to Harley.

"Rich? What happened?" Trembling with the effort, Ada clutched his shirt.

"You're safe, darlin'," he murmured. He covered her shaking hand. "It's over."

TJ rose and stepped to the blood spattered railing. He looked down. "My God," he uttered softly. Rich shifted in order to see between the wooden posts.

Below and to the left, Will Steiner sat on the ground. Off to one side lay Rich's M14, and Nick, having arrived seconds behind them, stood between the man and the rifle. Steiner's elbows were braced on drawn up knees, and he stared down, clutching his head between his hands.

Rich's gaze shifted to the body sprawled nearby. The velocity of the M14 round at such close range destroyed his features, making Harley unrecognizable.

The sun blazed down, warming his ice cold skin. Rich looked away.

TJ knelt and rested a hand on his shoulder. "I'm going to go help Nick. Jake will be here in case you need anything."

Rich nodded silently and held out his arms to Ada. She curled against him, and amidst the blood and gore, they clung to one another until Jake came and led them away from death.

*****

Late afternoon sun slanted through the windows at Pine Bluffs PD and highlighted Will Steiner's bowed head. He slumped in a chair, clutching a steaming cup between his hands.

Along with TJ, Rich entered the room and nodded when Nick indicated a chair not far from Steiner. He'd showered at Ada's after they'd taken her home. Cassi took over Ada's care and before he left the cottage, Ada was sound asleep in her own bed.

He'd brought several changes of clothes, intending to stay at Ada's at least for the time being. She wasn't getting out of his sight, he'd make sure of that. When he'd burst through that door, and knew in a split second she could be dead, Rich came to a decision. Maybe not at that *exact* moment, but not long after.

"Mr. Steiner." Nick took a seat across from his subject and TJ remained standing. "Can we get you anything else?"

Will's eyes remained on the cup in his hands. "No, sir. This will do for now," he said softly, and took a careful sip. He sat the cup down, then lifted his gaze to meet Rich's.

Rich didn't quite know what he'd expected, but the emptiness, the pain, radiating from Steiner's steady gaze shocked him to the core. He looked away, suddenly unable to cope with a rising tide of emotion.

Nick took charge.

"Mr. Steiner," he began. "You've been advised of your rights, do you understand them?"

"Yes, sir."

"I'd like you to tell us as best you can what happened today at Rich McConnell's, starting with your arrival at the residence. I may have questions and interrupt as you proceed, and I would like to record your statement."

"Am I being charged?" Will's voice shook.

"Not at this time," Nick said. "I advised you of your rights as a precaution. After we hear what you have to say, I'll have information to present to the Erie County DA's office. I will tell you, Mr. Steiner, I don't anticipate charges being brought against you given what we already know. Your testimony will help clarify details for our presentation. Are you ready?"

Steiner nodded. His expression never changed, but Rich noted he squared his shoulders and straightened in his chair. His face remained impassive, and he focused on the Marine Corps emblem visible on the back of his hand.

Will took another sip of coffee. "I don't mind the recorder," he said, and began to talk. "I needed to see Rich one more time. I'd tried, several times lately, to work up the nerve to say what I had to say." For a brief moment his eyes lifted to Rich's, then slid away. "I didn't know there'd been trouble."

"Trouble?" Nick asked.

"Yeah, the stuff that happened with Ada Blaine. I didn't know any of that. I knew Rich was seein' her. I'd seen them together."

Nick interrupted. "Did you follow Mrs. Blaine onto the lake in a kayak?"

Will's eyes widened and he stared at Nick. "No, sir." He emphasized. "I wanted to try the sport, and Lake Erie scared the sh... scared me. So I asked around and was told the lake here in Pine Bluffs was great. I just happened to be there that day."

"One more question," Nick said, then supplied a day and time. "You ran into Rich McConnell in Erie, correct?"

"Yes."

"What brought you to Erie that day?"

"I was looking for work. You can check with the place I applied."

"I'll need the name of the company and who spoke with you."

Will frowned. "The company was a delivery service. I have the details and the guy's name I spoke to back at my aunt's place." He shook his head. "I just can't think of it now."

"Get it to me when you can. Continue."

Rich listened as Steiner relayed how he arrived at Rich's place and what transpired. When Nick asked for confirmation, Rich nodded agreement. So far, what he'd heard was right on. Leaning forward, Rich rested both elbows on the table. Now he'd find out exactly what happened.

"I left," Will continued. "I'd parked up the road a bit and was getting in my car when I saw Phillips stop at Rich's. Man," he said, shaking his head. "It made me sick inside. Harley Phillips was bad news. I only met him once and he was a complete whack job."

"So you knew Harley Phillips?"

"I knew *of* him. His stepsister, Dodie, said he thought he owned her and to watch out for him. After she told me some of the crap he'd pulled. I steered clear of him."

"Why did his arrival at Rich's upset you?"

"By then I'd heard about the threats to Rich and Mrs. Blaine. I developed a good set of instincts inside." He looked at Nick. "You know what I mean?"

Nick nodded, and Will continued. "I put two and two together, and I couldn't walk away without warning Rich."

TJ flipped on the lights. The sky outside had grown steadily dark and sheets of rain pelted the window. He crossed the room to a coffee machine and refilled Steiner's cup. Will nodded his thanks and lifted the cup for a quick sip.

Nick waited patiently. When Steiner sat the cup down, he urged, "Let's continue."

"I was in my car, heading the other way when I saw Rich walk outside and look up the road. Guess he didn't see me, because by the time I'd turned and drove back to his place nobody was around. I went to the door and that's when I heard them."

"Who did you hear?"

"Harley and Rich. I knew right away something bad was goin' down." Steiner gave a detailed description of the exchange he'd overheard.

Rich's insides burned as Will talked. Word for word, it was almost exactly as it had occurred. He nodded agreement when Nick asked him for verification.

"Then I saw the M14." Will's gaze rose and locked with Rich's. "It'd been a while, but once, way back when, I was a sniper, an expert with the weapon. There it lay, complete with ammo on a bench inside the door."

Nick held up his hand and turned to Rich. "You left the gun there, Rich?"

Rich blew out a long breath, probing his memory. "I did," he responded finally. "I laid it down when Steiner... when Will came to the door."

Something flickered in Will's eyes, and Rich realized it was the first time since the Corps he'd called Will by his given name.

"Then Harley arrived," Rich continued. "I went to look outside. When I returned Ada and Harley were missing. I forgot all about the rifle and... Well, you know the rest."

Will picked up at that point. "I knew I had to do something. So I grabbed the M14 and ammo and went back outside. I could hear their voices out behind the place, so I made my way back there. I saw Phillips as soon as I turned the corner. He had ahold of Mrs. Blaine and had a knife to her throat."

Will's eyes darkened, and he pulled at the collar of his shirt. His steady gaze met Rich's. "I loaded the rifle and waited. When he leaned back far enough for a clear shot, I took it."

The rain pounded on the window, and overhead one of the

fluorescent bulbs buzzed and flickered. Will Steiner stared at the Marine Corps emblem on the back of his hand.

Rich quietly rose and left the room.

Chapter Thirty-Eight

Ada lifted her glass and swirled the contents before she sipped. "Did you know," she asked Rich, "that this is called a burgundy glass?"

"We're not drinking burgundy," Rich replied.

"We're not," she agreed. "This is a lovely pinot noir. Thank you, Richard, for knowing I'd want something stronger than the gallons of tea Cassi's been pushing all day.

He laughed. "You're welcome."

"Anyhow," she went on, "this glass is taller than what you'd use for a burgundy, and has a larger bowl."

"Good to know," Rich responded. He placed his drink aside and wrapped one arm around her. She slid close, seeking the warmth and comfort he offered. With one finger he gently touched the tiny cut on her face. "How are you feeling?"

"Much better," she murmured, and took another sip of pinot noir.

The rain ended shortly after Rich returned from Pine Bluffs PD. Clouds obscured the setting sun and runoff trickled like soothing music through downspouts. She'd insisted they sit outside, despite the downturn in temperature. Cassi had hovered all day, and to Ada's surprise and concern, her niece tended to burst into tears whenever she attempted to talk about the 'stand off'. An impromptu label Ada came up with for what happened.

Since Rich's return, it appeared she'd traded one 'hoverer' for another. Though it was nice to have a handsome, strong man hover. After today's frightening experience, he could continue to do so for a very, very long time.

They'd escaped to her porch and snuggled beneath a throw to keep warm. The air had a distinct chill, but a hearty wine, a fleece throw, and a hot blooded man beside her made watching night shadows fall quite comfortable.

Leftover tension slipped away, much like the fading light. She needed her place. Needed to gaze at Pine Shadow Lake, to smell her dripping gardens, and to know she could now walk there without fear. Things she'd taken for granted before a bullet blew her teapot to smithereens.

She turned to Rich. "Will he be in trouble? Will Steiner." She tilted her head to observe Rich's expression.

"Nick all but promised the DA wouldn't press charges. The gun wasn't his, and what he basically did was self defense. No, he'll not be charged."

She took his hand and rubbed it against her cheek. "You're not sure how you feel about all this, are you?"

Rich brought her hand to his lips. A gesture she'd come to expect from the man and his charming old fashioned ways. He pressed his lips to her palm and her heart melted. "Sooner or later, I'll contact Will. There's unfinished business to address. For now, I'll let it go and be thankful our paths crossed again." He heaved a deep sigh. "As for Harley, there's not much to say. Should I have caught all the signals? Maybe. He knew about the note and about your land being torn up, and he knew because he was responsible for both. I'm very thankful Harley was a piss poor shot."

"Me, too," Ada added. "Where did he get the rifle?"

"Believe it or not, he got the rifle from Dodie. Apparently Will called her after he was arrested and told her to keep the rifle he'd stashed in the trunk of her car. At some point she gave it to Harley. Could be that was the connection that finally set him off. Speaking of connections, TJ was sharp to make the one between your brake failure and Harley's injury. He's a good cop."

Ada agreed. She lay her head on his broad shoulder. "What about the bartender from North East? I assume he's off the hook, too?"

"I believe the only thing he's guilty of is a bad attitude and a fondness for drink."

"Mmmm. So, our lives can get back to normal."

"Amen to that. The past is over, done with. I can't change a thing. In some ways I'm glad I didn't know Dodie came to a bad end. With Gary's help, I learned to accept the decisions she made were hers and hers alone. As far as my life now, I'm hoping for a change."

She lifted her head and turned, looking into his eyes. A tug of apprehension curled deep inside her. Now the danger was past, maybe Rich felt the need to step away. To put some distance between them.

Her heart would break if that was the change he wanted.

He framed her face with his hands and brushed his lips to hers. "I've fallen in love with you, pretty lady. Will you marry me?"

Ada's heart turned over with a distinct thud. She started to reply... twice... and finally just folded her lips together and nodded as tears filled her eyes.

The fleece throw fell away as Rich pulled her into his arms and pressed his lips to hers.

"Well, well," Nick's voice made them reluctantly pull apart. "They just wanted to come out here and neck, Cass." He reached behind him and pulled Cassi through the door. "They didn't even hear me ask if they wanted some of Aunt Mary's pie."

Wiping her eyes, Ada laughed. She settled against Rich, turning slightly to face Nick and Cassi as Mary and Tom appeared at the door.

"Miserable night for necking," Tom remarked.

Rich tucked the throw around them. "That's your opinion, old man. It's cold out here. See this?" He lifted a corner of the fleece. "When's the last time you snuggled with your lady under a blanket?"

"Most every night," Tom said with a wink. "I consider it one of the perks of being married to a beautiful woman." He slipped his arm around Mary, then kissed her. "I don't have to sneak out and neck on dark, chilly porches."

"I agree with you, Tom," Rich said. "That's precisely why I just asked this pretty lady to be *my* wife." He shifted his gaze to Ada.

Silence descended. A chorus of night creatures along the lakeshore and the dripping eaves softened the night as Ada gazed into tawny eyes filled with love. "My answer is yes," she whispered. And as tears rolled down her face, she repeated, "Oh yes."

*****

The aroma of blueberry muffins hung in the air as Rich poured his second cup of morning coffee. "Can I have one now?" he asked as Ada skillfully popped the muffins from the hot pan onto a cooling rack.

"Help yourself," she said "They're best hot."

Rich scooped two onto a plate and leaned in to kiss the cook on his way past. Balancing plate and cup, he slid open the door and stepped outside. The morning sun was fast erasing all traces of yesterday's downpour. Choppy waves on the lake would settle by midmorning, a perfect Memorial Day.

Ada joined him. "Beautiful, isn't it?"

"Picture perfect," he mumbled around a mouthful of muffin. "Are you sure you're up to Mary and Tom's picnic today?"

"I wouldn't miss it." She stepped from the porch and strolled toward her gardens. "I'm looking forward to Tom's summer season kickoff barbecue. It'll give me a chance to thank everyone who took care of things for me the past few weeks."

"You've got good friends, honey."

"I do." She smiled, then turned and looked. "Last night you asked me to marry you."

"Um mm. I did. If I remember correctly, you said yes."

"I did." She took a step toward him and hooked her arms around his neck.

He kissed the tiny nick on her cheek, her forehead, and her lips. "I love you, Ada."

"I love you, too, Rich. With all my heart. I'm sure you know you'll have adjustments to make."

He grinned. "Right back at you, darlin"

She settled in against him. "There are few thing's I've really wanted in life," she began. "Now I've discovered there are some I simply can't do without."

"Such as?"

"I want to wake up with you every morning, just like today. I want to cuddle with you under a blanket on cool evenings, just like last night. I want to grow old with you. I love you Rich, and I want you for the rest of my life."

"Easy adjustments," he murmured. "I can live with them."

Surrounded by the soft scent of lemon, he kissed her.

*****

The McGraw Memorial Day picnic turned into a dual celebration. While Ada and Rich accepted congratulations from friends, TJ sipped fresh lemonade. He scanned the gathering crowd, smiling when he spotted his dad wearing a long white apron and manning the grill.

"Hey, cousin," Nick said, strolling over with a cold beer. "What happened to the whole weekend off?"

TJ shook his head. "I got four hours OT on Saturday," he said, checking his watch. "Then someone called off sick Sunday and they asked if I'd come in second shift that day and work early today. I agreed and the sergeant took pity on me and let me bring a state car home last night. I'm assigned this area and can hang out until I get an incident."

"Decent sergeant," Nick said, and took a deep pull of beer. He pointed with the bottle toward Rich and Ada. "Great news, huh?"

TJ turned just in time to see Rich lean over and kiss Ada. They sat on a blanket in the shade of a towering maple. "I saw it coming, but yeah, I couldn't be happier for them." He frowned at the frosty bottle in Nick's hand. "Quit flauntin' the friggin' beer, will ya'."

Nick laughed, and broke into a wide grin as his wife approached with an old friend. "Hello ladies," he drawled.

TJ glanced over his shoulder and almost dropped the tall icy glass in his hand.

"Hi, honey." Cassi wrapped her arm around Nick's waist. "Look who just showed up."

TJ looked directly into Lanie Delacor's green, green eyes and his throat went dry. He nodded hello and, tipping his lemonade, drained the glass.

Lanie arched her brow and looked him over, head to toe. "Picnicking or working, Trooper McGraw?"

"I'm on duty, and happened to be in the area."

"Ah. Our tax dollars at work."

Cassi edged between TJ and her friend. "Lanie, you wanted to congratulate Aunt Ada and Rich. Let's go find them."

"You know," Nick said as his wife pulled Lanie away. "She thinks you have a great butt."

"What?" TJ pulled his eyes from Lanie's compact little body encased in tight red shorts and a navy crop top. "Yeah? She said that?"

Nick nodded, grinning.

TJ frowned and checked the time again. "I've got to run. And about Miss Delacor? Not my type. It'll be a cold day in hell when I fall for a woman like Elaine Daphanie Delacor."

Look for *Deadly Triad Book Three: Deadly Encounter*

About Nancy Kay

Nancy Kay resides near Lake Erie in Western Pennsylvania with her husband, a former member of the Marines and the Pennsylvania State Police Department, thus providing valuable insight for her stories. At various times in her life she has worked in banking, as a veterinary assistant, and as an aerobics instructor. She pursues a healthy lifestyle and enjoys her part time job in an exclusive lingerie boutique. As a member of Romance Writers of America and three affiliated chapters, she keeps involved and informed while pursuing her writing career. Her stories are set in small towns and inland communities scattered along the shores of the Great Lakes amongst rolling grape vineyards and glorious sunsets. They focus on romance, intertwined with the love of hearth, home and family, yet are sprinkled with suspense, danger and intrigue.

Learn more about Nancy at **www.nancykayauthor.com**.

Made in the USA
Charleston, SC
28 March 2013